Heartbreak

The Lenka Trilogy

Part 1

John Righten

ACKNOWLEDGEMENTS

My thanks once again to Kate, Jacky and Fran for translating my novel into the Queen's English. To Viki for her creative cover design, and Chris and Davy for creating the Rogues website.

Dedication

To the Rogues we lost along the way.

Tom 'The Bomb'
Born (nobody knows) to 4 July 2019

This book contains adult content.

For reviews and comments on The Rogues Trilogy: *Churchill's Rogue*; *The Gathering Storm* and *The Darkest Hour,* The Lochran Trilogy: *Churchill's Assassin*; *The Last Rogue* and *The Alpha Wolves,* and The Lenka Trilogy: *Heartbreak*; *Resilience* and *Reflection,* go to

https://www.rightensrogues.co.uk
facebook.com/theroguestrilogy
twitter #rightenrogues.co.uk
Instagram @rightensrogues

ISBN: 9781093981926
ISBN-13: 9781093981926

"More than this"

Roxy Music

Chapter 1: Rogue Operator

3pm, 16 July 1995, Adriatic Sea, off the coast of Dubrovnik, Croatia (formerly part of Yugoslavia)

'Captain, the Cheshire Regiment have reported that there is a truck on the road to Tuzla,' said the radio operative.

'We're witnessing the largest exodus of civilians since WWII. Did you expect them all to be riding donkeys?' Captain Carlisle stepped forward. 'Still no reports of any males among the families?'

'Only young boys and old men.'

'The Bosnian Serbs may have promised safe passage, but that bastard General Mladić is up to something.'

The sound of rotor blades grew louder, as one of HMS Chatham's Lynx helicopters landed on the helipad.

'Who's on it?' asked the captain.

'Maximum security; no names,' replied Lieutenant Cole, who was standing beside the captain.

'Thankfully, not the admiral then. Royalty, I expect. With any luck the Queen Mother; superb company. Check that we're OK for gin, Lieutenant,' said the captain.

The radio operative lowered his voice. 'Sorry Captain, the truck . . .'

'What of it?' snapped his superior.

'It's parked on a bank . . . ,' he said and turned to look up at his commanding officer, '. . . pointing in the opposite direction, towards Bosnian-Serb-held territory.'

'What!' said the captain, peering at the screen in the communications room of the naval frigate. The grainy, black and white aerial footage was transmitted by a US Tomcat monitoring the train of refugees and NATO trucks fleeing from the town of Srebrenica. 'Jesus, who the hell is mad enough to enter a war zone? The MiG-29s will descend on it like vampires.' He glanced across several screens on the control panel. 'Where are the two MiGs now?'

'They're continuing to harry the refugee convoy,' continued the radio operative.

'If they open fire right in front of us, it's World War III,' said the captain.

'The Bosnian-Serbs are not crazy enough to give that order with UN troops all around, are they?' said the lieutenant.

'Whether they give the order, or one pilot has an itchy finger, the outcome will be the same,' said the captain.

The radio operative monitoring the truck zoomed in, then spoke again: 'Captain, smoke is starting to pour from the exhaust.'

'That's all we need,' said Captain Carlisle.

'Could it be one of the Rogues?' asked the lieutenant.

'Leave conjecture to the pen-pushers in Whitehall,' replied his superior.

Another radio operator turned her head. 'The vehicle is registered to a charity, Nurses Abroad, and said to be carrying insulin for a children's hospital in Mostar.'

Captain Carlisle paused. 'It can't be a Rogue. They're either dead, in straitjackets, or on the run.' He leaned further forward to view the live feed. 'It has to be some other kind of lunatic.'

A woman strode over to the two men and peered at the screen. 'One Rogue retired,' said Commander Stanford.

Sunlight entered the room, causing the officers to turn towards the open door.

A dapper-looking rotund man in his fifties, with wild grey hair, entered.

'Bloody hell!' said Captain Carlisle. 'We really are on the edge of Armageddon if you're here, Foxy.'

'I've had friendlier welcomes,' said Viscount 'Foxy' Foxborough. 'Captain, Commander,' he nodded as he strode over to the control panel.

'I take it you know the driver?' asked Commander Stanford.

Foxy said nothing, and peered anxiously at the screen.

'It's edging forward,' said the radio operative, sitting up.

3pm, 16 July 1995, Bosnia and Herzegovina (formerly part of Yugoslavia)

The engine of the matt-black, twelve-wheel Roadrunner T45 truck roared angrily, as its gears began to stir its pistons into life. The driver eased the engine into second gear as it crawled along the bank at an angle to the crowded road. The driver worked the accelerator and gear stick smoothly changing it up to third gear and then fourth within a distance of 100 metres.

Hundreds of weary heads began to lift, as the gleaming unmarked truck quickened its pace as it thundered up the bank towards the makeshift roadblock. Dutch UN troops began to shout, '*Hou op!*' (stop!), and a few refugees waved their arms. The truck was deaf to their pleas.

A little boy's hand slipped from his mother's, as he stumbled down the bank into the path of the climbing truck. The driver pulled sharply to the left, hitting a branch and shattering the windscreen.

The truck ploughed through the field, before turning right to once again scale the bank.

In a troop carrier parked 300 metres ahead, the

commotion alerted two Serbian troops who were lighting their cigarettes. The truck was coming right at them. They leapt from the vehicle, towards the abandoned field of rapeseed. The baying roar of the on-coming truck's horn startled the Serbian soldiers as they fumbled to find the triggers of their submachine guns. Now only metres away, the two soldiers disappeared into the yellow-carpeted fields. The truck steered to the right as it finally burst onto the road.

It punched arrogantly through the barrier of the roadblock, as if it were balsa wood. The two soldiers scrambled back into view and ripped back the triggers of their sub machine guns as the vehicle sped past, releasing their deafening rage.

Bullets ricocheted off the armour plates that shielded the truck's wheels but continued upwards shattering the driver's side window. UN troops and civilians dropped to the ground or disappeared into the fields of yellow to the right. With the road a hundred metres ahead packed with refugees, the driver kept the accelerator flush to the floor while veering the truck left at the fork in the road and onto the empty road leading towards the Gradina Hills. The MiGs veered away from the exodus of civilians and UN troops towards the barren road, before screeching directly over their next target.

'The MiGs are turning full circle heading towards the train of refugees again,' said the radio operator. 'Even lower this time. They're practically scraping the ground.'

'Anti-aircraft missiles?' asked Foxy, solemnly.

'We're too far away,' replied the captain. 'Even if we weren't, No 10 would have to sanction it.'

'Only after they talked to the White House,' added Foxy, shaking his head. 'Can you remove their warheads?'

'We have dummy missiles for range practice, Sir,' added the lieutenant.

'They still have guidance systems?' asked Foxy.

The lieutenant nodded.

'But if they're unarmed and can't reach their targets, what's the point?' said the captain.

Commander Stanford interjected, 'The missiles may

not reach them, but their guidance systems will lock on to the MiGs. When they do, it will send the aircrafts' defence systems in the cockpit into orbit. They will withdraw, we can abort the rockets and let them fall into the sea.'

Captain Carlisle frowned. 'High risk. If the MiGs shoot them down first, or if anything blocks our signals to the guidance systems, we'll all be sitting on the bottom of the sea.'

'Once the truck is destroyed, I have no doubt they will turn on the refugees,' said Foxy. 'Launching your missiles may be our only hope of averting war, Captain.'

'The MiGs are zooming in on the truck now,' said the radio operative.

'Load dummy missiles,' ordered Captain Carlisle.

'Four MiG fighters are reported to have taken off from Belgrade's Surčin Airport,' said another radio operative.

The ship's sirens screamed as the crew scrambled to their stations.

'Missiles loaded. Green light!' said one of the

operators.

'Launch missiles,' ordered Captain Carlisle.

Within seconds, two Sea Wolf anti-aircraft missiles were screaming through the skies towards land.

Everyone in HMS Chatham's control room watched the game of death played out on the black and white screen in silence.

Counting down the seconds behind the cracked face of the Rolex watch, the driver of the truck kept the accelerator flat into the pool of blood on the floor.

'The MiGs are less than a thousand metres from the train of refugees,' said the radio operator, swallowing quickly.

The British officers stared at the two advancing Russian-built grey-winged insects on screen, while Foxy squinted at the grainy, small black box in their flight path. He lifted his hands and clasped them in front of his face, resting his fingertips on his nose.

'Captain, the MiGs are rising,' the radio operator said, reading the rapidly increasing numbers by each speeding insect.

As the caravan of refugees began to disappear over the horizon, the two swooping silhouettes became more distinct. The driver peered up at the broken rear-view mirror to be met by glacial-blue eyes. The first strafes from the MiGs' autocannons ripped through the abandoned fields and tore up the road ahead. The roar of the aircraft above the truck's cabin was deafening. The MiGs had missed, but now they had their line. The driver ripped the scarlet bandana wrapped around the Redfield telescopic sight on the dashboard and pressed it against the shoulder wound. The accelerator pedal disappeared beneath the bloodied boot.

'They are coming around again. Both MiGs are locked on the truck,' said the radio operator. The calm demeanour of the officers in the control room was exposed by their still, grey faces.

'Both missiles have entered Bosnian airspace. Two minutes to impact,' said the radio operative coolly. '90 seconds. 80 . . . Sir! One MiG's broken off.'

'Abort!' ordered the captain, calmly.

The ship's klaxon fell silent, as both Sea Wolf missiles fell from the sky into the sea. With the convoy of refugees edging off the black and white screen, all eyes returned to the small white rectangle and the single, lethal, grey fly heading towards it.

'The guy in the truck is ploughing ahead,' said the captain, shaking his head.

'The truck is heading for the mountains, but the forest is not dense enough and it will still be visible from the air,' said the radio operative.

'God help him. Whoever he was, he had the biggest pair of balls on the planet,' said Captain Carlisle, crossing his arms.

Commander Stanford shook her head. 'Balls?'

Foxy gripped the top of the chair in front of him.

'That's one cooked goose,' noted the captain, as he watched the final attack on the screen. 'At least he saved those poor bastards on the road, though.'

Commander Stanford turned to the British diplomat. 'I guess that was the plan, Foxy, but at what cost?'

Foxy pressed his hands against his face and closed his eyes. 'MiG missiles launched!' said the radio operator.

The truck's driver breathed slowly, to ease the flow of blood seeping into the bandana as the MiG reappeared above the Majevica Mountains to the right. It began to turn towards its easy prey, covering the exposed valley in seconds. The driver watched as two flashes obscured the MiG's wings as it released its lethal cargo. Two S-24 rockets raced towards their target. The blistering sun was replaced by darkness.

All was silent inside the control room on the HMS Chatham. The radio operator looked up at Captain Carlisle, who turned to Commander Stanford, who was shaking her head and staring at Foxy.

Foxy slowly dropped his hands from his face, slipping one inside his tweed jacket to retrieve a silver flask. Slowly, he unscrewed the top and raised his trembling hand to take a long swig of *Talisker* single malt.

Captain Carlisle turned to Foxy, and to the surprise of his exhausted crew, he began to clap slowly. 'A tunnel! A bloody tunnel!'

Chapter 2: One for the Road

Midday, 3 July 1990 (five years earlier), Cork, Republic of Ireland

'Yes, Teresa, there are many religions: Judaism, Hinduism, Islam. Even our religion, Christianity, is split between Catholics and Protestants,' replied their teacher, Lenka Brett, who ran the orphanage with the support of her great aunt Marisa and her guardians, Estelle and Foxy.

In the living room of the orphanage were thirty children aged between three and eight years old. The other half of the orphanage consisted of twenty-eight children, whose ages ranged between nine and seventeen. Their class, held after lunch, would be her last for at least a month.

'They will go to hell though and only us Catholics will go to heaven,' added Patrick, aged seven. 'Canon Moore said so when you took us to Sunday mass in St Mary's Cathedral last week, Miss. He says he talks to God, so I guess he knows his business,' he added, huffily.

'Well, it's not for me to say any different to Canon Moore, but whether we go to heaven or hell, also depends on how we live our lives. Are we kind to others? Do we help and protect the vulnerable? These things are just as important.'

'You are kind, Miss Lenka,' shouted Christine, 'you are going to help those children in Romania.'

Lenka peered over to the VHS videocassette recorder by the television. On top of it sat the tape containing the harrowing eight-minute television footage of the children in a Romanian orphanage, which Estelle had shown her two months earlier.

'I wish you didn't have to go, Miss,' said Christine, quietly.

The children's faces fell, though their eyes remained on their teacher sitting on a chair in front of the blackboard.

'I won't be away long, three to four weeks at most,' reassured Lenka. 'And Robert McNamara from St Bercthun's telephoned me this morning to say he's coming to help Margaret with my classes while I'm away. Margaret's a wonderful teacher, but she's delighted that Robert has offered to help over the next few weeks. He's a good man.'

'The children in town say he's very kind and delivers toys to their parents for them when they're ill,' added Josie, aged six, nodding proudly as if she had helped deliver them.

'He's a cripple, though,' shouted Davy, who was seven, as his hand shot into the air. 'He won't be as good as you in goal when we play hurling after mass on Sundays, Miss.'

'He had polio, which has afflicted some of the children under our roof over the years. Robert is someone we should admire. He worked hard and has become an excellent teacher. He's conquered huge battles, so do not judge him merely because of his disability.'

Davy dropped his arm, and nodded. 'Yes Miss, sorry, Miss,' before mumbling, 'I'll judge him on something else.'

'Concanon's a vicious *basturd*,' muttered Peter, aged eight.

'Peter, say sorry for swearing, or I'll send you upstairs to Marisa. She'll sort you out.'

'Sorry, Miss,' said Peter loudly. 'Miss Ryan is good at ca . . .'

'Yes, I know what Marisa is good at. And as for rumours about St. Bercthun's headmaster, Mr Concanon, remember to judge someone by their actions and not by what you have heard about them.'

'He put three children in hospital this year, swinging his big belt,' retorted Peter.

Lenka sighed, knowing that this was true. 'Right, I'm leaving first thing in the morning, so I'll say goodbye now,' though she knew that most of them would delay going to Sunday mass to wave her off in the morning.

Suddenly, all the children, apart from Hannah in the wheelchair beside her, uncrossed their legs and raced towards her. As each child struggled to get close enough to embrace her, Lenka just managed to stop her chair from tipping backwards.

Margaret entered the living room and hesitated before clapping her hands. 'Right, come on, Foxy and

Estelle have lunch on the table.'

As she began to herd the children out, she nodded at Lenka and smiled. It was only when they had received Robert's offer of help that Margaret had confessed that she had been terrified of managing the classes on her own.

Hannah held out her arms, as Lenka bent down towards the wheelchair to give her a hug. The seven-year-old girl, who had been abandoned after she was diagnosed with spina bifida, whispered, 'We love you.'

Lenka kissed the girl gently on the cheek and said softly, 'I'll be back. Make sure the boys are nice to Robert while I'm away. They listen to you.'

Lenka wheeled Hannah into the dining room and manoeuvred her into her usual space between Peter, who was seven, and Davy. She then placed a *Ladybird* copy of *Gulliver's Travels* by each child's plate, along with an exercise book.

'I have told Margaret and Robert that I have given you some homework to do while I'm away. It's not much, but each exercise book has a list of questions that matches your ages and abilities. In your answers, I also want you to express what you think about the story. Is it simply a story about a giant or is it something more?'

'Why?' asked Philomena, aged eight.

'Because you're not robots.'

'And to make sure two or three individuals don't copy other children's answers,' continued Philomena.

'Sometimes, Philomena, I think you should be teaching my classes rather than me.'

'What's the pay like, Miss?' replied the smartest and sassiest pupil in the class.

'Don't be cheeky, Philomena,' countered Lenka, suppressing a smile.

Lenka stood behind Peter and Davy. 'Did you get that?'

'Yes, Miss,' the boys sighed loudly, before Lenka ruffled their hair, releasing giggles.

'There'll be no point in copying Peter, anyway,' said Davy. '*Sur* he's as thick as I am,' as both boys began to elbow each other.

Hannah glanced critically at the boys.

'Okay, we won't copy,' said Peter, biting into a slice

of soda bread topped with blackcurrant jam.

Lenka moved along and bent down to whisper into the ear of Ellen, aged six: 'Do your best.'

The black-haired girl nodded and said quietly, 'I won't copy, again. I will do my best, Lenka. I promise.'

'Then I can ask no more of you,' said Lenka, before adding, 'Do you want to join Hannah for the additional reading class before breakfast when I get back?

The little girl beamed up at her teacher, nodded and smiled at Hannah, and started to swing her legs.

Four hours later. 'Lenka, do you really think you can drive a truck across Europe on your own tomorrow?' asked Estelle.

'Look, the paperwork covering the medicine and medical equipment that we can take into Romania is only valid for a few weeks. Unless we find another driver in the next twenty-four hours, then I have no choice but to deliver the aid on my own,' said Lenka.

Foxy who had had his chauffeur, Cedric, drive him up from London to Holyhead to catch the earliest ferry and race straight to the house – bypassing the cellars of The Imperial Hotel for once – shook his head, angrily. 'We can hire a bloody driver.'

'Mind your language, Foxy, and remember *yer* sitting in my bedroom and above us is the blessed Holy Mother, herself,' snapped Marisa.

Foxy lifted his eyes to the picture of the Madonna and child above the bedridden but still formidable elderly woman's bed.

Lenka smiled. 'It's not like hailing a cab, Foxy. We have to find someone who is not only fit and competent, but also trustworthy. People in the town and orphanages across Ireland, including the North, have secured food and clothing, and I have given them my word that every single item will reach the children.'

'My chauffeur has volunteered his services,' retorted Foxy.

'That's very kind of Cedric,' said Lenka. 'No offence to him, but we need a younger driver. *Vigour* is required to cope with the long journey ahead.'

Estelle and Foxy glanced at each other; both were unsure that the young woman with a weak heart had what she claimed was needed for the journey ahead.

Foxy began to traipse around the room. 'That bloody Joseph McNamara,' he growled. 'Why would he offer us not just one, but two experienced truck drivers, only to withdraw them on the eve of departure?'

Marisa sighed. 'Sadly, it looks like his offer of help was just a way of getting his own back on me.'

'Damn the man!' roared Foxy, leaping up. 'I'm going over to McNamara's house now to beat some kindness into him.'

The three women looked at their angry friend, before turning to each other.

Lying in her bed in the centre of the room, Marisa lifted her hand unsteadily to clasp Lenka's. 'When it all goes wrong, men lose their heads. It's always the women who are left to find the solution.'

Downstairs there was the barely audible sound of the knocker tapping the brass base on the front door.

'Foxy, I will be fine,' said Lenka, walking towards him. She lifted her hand and pressed it lightly against his blotchy cheek. 'Thank you for asking your contacts in the armed services for a volunteer. Fingers crossed. Everything else is in place.' Foxy inhaled deeply, looking at his ward solemnly as he pressed his hand against hers. 'I'm twenty-four and not an ingénue in some tawdry romantic novel. I keep telling you that your little girl has grown up,' she said as she rested her forehead against his.

'You've been telling me that since you were four,' grumbled Foxy.

'Then it's about time you started to listen,' whispered Lenka.

Estelle walked over and placed her hand on Lenka's shoulders. 'We know you're a woman, and a pretty determined one at that, but we don't know what you are going to meet out there. I'm as worried as Foxy, and with your heart . . .'

Lenka clutched her guardians' hands, stepped back and looked kindly at their solemn faces. 'Bloody hell! Grow up, you two. I have my heart pills. I'll be fine. I'm not entering a war zone. It's all official. I'll be back within a month.'

'Yes, it's official,' grumbled Foxy. 'But the

Romanian authorities are furious about the international coverage of the state of the orphanages. They say it's scaring away investors. If anything happens, don't count on them to come to the rescue.'

There was a louder rap of the brass knocker on the front door.

Lenka squeezed their hands tighter, before releasing them. She turned to Marisa: 'Can you try to put some steel in their spines, while I go and see who's at the door.'

When Lenka reached the bottom of the staircase, Davy, one of the children, had already opened the door and was dragging the caller in by the hand. The boy shouted over to Lenka, 'It's Bobby McNamara.'

The visitor looked up nervously. 'I'm very sorry to disturb you, Lenka. I know you're busy. I came in person to apologise on behalf of my family, and see if there was anything more I could do to help?' The mousey-haired man smiled awkwardly, always aware of his misshapen body, crippled by polio. 'But perhaps,' he hesitated, 'after what has happened, a McNamara is the last person you wished to see.'

'Don't be silly, Robert, you are always welcome here. Whatever your grandfather does has no bearing on our friendship with you and the rest of your family. Now, come inside and have some tea.'

'I'll stick him in *da* kitchen, Lenka,' declared Davy, seizing the visitor's arm and dragging him into the hallway, nearly causing the man to drop his walking stick.

'Thank you, Davy, but I think Mr McNamara would prefer it if you *showed* him to the kitchen,' advised Lenka.

Five minutes later, Lenka handed Robert a mug of tea as they sat at the kitchen table.

'Now relax, everything will be fine. We are very grateful for your offer to help Margaret with the teaching while I'm away,' said Lenka.

'But the driving?' added Robert.

'Foxy will pull out all the stops to find a driver, and when he puts his mind to something it's as good as done.'

'I've only ever seen him in town, when he's stopped

24

at The Imperial Hotel to purchase cases of champagne. He always has everyone running around or in fits of laughter. The man's a whirlwind.'

'A hurricane would be a more appropriate metaphor,' boomed Foxy, bounding into the kitchen. Foxy flopped into one of the black leather armchairs that he had had installed in all the communal rooms in the house. He put his hands together as if in prayer. 'Start planning what to do with your inheritance, as I am going over to your grandfather's house tomorrow. He is shortly to meet his maker – that's of course if Marisa is right, that there is an afterlife, and the devil really does exist.'

'Once again, I'm sincerely sor . . .'

'Don't worry,' interrupted Foxy. 'Lenka is right. The sins of the grandfather are not inherited by his grandchildren – or something like that. As Lenka said, we are very grateful for your offer of help.'

'I wish I could be of more practical use and had a driving licence,' continued Robert. 'I take it that if you find someone suitable all the paperwork will have to be amended?'

'With my connections, it would not cause undue delay on our side,' replied a disgruntled Foxy. 'But of course, that's once we have found a competent individual with three to four weeks to spare who can drive a truck.'

'What about the aid? Are the food and medical supplies still valid?' continued the man, who was twenty-three, but from a distance could easily be mistaken for an old man by his laboured movement.

'The food is either tinned or in powder form, so no problem,' said Lenka. 'But some of the medicines expire in less than a month.'

'I have savings of my own. It's not much but it may help in hiring a driver or to purchase fresh medicines,' continued Robert. He lifted an envelope from inside his thin grey raincoat and pushed it along the blue and white checked tablecloth towards Lenka. 'It is all I can offer for now, I am afraid. However, I would be delighted to make a contribution on a monthly basis, to cover the additional expenses you have incurred due to the delay.'

Lenka lifted the envelope from the table and placed

it back inside Robert's coat pocket. 'We have money, but thank you for the offer.'

'My grandfather is a bitter man. It's sixty years since Marisa broke off their engagement. To be honest I was more surprised by his offer to help in the first place, than I was that he withdrew his support this morning.'

Robert saw the letter that had arrived in the first post, which lay opened on the table. He recognised the writing.

Miss Brett,

I am withdrawing my offer to supply drivers for tomorrow. A country should look after its own and not look to me for help.

Marisa must live with the knowledge that her cruelty to me will now cost the lives of children.

J McNamara

Robert closed his eyes tightly and sighed. 'Has Marisa seen this?'

'No, your grandfather clearly wants to inflict as much pain as he can on her, and I will not be his conduit.'

Foxy leaned forward in the armchair. 'Something else troubles you, young man?'

Robert's hands began trembling so much that he only just managed to place his cup and saucer back on the table. 'As you know I teach in the local school, St Bercthun's . . .'

Foxy raised his eyebrows repeatedly, as he did when he was about to put a friend in an embarrassing position. 'Isn't that the place you refer to as St Birch '*em*, Lenka?'

'Yes, it is, and thank you for pointing that out in front of its best teacher,' replied Lenka, who was used to Foxy's mischievous nature. 'But my issue is with the headmaster, Mr Concanon, and his free use of the belt on the children, not with his staff.'

'I approached Mr Concanon after school yesterday to request a sabbatical, to cover my time here. He dismissed me immediately,' said Robert.

'I'm so sorry, Robert,' said Lenka.

'You're clearly an intelligent man so you should have no problem in securing a new position in an excellent school,' added Foxy.

Robert looked at his limp right arm and spindly legs. 'I have tried, but no one wants a cripple. It was only due to my late parents' influence that I secured a teaching position at St Bercthun's last year.' He clasped his hands to stop them trembling.

'If you wish to withdraw your offer to help us here, I completely understand,' said Lenka, with a sympathetic smile.

'I do not. We have grown up together, and you know that I am neither a strong nor a brave man, but I have never broken my word.'

'So what is it?' continued Lenka.

'I realised that Mr Concanon's reaction will be nothing to that of my grandfather when he hears that I am to teach here.'

'I take it, that he would not only throw you out of his house but cut you off without a penny,' added Foxy.

'I do not fear his wrath, or am cowed by the threat of being disinherited, and I have enough money to pay for a room above Kennedy's Bar in town. My fear is that he will throw his wealth and influence behind those who wish to close this orphanage down.' Robert looked solemnly at Lenka and Foxy. 'In light of what I have just told you, you should seriously reconsider your charitable offer.'

'Charitable?' said Lenka, glancing at Foxy.

'You know that I'm unhappy at St Bercthun's as I do not condone the headmaster's use of violence on the children, so you graciously accepted my offer even though you have other, more beneficial, options.'

'You underestimate your qualities, Robert,' said Lenka. 'English and science are my forte, art and music Margaret's and history and geography are yours. Margaret and I do our best, but your presence would fill a huge gap in the children's education.'

Robert looked anxiously at Lenka. 'Please do not think that I am trying to manoeuvre you into withdrawing your offer because I now fear for my position and future wealth. The simple fact is that either of your guardians could easily assist Margaret over the next few weeks.' He tried to steady his trembling hands by pressing them on his knees.

Robert turned to Foxy. 'I am sorry, Mr Ar . . . sorry, Foxy . . . but as I have explained, you do see that my presence here could only bring more trouble?'

'You're right. I could assist Margaret in some small way,' sniffed Foxy. 'But having to reside here, poses an even greater threat to the orphanage than your vinegary grandfather.'

'How?' asked Robert.

'I'm as camp as Christmas,' continued Foxy. 'And if the authorities heard that a homosexual taught here, they would have me arrested as a paedophile. All nonsense, but unfortunately bigots often secure positions of prominence. My fear is not that I would be incarcerated, perhaps even castrated – though sadly, that would be as pointless as trying to immobilise a car by removing the fluffy dice from the mirror after its tyres have blown – but that the authorities would finally have their excuse to shut the orphanage down.'

'Foxy,' said the astonished Lenka. 'You must be careful about what you say. Homosexuality is still a crime in Ireland, and you've put Robert in a terrible position.'

'Have I?' asked Foxy, staring at the man.

'Sir . . . Foxy,' spluttered Robert.

'Just Foxy for now. The government will only confer the title in absentia when the embarrassment factor has passed, and I'm either interned in a casket or my ashes are polluting the heavens.'

'Err . . . yes,' replied Robert, not sure what to believe. 'I am shocked at your honesty, and clear disregard for your own safety. I certainly have no issue about your sexuality, nor for that matter do I have any justifiable fear for the children's safety.' He grasped his hands together. 'Indeed, I am honoured, Sir, that you decided to take me into your confidence, having only just met me.'

Lenka looked at her guardian sourly, shaking her head. 'You really do push the boundaries, Foxy. You will end up in jail one day or worse.'

'Worse!' challenged Foxy.

'I'll sneak into your hotel room and run a lawn-mower over that wilderness on your head posing as hair.'

Foxy clutched his hair with both hands and feigned

32

a look of horror.

The young man straightened up. 'Lenka, I would very much like to teach here until your return. That is providing you are still happy to have me knowing the risk posed by my grandfather?'

Foxy glanced at Lenka, nodding. 'Your call as always, Lenka, but for what it is worth, the young man has passed my test.'

'Test?' replied Lenka, shaking her head. 'What test? God, you're infuriating. You would try the patience of St Peter!'

Foxy shrugged like a little boy with a catapult standing by a broken window. 'I was testing his good character. If he had run off and denounced me to the authorities, I would be on my way to jail, but the children would be well rid of him. Instead, he has shown himself to be a fair and decent man. The children will be in good hands.' He clasped his hands over his bulging, emerald green waistcoat, looked up at the grandfather clock and decided it was time for something stronger than tea.

Lenka sighed, before turning to Robert and holding

out her hand to the young man. 'Welcome. I'm still looking for a driver, but I have secured an excellent teacher.'

Robert gingerly shook her hand. 'Thank you.'

She peered into Robert's flickering green eyes. 'Did you honestly believe that I would have the children taught by the biggest child in the class.'

Robert smiled as Foxy huffed. 'I confess, I'm not looking forward to telling my grandfather.'

'Oh! Leave that delightful pronouncement to me,' said Foxy, uncrossing his arms. 'I will help him to dig deep into his soul and find some modicum of decency that he never knew existed.'

'You behave, Foxy!' came a voice from upstairs.

'That was Miss Ryan,' said Robert feverishly. 'Oh no! I'm so sorry. I should have gone upstairs to pay her my respects. But I have to go now, as I have promised to prepare tutorials for my replacement on Monday. Please tell Miss Ryan that I was asking after her and that I will pay my respects to her properly, next week.'

'I will tell Marisa,' said Lenka, helping Robert to his

feet.

Foxy nodded to the younger man, as he raised a freshly poured glass of Haig whiskey in his direction.

Before Lenka and Robert reached the front door, they were met by the dead thud of the doorknocker. The young man stumbled, but Lenka caught him.

Lenka opened the door to find a clean-shaven man, in naval uniform, occupying two-thirds of the frame. His stern face instantly broke into a smile when he saw the blonde-haired woman. He removed his peaked cap, slipped it under his arm and quickly swept back a comma of black hair that had fallen above his right eyebrow.

'You are Miss Lenka Brett?'

Lenka nodded.

'I am Captain Simon Trevelyan Syrianus, ma'am. I believe you're looking for a driver.'

Chapter 3: "Say Hello, Wave Goodbye"

7.30am, 4 July 1990, Cork

Lenka crept into Marisa's bedroom. 'I was waiting until you were awake, so when I heard the radio I thought I would come in to say goodbye.'

'I love the pop tunes; Soft Cell I think this is and a beautiful song before that by a lovely lady calling herself Madonna in honour of the Virgin Mary. The song is all about the importance of chastity.'

Lenka looked wryly at Marisa. 'Is it really? Interesting that you listen to Radio Caroline on your little transistor radio, a pirate station that plays songs banned on Irish radio.'

'Banned! That's terrible!' replied Marisa, making no attempt to change the station.

Lenka placed a cup of tea and a plate containing soda bread, a knob of butter and a dollop of the Tate & Lyle thick lemon shred marmalade that Foxy had brought with him, on the table beside her grandmother's bed.

'Hmm,' murmured the elderly woman, savouring the smell.

'Foxy dotes on you,' said Lenka. 'He knows you love his little treats from Harrods.'

Marisa edged herself up on the bed and began to butter the bread. 'He once drunkenly confessed that his "three ladies" were the only decent thing in his life.' She put the knife down and held out her hand. Lenka took it and sat on the edge of the bed. 'How are you feeling?'

'Determined, though apprehensive,' said Lenka, before grinning, 'and excited.'

'All those feelings at once,' said the old woman, smiling. 'How wonderful.'

'Like you, I've never gone beyond Dublin, so add terrified to my mix of emotions.'

'You'll be fine. You come from a long line of adventurers, and thankfully there are no wars where you're going.'

Lenka smiled. 'Robert McNamara will be coming later. Are you sure you are okay with that?'

'Robert's always been a good boy.'

'His grandfather may come here to drag him home.'

'Let the twisted old sod try.' She gently tapped Lenka's hand. 'I put him in his place before and I will do so again. More so, after what he has done to you.'

'I've told Robert that if he has any trouble with the children to send the culprits up to you and you will sort them out.' Marisa nodded. 'But, Estelle says she's happy to stay for a few more days and help out here if you need it.'

'Tell Estelle to hurry back to her *halt culture* shop on the King's Road. I'll sort any trouble-makers out.'

'It's pronounced, *Hau . . . te Cou . . . ture,*' Lenka said before breaking into a wide smile

'She'd be angry if she heard me. Unlike *yerself,* I was never any good at languages. She always loved fashion, but to turn a passion into a thriving business is *grate*. I'm so proud of her.'

Lenka pulled open the drawer of the bedside table and reached to the back. She pulled forward what was there, exposing a set of playing cards. 'And even though you always give your winnings back, you shouldn't encourage the children to bet their pocket money against you once you've told them off.'

Marisa huffed. 'So you know about my little vice.'

'Hmm,' said Lenka, with a nod.

'Everyone thinks that my brother, Sean, and your grandmother, Lenka, had the monopoly on roguish behaviour. *Sur* I'm entitled to a little fun, am I not?'

Lenka laughed and gave Marisa a gentle embrace.

'Go now, before I embarrass *meself* and cry like a baby,' said Marisa, finally releasing the young woman. 'No, wait, talking of your grandmother, you should check the attic and see if there is anything among her possessions that's worth taking with you.'

'She had a leather jacket that I've always loved.'

Marisa shook her head. 'I should have said something earlier, as whatever you find will probably have a terrible musty smell and be covered in mildew. But it's thick leather, with a good lambswool lining that I added, so worth salvaging. *Yer* grandmother told me that it was made from reindeer hide. Mind you, it was Christmas and she liked to shock me. It's been repaired a number of times to sew up the bullet and stab wounds. I'll wash it with *turps*' (turpentine), 'if you bring it to me.'

'Don't be silly. I'll have plenty of time to clean it when it's the Brit's turn to drive.'

'*Sur* he's handsome. I thought it was Cary Grant when you brought him up to say hello.'

'Behave!' said Lenka. 'And nothing is going to happen.'

Marisa raised her grey eyebrows. 'And how do you know that?'

Lenka leaned forward. 'Because he calls me ma'am.' Marisa laughed, as she squeezed Lenka's hand. 'I'll take a quick look in the loft,' said Lenka, as she released her grandmother's hand. 'I'll send postcards every day.'

'Your father used to tell me that he would never send me postcards, as he'd be home before they arrived.' She smiled warmly at the young woman sitting on the bed and whispered. 'But he always did.'

Ten minutes later, Lenka entered the loft, which her grandmother had used as a study. There were black and white group photos of children covering the wall opposite the front window. Each was carefully organised in date order, spanning the twenty-six years her grandmother had spent helping Marisa manage the orphanage. There were also two very faded lithographs marked *Krakow, 1913*. Despite the large number of children, you could not miss the four-year-old girl with black hair and penetrating dark eyes, on the far left of each picture. With her jutting jaw, her grandmother projected more of a commanding presence than the two orderlies hovering over the group.

As always, Lenka's eyes finally rested on the picture at the centre of the montage marked *May 1943*. On the left was a strikingly handsome woman, whom she knew was Marisa. Her pose was assured, indicating that she had already assumed the mantle of matriarch. She was holding eight-year-old Estelle's hand. The oval-faced, young girl, with a black bob, was wearing a black and white polka dot dress that Marisa had made her for her birthday. She looked remarkably like her idol, Audrey Hepburn.

To the far right of the photo stood her grandmother. In her mid-thirties, she was waif-like in appearance, only an inch or so above the tallest of the thirty children amassed in the centre of the photo.

Silver strands were already invading her short black hair. Her wide eyes were dark and piercing, and her facial features uncompromising, apart from one – her smile. Beside her, holding her hand, stood a little boy, her son, Lochran 'Lock' Ryan. The five-year-old boy's smile was broader than his mother's and mischievousness oozed from his freckly face.

Lenka kissed her fingertips and place them on the boy's black and white face.

Beneath the photographs, on the top of a fully stacked bookcase was a cigar box containing more photographs. Lenka had gone through it very carefully, several times. The photos were of two boys, taken some thirty years apart. Both had jet-black hair, cut in a 'short back and mummy done it' style. The serious looking one with dark eyes that she knew to be grey-green was her grandfather, Sean Ryan. The other boy, she recognised from the photo above and those on the sideboard in Marisa's room, was his son, Lock. She knew she had his smile, but from the photo of her parents, which she kept in her purse, her blonde hair and porcelain skin were inherited from her mother.

Though there was no evidence that she had inherited the anomaly that the men shared, of their eyes changing to glacial-blue when threatened.

Lying at the bottom of the box was a gold ring. She glanced over at the battered, black, leather jacket hanging on the back of the door; the one her father was wearing when he died. For some reason that Marisa was never able to explain, she had insisted on keeping the jacket, and proceeded to clean the mud and blood from it. She spent weeks sewing up the slashes and adding patches but looked blankly at those who asked her why. That was when Marisa had found the bloodstained ring that Lochran had tucked into the tiny pocket he had sown into the collar. Lenka returned her mother's engagement ring to the box and gently closed the lid.

Lenka removed the key from under the rug by the door and walked towards the larger pine trunk beneath the window. She unfastened the padlock and raised the lid. Inside were various jumpers, canvas trousers, mothballs and a sheathed, US marine issue, Ka-bar knife. There was also a beautiful, oak box containing replies to requests for help. Prime Minister Winston Churchill and US President Theodore Roosevelt were among the dignitaries who had responded, offering books for the orphanage where her grandmother was raised in Krakow, as well as for Marisa's library. There was also a beautifully handwritten letter from Mahatma Gandhi offering his prayers.

At the bottom of the wooden chest was her grandmother's black leather jacket. Thankfully, it was neither damp nor smelly. She stood up and tried it on. Judging by the fit and length of the sleeves, her grandmother was smaller than her and slighter in build. The buttons were tight but left undone and with the belt tied tight, the fit and length were good enough. The thick leather and Marisa's additional lining would be welcome, as the temperatures in Bucharest were said to drop rapidly at night even though it was the height of summer.

As she slipped the jacket off, she noticed in the sunlight for the first time a footprint on the left side of the window ledge. On closer inspection, she saw that it had been made by a small right shoe. Perhaps made when her grandmother had tried to shut the window.

Lenka stood back to peer up at the top of the wardrobe to the left of the window. The corner of a book peeked out. She stood on a chair and placed her right shoe on the footprint, easily covering it, and lifted herself up to reach the book. She grabbed it and jumped down.

'Lenka, it's time to go,' shouted Estelle, from the path that stretched from the house to the road. Lenka threw the book into her knapsack and hurried to join the others downstairs.

Minutes later, Simon started the engine of the battleship grey 2.5 litre van. With a laden weight of 7.5 tonnes, it bordered on the limit permissible to be driven by someone with a standard driving licence. Lenka and the excited children watched as the truck reversed into the barn to load the last of the supplies.

'The good-looking Brit is going with you,' added Shirley, who was eight years old.

'Looks are immaterial,' said Lenka.

'Yes Miss, he's going to help the orphans because he's kind and not because you're very pretty,' said

Michael, who was also eight, before he started to giggle, immediately joined by his classmates.

'Calm down, all of you,' said Lenka, extending her arms and pointing her fluttering fingers downwards. The children giggled and nudged each other, as Lenka shook her head. 'Come on, all of you. Go and help the Captain load the last of the supplies.'

Foxy and Estelle joined Lenka in the doorway, as the children scampered off.

'Hollywood looks, our Captain,' noted Foxy. 'Every inch the hero. He may only have been here a few hours, but he spent all evening bombarding me with questions about you,' said Foxy. 'The poor man is clearly besotted with you,' he added, standing beside her.

Lenka looked nonchalantly at her guardian. 'And of course, you're not one to exaggerate,' she said, tweaking his ruby cheek.

'A flick of the hair, a flash of a smile or exchanging glances can be all that is needed to change a man. Trust me; I know something of such matters, for I too am a man.'

Estelle laughed. 'Kind of you to share that secret.'

'Mum's the word,' nodded Foxy, tapping the side of his nose. 'Seriously, Lenka, he wanted to know everything about you. He wanted to know about your parents, and even asked about their nemesis, The Alpha Wolves.'

'Foxy, the world I live in is small. I have not travelled or engaged much with anyone beyond the confines of our little town.' Foxy crossed his hands over his waistcoat and waited to be admonished, as his ward had done many times before. 'I would be the first to say that I'm unworldly, but I am not naïve. When it comes to men, they often mistake lust for love.' She smiled at the man playfully twiddling his thumbs. 'Your drunken confessions over the years have taught me that.'

'Ouch!' cried Foxy, as he launched his arm melodramatically across his forehead. 'Woe is me! I am undone!' he howled before heading off to talk to Cedric who was sitting in the Bentley.

'And you, Estelle,' said Lenka turning to her guardian and best friend. 'Care to share your thoughts on the subject?'

The German woman smiled. 'I noticed the glances you gave our dashing Captain at the dinner table. You may be about to enter another new world,' putting her arm around the younger woman's shoulders as they set off towards the door, 'but be careful. Your heart is fragile and with love, comes pain.'

Father Kent from St Anne's Church, in Cork City, who also stood in for the elderly and increasingly frail Father Maze to say mass in the local church, St Bercthun's, drew up in his faded green 1945 Morris Minor.

'Ah, Viscount, good to see you again,' said the priest, extending his hand, which Foxy shook warmly.

'Of course it is. But it's good of you to say it, for you speak on behalf of your church,' bellowed Foxy, looking up at Marisa's window. 'Do you hear that, dear lady, the Church welcomes my presence.'

Upstairs, the elderly woman smiled, as she continued to darn little Tommy Murphy's sock. 'Godless pagan!'

'*Sur* how is Marisa today, with Lenka going '*en* all?' asked the priest, addressing Estelle.

'Stoic as one would expect, Father,' said Foxy. 'She'll be pleased to see you today. Your prayers provide her with solace.'

'Your country has brought considerable pain to our island, but there is no denying that your presence has raised Marisa's spirits over the years despite the tragic loss of her brother, his son, and the terrible death of Lenka's grandmother in England.'

'You never knew any of them, did you?'

'Sadly, I joined the parish after their time.'

'Lenka's grandmother knocked your predecessor Father Hanrahan's teeth out with a frying-pan,' said Foxy, making no attempt to hide his glee.

The priest grimaced. 'So, I have been told. On the day of his departure, I did ask Father Hanrahan if it were true or a tale contrived for the Rogues' comics, but he was having trouble with his dentures and I found him hard to understand.'

Foxy smiled. The priests were very different men, and it was hard to believe that they preached from the same gospels.

'Oh, it's true, Father. I was there,' said Estelle. 'Your predecessor, with the authorities in tow, was attempting to shut down the orphanage.'

'It still bridles with my superior, Canon Moore, and the authorities that you refuse to send the children to St Bercthun's,' the priest replied before smiling at Lenka.

'You know, Father, that as long as its headmaster wields his belt, I will never allow it,' said Lenka. The priest shrugged and nodded. 'However, Father, since your arrival, the Church has been less strenuous in its efforts to shut the orphanage and that has lowered the stress levels for everyone here, especially Marisa. I thank you for that,' she said before turning to walk back into the house.

The priest smiled. 'Viscount, would you be our guest to ring the bells of St Anne's at our Easter service?'

'Nothing would give me greater pleasure,' replied Foxy, unenthusiastically. 'Drink, Father?'

'Grand, but after I've delivered a blessing on the

vehicle before sending it on its way.'

Foxy looked up at the clouded heavens and sighed.

Lenka reappeared at the door, holding her rucksack and the battered leather jacket. 'Father, will you say mass for Marisa this morning? She would appreciate it.'

'I'll be back to deliver the sacrament later, but I'm here to give you a blessing, for you and the good captain are doing the Lord's work, Lenka.'

Foxy turned towards the house. 'I'll make a telephone call and check when the Age of Enlightenment is due to arrive.'

'Ignore him, Father,' sighed Lenka.

Father Kent whispered. 'He's godless for *sur*, but after all the support he has given the orphanage and helping Estelle to raise you to be a fine woman, the Lord will, I'm sure, find a place for him in heaven' – before tilting his head, 'which will annoy the *bejasus* out of him.'

Simon returned, pulling up in the van alongside the Bentley. Lenka introduced him as he stepped down from the vehicle.

'Pleased to meet you, Captain. Did you come by the cattle boat?'

Simon looked quizzically at Lenka.

'The ferry,' she replied

'No, Father. I had a rather bumpy flight from Brize Norton.'

'However *yer* came, please bring Lenka back to us,' the priest said as he shook the officer's hand.

'I will bring her back in one piece, Father,' said Simon.

Lenka straightened up. 'Listen, both of you. I'm not a package with a label marked "Fragile" slapped on my head.'

'We know that Lenka,' said the priest. 'But you're a . . .'

'A grown woman, who until yesterday was going to drive this van on her own.'

The officer bent her heads towards Lenka and smiled. 'The Father was only trying to . . .'

'Retain his footing, because like you, he is on dodgy ground, Captain,' snapped Lenka.

Some of the children watched from the porch as they

shared a plate of biscuits that Peter had swiped from the breakfast table. Philomena nudged Davy, 'I love a domestic.'

'*Yer*, mean yer love the cleaner,' said the bemused boy. 'Mrs Hebbert's near ninety!'

'I think Estelle's a Lederhosen too,' said Christine.

'A lesbian,' said Philomena, shaking her head.

'You're getting all muddled, Christine,' said Davy. 'Lederhosen is what German lesbians wear when they go dancing.'

'And it's a sin,' Patrick added with a curt nod.

'When I get a girlfriend, *sur* I might give this lesbian *ting* a go,' said Peter.

Philomena grunted. 'Idiots! I mean the Captain fancies Lenka, and she's marking out the boundaries.'

'No she's not!' said Peter. 'She's just *bolloxing* him. Like she does me when I don't do my homework.'

Hannah looked questioning up at Philomena. 'How do you know all this, Ena? You're only eight?'

'I read books, Hannah. Anyway, you've read *Pride and Prejudice*, too'

'*Two* . . . There's a follow up?' said Davy, before

Philomena pushed him.

'Yes, I read it,' replied Hannah. 'But I don't remember Elizabeth Bennet being that angry with Mr Darcy.'

'Grown-ups dance around each other,' said Philomena. 'Then if they don't squash each other's toes and both grin a lot, they fall in love. Text book, just like Miss Austin's novel.'

The two boys looked over at the couple arguing, as the priest had backed away. Simon had raised his palms up in an attempt to placate Lenka, but only succeeded in increasing her wrath.

'I don't see much smiling,' noted Christine.

'It's more like *War and Peace*,' said Davy. 'Not that I've read it.'

'But without the peace,' giggled Peter.

A few minutes later, Father Kent began sprinkling holy water over the bonnet of the truck, followed by a few words from the bible in the traditional Latin. Then he climbed into the driver's cabin and hung a St Christopher medal over the rear-view mirror before stepping down.

Foxy returned to the doorway with two tumblers, each containing a four finger measure of single malt and handed one to Father Kent.

Lenka gave every excited, jumping child a hug, and bent down to embrace Hannah, before climbing into the passenger seat. A huge cheer went up as Simon turned the ignition. Nothing happened.

Foxy raised his glass up to the sky. 'Dear Lord, where would we be without you?'

After a few more false starts, the truck finally pulled away leaving a trail of laughing children running in its wake.

Estelle pushed the door of Marisa's bedroom open and peered in.

'You've said your goodbyes?' asked Estelle, seeing that the elderly woman was awake.

'We did,' Marisa said and smiled, placing the darned socks on the bedside table.

Estelle sat on the edge of the bed and took the old woman's hands. 'Are we doing the right thing in letting her go?'

Marisa smiled as she wiped a tear from Estelle's

face. 'Come here.' Estelle nodded, and leaned towards her 'mother' who held her gently in her arms. 'You make it sound like we had a say in the matter.'

ROMANIA
1990

Chapter 4: The Rollicking Magician's Friend

2.40pm, 4 July 1990, Vienna, Austria

'You have a truck, yet you flew here?' said the tall black man, approaching Lenka and Simon on the runway of Vienna International Airport.

'I have generous and influential benefactors,' replied Lenka. 'Foxy said he had a contact who would help us along the way. You must be Kenneth Clayton,' said Lenka with a smile, extending her hand.

'I am,' he replied, before her hand disappeared within his. 'Some people call me Kenny, but friends call me Klay.'

The Glaswegian, a former sniper in the Parachute Regiment, was six-foot-three in height, but his build dwarfed that of the British officer, even though he was only an inch taller.

'When I asked for the register of flights coming in this morning that could carry a truck, all there was, was a British military troop carrier. I take it that Foxy had a hand in it. He contacted me yesterday morning and asked me to collect you. Did you grab any sleep on the flight?'

Simon nodded, but Lenka shook her head. 'I'm a country school teacher working in an orphanage. To be honest, all this is overwhelming.'

'I'm Captain Simon Trevelyan Syrianus,' said the British officer, extending his hand. 'I . . .' before he noticed Lenka's glance. '*We* have a number of questions, for although we know where we're going, we know little of what lies ahead. So forgive me, as you're about to be bombarded with questions.'

'Fire away,' said Klay, as they headed across the tarmac towards the main airport building.

'You're familiar with Romania, I take it?' asked Simon.

'After I left the army, I carried out a number of covert aid missions behind the Iron Curtain before it fell. I'm familiar with Eastern Europe.'

'Are we heading east together?' asked Simon.

'Not just us; we will be joining others as part of a larger aid convoy.'

'Won't that slow us down?' asked Lenka.

'In recent weeks, aid vehicles have been hi-jacked in Hungary and Romania and robbed of their cargo,' continued Klay.

'Why?' asked Lenka.

'Drugs of any description have a high value on the black market.'

'Any description?' queried Simon.

'Even horse tranquilisers are in high demand, though not for use on horses,' added Klay.

Lenka looked nervously at Simon, who appeared unmoved. She continued, 'You're a friend of Foxy's?'

'I would like to think so. He's one of those mysterious characters from the Foreign Office who pops up in the middle of a conflict. I first met the "Rollicking Magician", as we call him, when my unit and I were on a reconnaissance mission in Afghanistan. We found ourselves surrounded by angry tribal leaders. Foxy appeared out of nowhere, and the next thing we knew we were being ferried onto an air force transporter by drunken tribesmen.'

'Aren't they Muslim?' asked Lenka.

'I'm sure that after a few hours in Foxy's company,

Billy Graham would be swearing and drinking like a trooper. Two years later, when we found ourselves in similar circumstances in Iraq, there he was again. Speaking in Arabic, with his natural bon viveur, he managed to gain the confidence of our captors. Having a mobile drinks unit inside his suitcase, and an abundance of Havana cigars helped.' Klay laughed. 'He's up there with Evel Knievel and Red Adair in legendary status – at least to those in the services. Rumour has it that in one corner of his luggage he has a refrigerated icebox, would you believe. All nonsense . . . or is it?' he asked quizzically.

'Oh, I'd believe any urban myth associated with Foxy. He's one of my guardians,' said Lenka.

'With this big fellow?' said Klay, eyeing up the other man. 'You have no need of a guardian.'

'After my parents died when I was a child, your Rollicking Magician and a lovely woman called Estelle took on the roles.'

'Lucky you – not for losing your parents,' he added quickly, 'but for having someone who is as outrageously good fun as Foxy to help raise you,' said

Klay.

'What supplies are you carrying?' asked Simon

'Four baby incubators, and enough bed frames and mattresses for a neighbouring orphanage. Anyway, as I said, yesterday I received a call from Foxy. God knows how he found me, or how he knew that I was taking aid into Romania, but he asked me to meet you here.' Klay scratched his chin. 'He dealt my self-confidence a body-blow, as I pride myself on being able to move undetected.' He shrugged, as he watched Lenka's vehicle being driven down the landing ramp. 'Right, let's park up in the secure compound at the back of our hotel.'

'We're all gathered in one place?' asked Simon, sceptically.

'Relax, Captain, we're not on manoeuvres. Foxy has booked us all into the Graben Hotel.' He laughed heartily. 'This is how posh people do aid convoys, I guess. Very plush indeed. The brochure on reception says it was frequented by Kafka and other luminaries. It's just a five-minute walk from the Hofburg, right in the centre of town.'

'Nothing but the best; Foxy's trademark,' added Lenka.

'The man has style,' continued Klay, 'and after you've settled in, let's continue the Foxy tradition and go to a bar I know in town. There's a *Rogue* there I'd like you to meet.'

'A rogue?' said Lenka, with surprise. 'Why use such a term?'

'It's a name given to those individuals who drive humanitarian aid trucks into known no-go areas. Independent operators who have no allegiance to any government, or major charity, but who can transport food, clothing and medical supplies to where they are most needed. It merits a capital R, I suppose. The character you're going to meet tonight is a fully paid-up member of the Rogue fraternity.'

'Of which you are a member, too,' noted Lenka.

Klay smiled back, and then he noticed Simon's look of disapproval. 'You've had combat experience, but this isn't a war, Captain.'

'I've no combat experience, but it's common sense to know more about where we are going,' retorted

Simon. 'Particularly, as you've mentioned "no-go areas".'

'The sector of Bucharest where the building's being turned into a children's hospice, is in the gypsy quarter. It's not really a no-go area, but there are frequent clashes, as the locals despise gypsies and the gypsies live by their own law,' said Klay.

'From your introduction, I take it you never secured promotion during your time in the service. Rank never leaves you,' added Simon, curtly.

Klay opened his dinner-plate-sized hands. 'Sadly, you're right. Because of my independent streak, I was judged not to be officer material.'

'Discipline is essential in any army, and it will be on the convoy to ensure the success of our mission.'

Klay nodded at the British officer. 'Captain, you and my roguish friend are going to get on like a house on fire,' he shook his head and smiled, 'only this one will be packed with explosives.'

'As we are not leaving until tomorrow, I have to head to a base in Germany. I will be back first thing in the morning.' He stopped. 'I need to talk to Lenka in private.'

Klay turned to Lenka. 'I'll be waiting for you in Arrivals.' As he walked away, he shouted, 'See you tomorrow in the hotel, Captain.'

'I have to put the delay to good use; I have unfinished business to attend to in Berlin,' said Simon, before smiling at Lenka. 'Will you be okay?'

'I'll be fine, but Berlin sounds all very cloak and dagger. Speaking of which, Foxy said that you were asking about my parents. Why?'

Simon hesitated. 'I was interested in learning more about you. I thought that having an insight into their characters would tell me a little more about yours.'

'You asked about The Alpha Wolves, too. Why?'

Simon looked towards the aircraft. 'That was an aside. I read in the papers about the Wolves and wondered if there was a link.'

'Wolves?'

'A group of mercenaries. Anyway, it's of no consequence, I just ran out of conversation.'

'With Foxy in the room, never.'

'Are you sure you're going to be okay tonight?'

'I was all set to do this on my own, remember.'

Simon was about to turn away, but stopped. 'When I arrived yesterday everyone, including your grandmother, thought my offer to co-drive was an ideal solution. But while they welcomed me, you did not.' He paused, and spoke softly. 'I've known you less than twenty-four hours, but you're a determined young woman and it's clear that despite taking soundings from the others, you call the shots.'

'And?'

He looked uncomfortably up at the gathering clouds, before dropping his head. 'I want to help you, but you barely lifted your head up from the map on the flight. Do you want my help? Do you even like me?'

'This is not about whether I like you or not, it's about making sure that we deliver everything we promised. I know nothing beyond books, and my life at the orphanage. So, Estelle, Marisa and Foxy's opinions *do* carry considerable weight with me.'

'But what do you think of me?'

'If you're fishing for compliments, you've picked

the wrong woman. I have inherited Foxy's cynicism and Estelle's suspicious nature. Add to that Marisa's world-weariness, and you're left with one unimpressionable woman. Now is that enough for you?' she asked, looking sternly up at the British officer.

'Yes, Miss Brett,' he replied, dejectedly.

Lenka smiled. 'We're making progress; at least you're not calling me ma'am.'

2.45pm, 4 July 1990, Cork

'Good afternoon my good man. My name is Viscount Arbuthnot Foxborough, and I wish to speak to the bastard of the house.'

Before the startled, elderly butler had a chance to respond, Foxy had stepped out of the clingy afternoon mist, into the hall and placed his brown, cowboy duster overcoat over the man's arm.

'I'm sorry, Sir, but did you say bas . . . ?'

'I did indeed. My apologies for putting you in a difficult position. Can you inform your master that . . . Forgive me once again; pray what is your name, my good man?'

'Michael, Sir.'

'Well Michael, inform Mr Joseph McNamara that I wish to see him, immediately. If that doesn't work, remind him of my original greeting.'

'I'm sorry, Sir, but my master does not welcome visitors.'

'No surprises there,' huffed Foxy.

'Send the bastard Brit in,' boomed a voice from the study.

The butler nodded dejectedly. Foxy placed his hand on the man's arm and whispered, 'My apologies again for my earlier profanity; adrenaline got the better of me, Michael.'

The butler raised his bald dome and presented his hand to receive the visitor's cane.

'I'll keep it with me, as I may need it later. Your master may be so pleased to see me that he plies me with his finest whiskey.' Michael smiled politely. 'If not, it's an excellent prop when the conversation requires pepping up.'

Foxy sailed forward at a pace that, as always, was

surprising for a man standing only at five foot ten but weighing seventeen stone. He spun a sharp left into the study and locked his eyes on the elderly man sitting in an armchair by an unlit fire. Foxy said nothing as he strode in and bounced into the armchair opposite Joseph McNamara.

'I didn't say you could sit, Englishman.'

'No need, for it is patently obvious that I can,' replied Foxy, removing a hip flask from his herringbone tweed jacket. 'I brought my own, in the knowledge that I would not be offered one.' He took a swig. 'I'd offer you some, but there's always the risk that you might accept.'

McNamara's reedy, six-foot-four-long body uncurled in the chair opposite. The ninety-year-old man's nose, ears and even his chin were pinched, like the features on a plasticine face that has been pulled rather than added. Liver spots dotted his pallid skin, whilst surprisingly, his hair was unkempt and matted. Thick locks of grey hair dropped randomly from his head, like sleeping snakes on a hydra. His tweed jacket had black, leather patches on the elbows, as you would expect on a farmer. But protruding out of his left cuff was a jewelled, gold Rolex from its exclusive Crown Collection.

The image the man wished to project was of someone who had amassed considerable wealth by working the land, but his immaculately clean, symmetrical fingernails betrayed him. His sunken, deep-set eyes surveyed the man sitting opposite as he ground his thin, yellow teeth, like a wolf deciding where in its prey to bury its fangs.

Foxy scanned the walls, which were lined with the heads of various animals staring out in frozen rage. There were spaces, but he knew they were for future kills rather than family photos; there were none in the room.

'A close relative perhaps?' said Foxy, looking across at the stuffed weasel on the sideboard. 'Enchanting.'

'Another over-educated Brit, who uses big words to bewilder the common man.'

'Uncanny! I'm a civil servant and work with politicians, so it's in my job description to bamboozle the ignorant. However, you do yourself an injustice, for you are far from what is generally described as "the common man". You are one of the wealthiest men in the Republic of Ireland, son of the shipping magnate and philanthropist, Tom McNamara. Apart from the 2,000 acres that your father, a kindly gentleman I believe, bequeathed to you, he also left you commercial maritime investments across Eire that on a bad day would still leave you a millionaire.'

'I've worked hard for my wealth,' spat the old man as his long fingers dug into the armrests.

'Nonsense. I made a few telephone calls. Your assets have depleted, though ever so slightly, since you inherited your estate.'

'Again, the Brits refuse to leave us in peace, always barging in and throwing their weight about,' scowled McNamara. Foxy patted his girth and smiled as he helped himself to a Cuban cigar, manufactured in the Dominican Republic, from the cedar box labelled *H. Upmann & Co* on the table. 'And take what little we have!' roared McNamara.

Having lit the cigar, Foxy blew a cloud of smoke towards the huge, horizontal glass cabinet above the mantelpiece, framed by an array of shotguns. Foxes, wild cats and stoats, all with glass eyes and frozen in attacking poses, stared down at him. 'Oh, please don't trouble yourself that I'm here to abscond with your possessions.'

He grimaced when he caught sight of the glass cabinet behind the door, not because of the horrific expression of the stuffed wild cat on the top shelf, but because of the cheap brands of whiskey bottles below it.

'If I had a sense of humour, I might find you amusing, but I don't,' growled McNamara.

Foxy smiled. 'Have you read the Rogues comics?'

'I don't read comics,' sneered the other man. 'Especially that trash.'

'Shame, an early version of you is in them. If memory serves me correctly, Marisa discovered that you took a belt to one of the children in her orphanage and that is why she broke off your engagement.'

Reddish botches of rage erupted from McNamara's cheeks. Quickly, they spread across his goblin face and coiled like a scarf around his sinewy neck.

'And you're the Brit, along with that German bitch, who helps support Marisa's *fuken* bastards!'

'Your kindly father used to be its chief benefactor, until his widely mourned demise.'

'Kids should stand on their own two feet.'

'And you inherited how much?' McNamara clenched his fists and edged forward. 'You are known as the bastard of Cork, I hear,' grinned Foxy. 'Said ironically, no doubt.'

'Unlike Marisa's brats, my parents were married.'

'Bastard is used in its broadest sense, I believe. However, the townsfolk will have to find a more derogatory term following your latest betrayal.'

'There are different faces a wealthy man presents to the world. When he's young, he makes himself seen in all the right places to gather influence. When he has reached middle age and has amassed his fortune, he turns his attention to erasing any black marks on his name made as he accumulated his wealth. He opens fetes, becomes a school governor and provides a little funding for the most public-facing charitable projects. When's he finally reached my age, he doesn't give a *shite* what anybody thinks, and not a *fuken* jot for being called a bastard.'

'World-renowned bastard, and now kitchen-sink sociologist. I am in the presence of a polymath.'

'And I am in the company of an Englishman, and therefore someone who has more of a right to be called a bastard than I.'

'With some credibility as several Cheltenham townsfolk say I bear a striking resemblance to a chambermaid who used to work for my father.'

'The Brits and their upper classes. You live beyond your means, knowing that by pulling the tails of friends in high places your debts will be paid or waived.'

'Good God man, you really do have me down to a tee. But I'm not here for an amateur diagnosis of the English class system but . . .'

'But to run me through with the blade concealed in the barrel of your cane.'

Foxy did not show it, but he was surprised that the man knew of the lethal device in his hand, for he had never exposed it on his visits to Ireland. 'You're remarkably well informed, but putting the city out of its misery by ridding it of you is not the purpose of my visit this morning.'

'Then why didn't you hand the weapon to Patrick?'

'You have a reputation for violence,' Foxy said, as he scanned the various shotguns mounted on the walls in the room, 'and particularly the use of firearms.'

'*Yer* right,' said McNamara, as he lifted the Webley Mk V1.38 service revolver from his jacket to point it at Foxy. 'And I have no love for the Brits.'

'I know that too, as you are the paymaster general for NORAID, an organisation we believe finances the terrorist activities of the Irish Republican Army.'

Now, it was time for the other man to hide his surprise.

'Be careful what you say, as *yer* might be "accidentally" shot as an intruder, as an honest man like my manservant would confirm. With the cane found beside your dead body with its blade unsheathed, there is not a court in the Republic that would convict me.'

'Court,' laughed Foxy. 'The Secret Service knows you're a leading IRA benefactor, so I doubt you will ever trouble the courts. A night-time visit from one of our James Bond types would deal with my killer.' Foxy wiggled forward on the Harris Tweed upholstered armchair. 'Now that both of us have played our hand, we turn to a different game.' McNamara glared at his uninvited guest. 'Time for you to make amends for breaking your word to Lenka.'

'Am I to play the role of the redeemed Scrooge in *A Christmas Carol* and distribute cheap presents at the orphanage, as you do?'

Foxy feigned outrage. 'The gifts for the children are from *Hamleys* I'll have you know!' Foxy pressed the button on the handle as the cane shot up. The steel tongue of the extended blade lightly licked the vein on the wrist holding the revolver. 'But it's not too late to make a philanthropic gesture, and you have contacts that I don't have, you soulless old bastard.'

8.35pm, 4 July 1990, Vienna

Six hours after Klay had collected the young couple from the airport, he led Lenka into the Zwölf-Apostelkeller, a bar three minutes from St Stephen's

Cathedral in the heart of the city. It was the cheapest student bar in the most expensive city in Europe. The underground bar had so many levels that the lowest one had straw plugged into the gaps in the brickwork to absorb the damp.

'I don't wish to appear priggish,' said Lenka, warily. She shook her head, as the drunken karaoke singer swaying on stage yelled into the microphone. 'But a nightclub? I haven't come all this way to party.'

'Well, we are not going anywhere tonight and probably not in the morning. The Hungarian authorities are now demanding a bond for each vehicle travelling across its border,' said Klay.

'Additional insurance, perhaps, if anything happens to us inside their borders?' said Lenka.

'More likely a lever to extract more money. It happens all the time. Aid convoys are often seen as cash cows. I telephoned Foxy and he has faxed payments to Budapest for our vehicles. The permits will be faxed here by midday tomorrow, if we're lucky.'

Lenka shook her head, as she peered over at the blue-neon lit bar. 'We might as well have one drink then. But why here?'

'To meet the driver I mentioned, who's joining us on the convoy.'

'The Rogue,' noted Lenka.

'One of them, there are a couple of others.'

'What are his qualifications?' asked Lenka.

'None, apart from a Heavy Goods Vehicle licence. He's volatile, winds up everyone he meets, and has no respect for authority.'

'He sounds the opposite of what is needed for this endeavour,' replied Lenka.

'When he's delivering humanitarian aid, he's cool-headed and the best I know.'

'Better than you?' added Lenka, tilting her head cheekily.

Klay smiled. 'I'd say we are on a par, but I edge him on looks.'

Lenka frowned. 'What time do you expect him to arrive?'

'He's already here, and has been for some time, judging by the empty chairs at the front.' Klay turned to the stage. 'And this time, he's murdering *Centerfold* by the J. Geils Band.' Klay broke into a loud whistle and began to applaud the man who appeared to be crying out in pain, before turning back. 'Oh, did I mention he likes a drink and can't sing for shit!'

The singer bowed, before falling head first off the stage into the front row.

'Encore! Encore!' yelled Klay, clapping furiously. He turned back to the unimpressed woman. 'See, what did I tell you, never dull. You can take Connor Pierce anywhere, the only problem is that the authorities will want to incarcerate him.'

'Oh Christ!' muttered Lenka.

Chapter 5: Message from Hell

2.20am, 5 July 1990, Vienna

Lenka had decided not to sleep in the hotel, but to stay with the vehicle and its precious payload. Simon had returned an hour earlier, but despite his protests Lenka insisted that he should sleep in a sleeping bag within the nose of the body above the driver's cabin, as it was his turn to drive in the morning.

Being awake in the early morning was not unusual for Lenka. It was the only time she had to herself, and she would often use the time to plan lessons for the children for the following day. Sleep when it did come was a joy, as her dreams were mostly of herself as a child talking and playing with her parents.

Splayed across the seats, Lenka checked the watch she had bought from Woolworth's in Cork especially for the trip. It said 2.20. The *Tiffany & Co* eighteen-carat gold watch that had once belonged to her mother, remained in a drawer in her room at Marisa's Arms.

She decided that it was no use fretting about going to sleep and set about making some notes on the day before – the most eventful day in her life. Lenka fumbled around in the glove compartment for a pen and a piece of paper but instead found her grandmother's diary. She switched on the overhead light, pulled the blanket and the shawl Marisa had knitted for her eighteenth birthday around her, and opened the faded brown, exercise book.

The inscription inside the cover read,

'To my granddaughter(s)'

She turned the page and began to run her fingers across the beautiful script.

12ᵗʰ January 1965

To my granddaughter(s),

If you are looking for guidance on how to act like a lady, ask Marisa or Estelle. If you want to know what to wear, then ask Estelle. What I am about to write in these pages deals with survival and how to be true to yourself – though talk to Marisa and Estelle as they have a lot to tell you, too.

I am off to England in the morning, and I'm writing this in a hurry. I am not a superstitious or even spiritual woman, but I have a sense that death has finally opened its arms and is impatient to embrace me. I care little for my own fate, as it was against the odds that I would reach fifty. I fear only for your parents, Lock and Kirsten.

Therefore, as I may never meet you, with the help of a half bottle of brandy, here are a few thoughts from your grandmother – death also saves me from being called 'granny'. It's probably also time I joined Sean and we can return to knocking sparks off each other – I am sure the Devil could do with a break . . .

A glaring light forced Lenka to turn her face away. The security guard peered sourly through the windscreen. He turned his torch up at the light above her head. Lenka had forgotten that no lights were allowed after midnight, in case it attracted 'undesirables' as the receptionist referred to thieves. He was looking at Connor at the time. She raised her arm, flicked the switch and returned the cabin to the night. The officious guard carried on with his hourly patrol.

Lenka fumbled around the dashboard until she pressed the button that opened the glove compartment and placed the book inside. She lay back down across the black plastic seats and pulled the shawl and the blanket up to her chin. *So, Grandmother had a premonition that she was going to die at the hands of Delafury.*

Lenka suddenly remembered that she had to take her daily assortment of heart pills and switched the light back on. Having retrieved them from her jacket she washed them down with a bottle of Evian. Her thoughts turned to Connor and the other Rogues, as she watched the moths ricocheting off the windscreen as they frantically threw themselves towards the light. As the beam from the torch in the distance began to return, she switched off the light.

She lay down. *Simon appears lost, even afraid, like a little boy standing alone in a noisy playground. But how would he react if I reach out to him?*

7.35am, 5 July 1990, Cork

'Have the children devoured all the chocolate from Fortnum & Mason?' asked Foxy.

'Not a crumb remains,' replied Cedric, who was waiting with Foxy's three suitcases in the grand hall of

The Imperial Hotel. Foxy shook his head as he patted his stretched waistcoat. 'With so many hungry mouths to feed, too often I forget my own needs, spartan though they are.'

The driver nodded courteously. 'You are a martyr, Sir.'

Foxy smiled at the irony in the voice of the man who had been his chauffeur for nearly twenty years. As they were about to step inside the vehicle, a police car pulled up behind them.

'Sir, we need to talk to you,' said a blonde-haired man, stepping out of the car. The man, who was in his early thirties and wearing a dowdy grey raincoat, raised his warrant card up to the Englishmen's faces.

'My apologies,' said Foxy squinting to read the name. 'But . . .' scanning the card, 'Inspector O'Brien, I have an urgent meeting, and the RAF has laid on a freight carrier to take me to England.'

'It's important, Viscount Foxborough,' continued the police inspector. 'I just need a few minutes of your time.'

'Again, my apologies, but I have diplomatic

immunity and I have to go.'

The police inspector looked apprehensively at the constable, before continuing. 'I am aware of your status, sir. But I just need to ask you a few questions.'

Foxy stepped back from the car and looked quizzically at the Garda officers. 'Has something happened to Lenka Brett?'

'Not that I'm aware of, Sir.'

Foxy huffed. 'So, what is it?'

The inspector scanned the quizzical expressions of passers-by. 'Can we go somewhere more private?'

'No, my flight is in thirty minutes; say what you have to say. My chauffeur is always earwigging my conversations anyway.'

Cedric gave his employer a sly look but said nothing.

The police officer continued, 'I really think we should go inside, before . . .'

Foxy lifted his hand. 'Say what you have to say, and quickly.'

The inspector stepped forward. 'We need to ask you a few questions concerning the death of Joseph

McNamara.'

7.40am, 5 July 1990, Vienna

'Morning!' yelled Connor, as he leaped down from the matt-white, 10-tonne turbo-charged box truck. He landed on the tarmac of the secure compound at the back of the Graben Hotel. Alongside him was Klay's 18-tonne, blood-red artic. Directly opposite and facing him was Lenka's battleship-grey van. He stretched his arms out wide and yawned loudly.

Lenka and Simon were sitting in the cabin of her truck, eating bacon sandwiches made from the hotel's breakfast buffet. They looked over and nodded curtly.

Klay appeared and put a tin mug in Connor's hands.

'Jesus! Thanks for reminding me that hot coffee heats up metal,' he said, as he passed the mug from hand to hand before taking a sip.

'Sorry, I didn't bring a child's dummy with me either,' replied Klay drily.

'Harsh but fair,' replied Connor. 'They're a friendly couple,' he said, staring at the pair in the van, thirty feet away. 'Who are they?'

'You met them last night,' said Klay.

'Did I make an impression?'

'Not as much as the one you made on the drunk asleep in the front row when you toppled off the stage on to him.' Klay took a sip of the first of many coffees that day. 'I suggest you put a pair of trousers on.'

Connor looked down at his shorts, which had a picture of the Sex Pistols' 1977 album cover of *Never Mind the Bollocks!* printed on the front.

'Wars have been started for less,' said Klay.

'Fair point, and I'm not one to cause offence as you know. Who's the woman?'

'And off we go. Lenka Brett, a teacher from Ireland.'

'And cornflake packet-head?'

'Our square-jawed friend is a British naval officer, Captain Simon Trevelyan Syrianus, her co-driver.'

'Christ almighty, I wouldn't know where to begin taking the piss out of all that. I'll stick to the clockwork soldier's features.' He paused. 'Hold up! I've got it. I'll call him anus.'

Connor proudly clattered his tin mug against his friend's, before draining it.

Klay noticed that Simon's eyes were trained on Connor. He raised his eyes to the restless black clouds. 'Great, we have medical aid, food, clothing and now Connor's brought the fireworks,' he muttered. 'We may not save the world, but it shan't forget us.'

Three hours later, beside the city's largest park, the Wiener Prater, a wealthy-looking, elderly couple sneered at the dishevelled troop, eating at one of the *Schell Imbiss* snack counters. Connor, having registered their disgust, thrust his hand into a dustbin, grabbed a half-eaten sandwich and shoved it in his mouth. The couple quickened their pace.

Lenka, who was checking a map draped over the log chair opposite the one she was sitting on, looked up at Klay. 'He's nuts.'

'Yes, but he has a clean driving licence – I think!'

'If I'm ever tempted to be bi-sexual, I'll just think of you, that will cure me,' laughed a stout, red-haired woman, approaching and nodding in Connor's direction. She had just taken a spin on the famous giant 65-foot-high Ferris wheel, and consumed four cans of Carlsberg extra strong lager, Special Brew, in the process.

Connor spat the contents of his mouth out and scraped ash off his tongue. 'I wouldn't recommend eating out in Vienna, Bazooka Joe,' he said, looking up at the woman.

She tipped her red baseball cap back as she handed him a slice of Sachertorte. 'Do the world a favour and shove that in your gob.'

Connor took a bite and grimaced. 'Christ, there's enough cocoa and sugar in this to smother the taste of diesel.'

Klay stepped forward. 'Connor, let me introduce you to a good friend of mine,' he said as he splayed his right arm out towards the redheaded woman. 'Connor, meet Holey Mary. Holey Mary, meet a lunatic.'

Connor released an exaggerated sigh. 'Excellent, another God-botherer. Starving orphans will be overjoyed when we turn up and start shoving bibles down their throats!'

The woman placed her fists on her hips. 'Holey, is

spelt with an e. I got the name because I throw on what's comfortable, rather than what's fashionable. The holes in my jumpers are part of the brand.'

Connor smiled at the middle-aged woman, whose red hair was styled into long, matted Rastafarian locks. He straightened up and peered down at her torn, dishevelled, grey-woollen jumper, which was full of holes. 'You're not going to net many fish with that.'

'Looks like I've caught and landed a big-mouthed cockney dick, instead. If you're going to judge me, you should also know that I'm Welsh and a dyke.'

'I've never been so insulted in my life,' said Connor.

'Really!' said Mary incredulously.

'Average,' said Connor as he lifted his hand and twirled it as if he were holding an invisible ball – 'I was born in Belfast.'

'Average. What does he mean?' asked Lenka, tilting her head up towards Klay.

Klay sat down beside her. 'I once challenged Connor on whether what he had just told me, was the truth or a lie. He made the same hand gesture and replied, "Average".'

'A lie then!' said Lenka, laughing aloud for the first time since she had left Marisa's Arms.

Connor glanced over at Klay and Lenka, muttering with feigned solemnity, 'I'm devastated. Potty-mouth here is gay. I really thought me and her had something special going.'

Mary stared with disdain at the two men, before turning to Lenka. 'Be careful, I know Klay, and his Rottweiler is probably no different. These two believe they can pull every glamorous young woman they meet by boring the arseholes off them with schoolboy jokes and embellishing the tales of their heroic deeds.'

Lenka said nothing, only rolling her eyes before returning them to the map.

'She's been peeking at our notes,' said Connor, looking aghast at Klay. He leaned down towards Mary. 'I'll have you know that I and my good friend here,' he said as Klay placed his hand on his chest and bowed, 'have never fallen out over a woman. You see Klay is attractive to women who prefer brawn above brains.' His friend bowed even lower. 'While, I am regarded as quite a catch, by women with little or no expectations.'

Mary stepped forward, so she was toe to toe with Connor. 'And my sexuality, any problems with that you big, dumb, gobby arsehole?'

'No, but even if I did, I don't have big enough balls to admit it. However, I might risk one though and express my views on the Welsh.'

'I don't do singles,' sneered Mary. 'But if you have a problem with me being queer, I'll kick both your nuts so far up your throat that you'll be able to clean them when you brush your teeth.'

'I'm charmed,' said Connor and turned to Klay. 'You dark horse – and I'm not referring to the colour of your skin or your proportions –'

'I could not sue you for slander on either,' said Klay, with a smile.

'But where have you been hiding this little beauty?' Connor said before he turned back to smile at Mary. 'You may be gay, but my heart will always be yours.'

Mary sniffed, as she turned to Klay. 'He's a flash cockney cretin, but I guess you can't be too choosy who you work with in this game.'

'Flash Belfast prick,' interjected Connor. 'However,

I was raised in London from the age of five.'

'Talking of not being too choosy who you work with,' continued Connor. 'What's the story on the twelve-wheeler lorry over there?' she said, peering at the matt-black, Roadrunner T45 truck. TURKEY SHOOT was daubed on both sides of the truck in large, white letters, slapped on with a paint roller, with the symbol of a skull and cross bones separating the words. It was by far the largest truck among the unusual assortment of vehicles that formed the convoy.

'Anarchists from London's East End. Hackney, I think,' said Mary. 'There's two of them, a young woman and a man. Both punk rockers. They keep themselves to themselves. In terms of mixing in with respectable society, they make me look like a member of the Women's Institute.'

'They must have two heads each,' noted Connor.

'Prick,' said Mary.

'What are they carrying?' asked Lenka, taking the woman's hand in hers and shaking it. 'I'm Lenka Brett. I'm sorry that I didn't introduce myself earlier. I'm just fretting over the route and exploring alternatives in case we get snowed in up the Carpathian Mountains.'

'You're thorough. We'll make a Rogue of you yet.' Mary noticed that the other woman appeared unsettled by the word. 'I'm Holey Mary. Pleasure to meet you. God you're beautiful. Anyway, don't worry about the journey; I'll get us there and back. It's the pricks we're driving with that are the problem.'

Connor gave them both a ridiculously exaggerated smile and began waving frantically in the background.

Simon appeared. As he was the only fluent German speaker, everyone had agreed that he should go to collect the faxed documents from the Hungarian embassy. He nodded as a gesture of welcome at Mary but did not smile. 'The papers came through, but they only cover the trucks for one day into Romania. They are being amended – for a fee – and we are to collect them from the Hungarian customs office on the border.

'We all got the same bullshit when we went to pay the additional fees this morning,' said Mary, looking at the other trucks parked up on the roads.

Klay shook his head when he saw the converted ice-cream van, *'Carry On Up the Balkans,'* he muttered.

'Fantastic!' said Connor, as he slapped his hand loudly on his friend's back. 'Don't worry. None of this is real! Someone dropped a hallucinogenic drug in our coffee.'

Having overheard the conversation as he approached, Simon turned to Mary. 'Do we know what the anarchists are carrying?'

'Apart from a huge chip on their shoulders, building material. That's all I know,' replied Mary.

'I'm going to check it,' said Simon, peering over at the black vehicle.

'No, when we first joined up in London, we all agreed to respect each other's contribution to the convoy, no questions asked,' said Mary. 'Trust is everything in this game.'

'I don't like it,' snapped Simon.

Connor and Klay glanced at each other, as they had to agree with the British officer.

Eight hours later, the convoy of sixteen vehicles had covered the 300 kilometres to the Hungarian border crossing at Klingenbach, though the converted ice-cream van driven by two Italian students, Carlotta and Martina, had broken down twice.

Connor and Klay leapt from their trucks and ran to the customs office. Frustratingly, though not surprisingly, they were told that the border documents had not been faxed through.

Minutes later, Simon approached the two men, who had opened two bottles of Carlsberg and were leaning against the wall of the customs office.

'Sober, now are we,' said Simon, mockingly.

'*We?*' asked Connor. 'Were you off your tits last night, too?'

'Funny man. You had better step up to the mark. If I had my way, you would not be on this convoy.'

'Don't worry your empty little head about me,' said Connor, straightening up. 'But I'm interested to know what you intend to do if I fail to reach your high standards?'

Simon leaned forward so their noses were only a couple of inches apart. 'Seems a waste of time waiting for you to fail, because you certainly will. Perhaps, I should teach you a lesson now?'

Connor smiled, as his fists tightened.

Klay stepped forward and parted the men with his arms. 'Guys, sort out your issues once the aid has been delivered.'

Simon held his arms up, turned around and walked back to Lenka's truck.

Two hours later, with the sun slipping behind the hills surrounding Lake Neusiedl, the documents began to judder out of the fax machine inside the Hungarian customs post. Lenka appeared, having gone into town for provisions with Mary and Joe, a postman from Seville, who was driving a mail truck donated by his employer.

Connor passed her the papers for her truck. 'Thank you, Mr Pierce. We were properly introduced, but that was last night and you were so drunk that I doubt that you will remember me. My name is Lenka.'

'Yes, last night is a little hazy,' said Connor, holding out his hand. She shook it, before returning to her vehicle where Simon was watching them closely.

Klay appeared beside Connor, who matched the

British officer's gaze. 'The Englishman is probably going to get even more agitated, if he thinks you've got your eye on Lenka.'

'Good-looking woman, but not my type.'

'She's exactly your type,' said Klay.

'Usually, but there's something about her. Weird, isn't it? Maybe it was the way she was whistling when she stood next to me to take a piss in the gents, earlier.' Klay rolled his eyes. 'Anyway, what about you?' asked Connor. 'Lenka's out of your league, but worth making a fool of yourself over.'

Klay shook his head and grinned. 'Don't laugh, but I've got my eye on a Brazilian.'

'Have fun while you're down there but be careful; the hair will grow back with a vengeance.'

'Hilarious! I mean as in the country.'

'It looks like our clockwork soldier has nothing to worry about then.'

'He won't have it all his own way. That woman has steel,' added Klay. 'If it goes any further, it will be on her terms.'

Connor ripped the tops off two more beer bottles

on the side wall of the border office and passed one to Klay.

'Handsome, though, our chiselled-faced action man,' said Connor, who raised the bottle towards Simon who continued to glare at him from the truck.

'I'd say by his accent and bearing, he comes from a wealthy family,' added Klay.

'Raised on a country estate. Best friend was a border collie called Hugo.'

'And when you're not around, he has a very affable manner,' continued Klay. 'Any young lady would be proud to introduce him to her parents.'

'Three years courting then a grand village wedding.'

'Within a year, the first of four rosy-cheeked children will appear.'

'Big lad too. No doubt hung like a horse,' said Connor, before taking another sip.

'Excellent career prospects,' continued Klay, before taking another swig.

'Colonel material,' added Connor, pointing the neck of the bottle in Simon's direction. 'No, correction, major . . . no, major general.'

'Then a highly successful parliamentary career.'

'Ministerial material. Followed around by a salivating buxom secretary.'

'Yes,' sighed Klay. 'But a respectably married man and a dutiful father. Yes, the man has the lot.'

Both men raised the necks of the bottles to their mouths, but Klay stopped and smiled 'Poor bastard. It must be hard, knowing that everyone hates your guts.'

'If I didn't hate every little thing about him, I'd feel sorry for him,' said Connor with a smile.

7.45am, 5 July 1990, Cork

'Did you make the call?' asked Foxy, looking towards Cedric as he returned to the table in the lounge of The Imperial Hotel.

'The pilot can wait an hour but no more.'

'That should do,' said Foxy, rolling the half-full brandy balloon between his hands. 'Right, Inspector. I will answer your questions – and remember that I have diplomatic immunity and I am here of my own free will – but first, I have some questions of my own. What are the circumstances of Joseph McNamara's murder?'

'I didn't say murder,' replied the inspector.

'You would not have attempted to detain me, Inspector O'Brien, if the old buzzard had dropped dead of natural causes.'

'You disliked the man?'

'With every fibre of my body,' Foxy said, peering down at the stressed buttons on his robin redbreast waistcoat. 'But the British Government has not yet found a way of turning me into a lethal weapon. How did he die?'

'Shot dead, while sitting at his desk in the front room of his mansion.'

'Did Michael or any other servants, hear or see anything?'

'No.'

'How did the assailant enter?'

'He didn't. A newspaper was stuck to the window of the glass door behind McNamara, with treacle. The nozzle of the weapon, which we believe had a silencer, had been placed against it.'

'Treacle?'

'A half-empty tin of *Tate & Lyle* Black Treacle was found in the gardens.' He paused, as he leant forward and clasped his hands. 'It's manufactured in the UK and, having checked, none of the local shops sell it.' The inspector scanned the suspect's face for a reaction.

'Fingerprints?' asked Foxy.

'None.'

'Any clues?'

'Despite dying instantly at his desk, we found blood from a cut on his wrist on the carpet by the armchair next to the fireplace.'

Foxy nodded. 'Nothing else?'

'Some earlier editions of the Rogues comics were found on his desk.'

Foxy smiled. *Duplicitous to the end; so that is how the old bastard knew of the weapon concealed within my cane.*

'But nothing else,' continued the inspector. 'The killer must have observed McNamara at his desk, placed the newspaper on the window pane a little off centre, so his target was still in view as he fired one bullet into the back of the man's head. A simple, but effective execution.'

'You are here because of my visit to the house yesterday?'

'Yes, and because you sliced McNamara's wrist with the foil inside the cane you are carrying.' Foxy propped his elbow on the edge of the chair and rested his head against his fingertips. 'While Patrick, his manservant, was bandaging his master's wrist, the furious McNamara told him how you had attacked him with a sword concealed in the stick you are carrying.'

Both men glanced down at the cane. 'And you believe I came back and shot him through the window?' continued Foxy.

'I didn't say that. Nevertheless, the details of your bloody clash with McNamara are hearsay. I want to hear your version.'

'I will tell you what happened, as I am intrigued to learn more, particularly as it may have implications for the safety of Lenka Brett.'

'Your ward?'

'Former. I have to remind myself that she is a grown woman, now.'

Twenty minutes later, Foxy had completed his version of the events that took place in Joseph McNamara's sitting room but had left out the details of the man's involvement with the Irish Republican Army. Inspector O'Brien asked the usual questions.

'Did the victim have any enemies?'

'Family and anyone who knew him.'

'Acquaintances?'

'Do those he employed count? Otherwise, look up the name of his accountant.'

'What was the state of his finances?'

'Plentiful, I would say. He was a known tightwad.'

'During your meeting, he made a telephone call to his bank and transferred a large amount of money to an as yet undisclosed bank account.'

'Really?'

'He also chartered a flight. I take it you have no knowledge of these transactions?'

Foxy refrained from incriminating himself and said nothing.

'Any knowledge of McNamara's former relationships?' continued the inspector

'Apart from Lucifer, no.'

'Did you see anyone suspicious loitering near the dead man's estate?'

'Not suspicious, but I thought I passed a strikingly handsome chap in the hallway; it turned out to be a mirror.'

Flippancy apart, Foxy divulged only what he knew to already be public knowledge.

'Do you have a telephone number I could call you on?' asked the inspector.

Foxy scribbled a number down on a napkin and handed it to the police officer. 'I sense from the tone of your questions that you believe I am not the killer?'

The inspector rose up and lifted his trilby from the table, leaving the brandy that Foxy had ordered for him without asking, untouched. 'I didn't say that. But I sincerely hope you are not McNamara's killer, as you have a licence to kill and I can't lay a damned hand on you.'

Chapter 6: Cutting through the Red Tape

8.50pm, 6 July 1990, Sopron (inside the Hungarian border)

'I think the bribes we are expected to pay on this trip are about to double,' said Klay, handing his battered Leitz Binuxit binoculars to Connor. He adjusted the focus until the portacabin and the well-lit mobile barrier came into view. 'Bollocks! A shadow post?'

'Looks like it,' sighed Klay. 'We're only twenty minutes' drive from the border.'

'Greedy bastards,' said Connor. 'As if we hadn't paid them enough for the faxed documents at the border.'

Lenka lifted the binoculars from Connor's hands. 'What's a shadow post?' she asked as she zoomed in on the staging post that rudely stood out in the darkness under the glare of four freestanding lights.

'A false border crossing set up in front of, or behind the main one,' added Klay. 'They pop up along various borders to extort money from shattered truck drivers desperate to get home having delivered their aid, and the likes of us, desperate to deliver our cargo.'

'How?' asked Lenka, counting at least three men in uniform manning the barrier, all heavily armed.

'By demanding an additional toll of all convoys entering Romania,' added Mary, pulling the cap off two bottles of Pilsner and handing them to Connor and Klay, before opening one for herself. 'And that's before we receive a similar demand when we reach the official border crossing in to Romania.'

'You've come across many of these?' asked Lenka, lowering the binoculars.

'It's rare in these parts, but common in other war-torn regions,' said Mary, taking the binoculars from Lenka's hands and adjusting the focus on the lenses. 'Charities, aid trucks, are all viewed as cash cows during war, famine and any kind of crisis situation.'

Connor turned to Lenka. 'Do you ever stop asking questions?'

'Unless I've straightened up the chairs after you've collapsed into them, no.' Before Connor could respond, 'I'm not paying them anything,' Lenka said, scathingly. 'All the money we have is to buy additional supplies for the orphanage.'

'I'm with you,' added Simon, who stood beside her scanning the fake border post, but without any visual aid.

'Quite right, Captain Sensible,' snapped Connor. 'But how do we navigate our way past our friends down there, who are armed to the teeth,' he continued, nodding towards the crossing.

'We go back to the official border post and inform them of what is happening here,' retorted Simon. He glowered at Connor, 'Or do you just grease every palm held out to you.'

'Anything for an easy life, you know me, Captain Braveheart,' said Connor, with a mocking grin without looking at the officer.

'They are probably all in this together, and if we go back and cause a stink they will, I have no doubt, impound our trucks along with their cargoes,' said Mary.

'What about lodging an official complaint with the Hungarian Government?' said Lenka. 'I have a good friend, Foxy, who would make them sit up and send the police or the military to close it down.'

'I have no doubt that with Foxy pulling their ears the authorities would shut it down immediately,' added Klay, 'as it's bad for the country's image. But it may take a day or more before anyone gets out of here.'

'I'm with Lenka,' repeated Simon.

'A bit premature, but I guess you've heard that phrase many times,' mumbled Connor.

'We're not paying them a brass farthing in bribes,' continued Simon, his nostrils flared.

'Listen, Syphilis,' snapped Connor, 'sometimes you have to play the game when there's no other option and lives depend on it.'

'You deride me again, and I will not be responsible for my actions,' said Simon, fists clenched as he moved towards the man.

'Then who does take responsibility for your actions, *Slimon*? Whatever moron programmed you?' scoffed Connor, assuming a defensive stance, his arms ready to parry the first punch. 'You're very brittle, Captain Silly-Arse. You'll break easily.'

'Guys, not here,' said Klay, stepping between the two men, again. Lenka slapped her hands against Simon's chest. 'When this is over, you two can find a pub car park and sort your issues out, but now we have to find a way to get past the road block.'

Lenka took hold of Simon's arm, but he did not budge. Connor shook his head. 'Okay, I'm happy to wait until we find a pub. Then I can have a celebratory drink after I beat several shapes of shit out of Captain Fantastic, here.'

'Let's all get some sleep, it's nearly midnight, and all this macho bullshit is getting on my tits,' said Mary. 'We can decide what to do in the morning.'

6.55am, 7 July 1990, Sopron, Hungary

The next morning Lenka slipped out of her sleeping bag in the hold above the driver's cab. She began to climb across the boxes towards the back shutter, with her black, leather jacket scrapping the roof. She reached down, lifted the shutter and was instantly blinded by the blistering light of dawn. 'You two are starting early,' she shouted when she saw Klay and

Connor each bashing the tops of their *Keo* bottles on the bumpers of their trucks.

'This is a nightcap,' replied Klay, stretching his arms. 'There's no rest for the extremely wicked.'

Lenka could hear shouting in the distance. 'What's happening down there?' she asked, as she lifted her hand over her eyes to cut down the glare of the rising sun and squinted in the direction of the shadow post.

Mary appeared and Klay handed her his Redfield telescopic sight, 'Nice jim-jams,' she said, nodding at the dancing teddy bears on Lenka's pyjamas before raising the infrared rifle sight to her eye.

Lenka shrugged. 'A Christmas present from my guardian, Foxy. He must have found an outlet that specialises in clothing for four-year-olds, five feet tall and above.'

'Ah, Foxy again. I must meet him one day,' said Mary. 'He sounds a colourful character.'

'You'd better put that on anti-glare when you do,' said Lenka, and smiled, as Mary adjusted the focus and zoomed in on the fracas on the road below. 'They're going nuts down there.'

'Officials are never happy in the mornings, as they wake up and realise what a shit job they have. But this morning, I think they may be a bit angrier than usual as someone has screwed up their holiday with their mistresses on the Volga,' laughed Connor.

'What do you mean?' asked Lenka, as Klay and Connor flopped down onto a trunk. 'And where did that chest come from?'

'All I did was keep watch up here,' said Klay. 'You can thank this man,' nodding at his friend, shaking his head. 'I did warn you that the man is a Rogue.'

Mary smiled. 'I would say our Rogues here, broke into the shadow post last night and liberated the place of its ill-gotten takings.'

Klay held out his arm towards Connor, who stood up and bowed. Then both dropped down on one knee and flipped back the lid of the chest as if they were showgirls at the London Palladium, displaying piles of notes in various denominations.

The cabin door of Lenka's truck slammed so hard that only the strap around her wrist stopped the binoculars landing in the dirt.

'You idiot!' roared Simon, marching towards Connor.

Connor rose slowly and smiled. 'I hope you had a lovely sleep, while I was sorting things out.'

This time Mary stood between the men. 'Pub car park remember, you pair of wankers.'

'We're supposed to work as a unit, Irishman,' snapped the British officer.

'Sorry, I'm a Rogue. I don't do teamwork. The clue is in the name . . . Ro . . . gue!'

'Without discipline a mission will fail. I know. I have witnessed the aftermath.'

Connor leaned forward. 'Really, your men turned on you and tried to shoot you? What a surprise.' He turned his head to the side and bent it forward. 'Now where exactly was that, our little Secret Squirrel?'

'He has jeopardised the whole mission,' snarled Simon, turning to the others. He then added coldly, 'He *will* get us all arrested.'

'Maybe, but not today, Captain,' said Klay, who had picked up the eyeglasses and was training them on the border post, which was being dismantled. 'If they are, as I would expect, genuine border guards from the official customs post a few miles back, then one of them has just brought his military career to an abrupt end,' he said, handing the binoculars to Simon. 'He's just thrown a haymaker punch at his senior officer, knocking him on his fat arse.' The big man shook his closely cropped head. 'Oh dear, and as I know from my own experience, that is not a good career move.'

Two hours later, the portacabin of the former shadow post was loaded onto a transporter and driven away. Klay made his way back to his vehicle, and stopped next to Connor, who was topping up the oil in his truck's engine. 'Do you have to keep ribbing the Captain?'

'I'd be a hypocrite if I tried to hide my dislike of the sanctimonious dick.'

'And the name calling?'

'Name-calling is childish and certainly not the best way to resolve a difficult situation.'

Klay raised his eyebrows, 'But . . .?'

'It's always an option, though,' Connor said, and smiled.

'We need to get on as we have a job to do. Perhaps you can park your dislike for him until this is over.'

'Okay, I'll try. But, he's an icy character and only rattled when ridiculed. He's hiding something, and I want to shake him up and find out what it is.'

'Why?'

'I don't trust many people, and if he wants us to work as a military unit, he will have to earn my trust. I don't give a shit about him judging me, but he has divulged nothing about himself or why he's here and that makes me uneasy.'

'He's after Lenka, and by joining her on this mission he hopes to win her over. And you're one to talk. You've done some pretty crazy things to impress women. Remember when you volunteered to be shot out of a cannon in the circus in Antwerp. You thought it might get you closer to Rosy, the circus' voluptuous ringmaster?'

'Yes,' grinned Connor. 'I got nowhere though.'

'Nonsense, you travelled at least a hundred and fifty feet.'

'One hundred and seventy feet; I bounced off the

net.' He sighed. 'I'll keep my distance, though.' He slapped his friend on the shoulder. 'But there is something about that clockwork toy soldier that isn't right.'

'We discussed that: he's too damn good-looking for his own good,' laughed Klay.

'Yes, that's it. The git!' said Connor with a smile. 'Beer when we cross the Romanian border?'

'Of course. Anyway, try and give the Captain a little leeway as perhaps he's trying to find his feet. Remember, he said that all this was new to him.'

'Oh, really?' said Connor. 'Okay, I'll try to build bridges. Maybe I'll ask Captain Bambi to join us for that beer.'

The Rogues returned to their vehicles. The engines shuddered into life and they trundled down towards the main road in the direction of Romania.

9.30am, 9 July 1990, Cenad (on the Hungarian-Romania border)

It took a day and a half before the convoy, along with hundreds of other trucks and cars, was allowed through by Hungarian border officials. Any elation was soon brutally extinguished by Romanian border police two days later, who informed them that it would take a further two days before they would be allowed to enter the country.

All the drivers, except Lenka and Simon, partied in the bar erected between the border posts. It shared ten per cent of its takings with the border guards on both sides.

7.20am, 10 July 1990, Cenad (on the Hungarian-Romanian border)

'Lovely morning, Princess, my little cuddly bundle of delight,' said Connor, as Mary emerged with a hangover from the back of her truck.

'Bollocks! I'm off for a piss,' she replied, scratching her head and backside in tandem as she passed.

Connor handed Klay a mug of tea and the men sat down on a log beneath a sign that read 'NO MAN'S LAND'.

'Do you ever have a hangover?' asked Klay.

'At the moment, I have a sledgehammer in my head on fast spin.'

'The echoes must be deafening.'

'You're always there for me,' said Connor drily. 'Did I disgrace myself?'

'Naturally,' replied Klay.

A startled, scabby black and white mongrel barked, before Mary leapt out of the bush where it had been sleeping.

Connor waved, and Mary extended her middle finger and raised it in response, before heading off towards some trees.

'I said the wrong thing at the wrong time, again?'

'Worse.'

'Pissed my pants?'

'Far worse.

'Shit my pants?'

'Far worse!'

Connor clapped his hands, 'Oh please tell me that I knocked *Slimon* on his ass?'

'You're not even close.'

Connor took a sip of coffee and shook his head. 'Ah, *Centerfold.*'

'You need to get that tune surgically removed from your head. You're not just murdering it, you're slowly

119

torturing it and us along with it.'

'The lyrics have personal significance.'

'An ex-girlfriend posed nude for *Playboy*?'

'The British equivalent, or near as, she made a porn video, *Bored Welsh Housewives of Pres-that-in!*'

'I'm not up on films. Was Meryl Streep in it?' asked Klay.

'Might have been as she's good on accents, though there weren't many speaking parts.'

The young woman, who co-drove Turkey Shoot, fell backwards, as she was climbing out of the driver's cabin.

'Morning gorgeous,' greeted Connor, as the punk rocker dusted the dirt off her canvas trousers and stumbled past the two men.

'Fucking cretin!' she replied, before disappearing behind a wall of rubble.

'Cretin is starting to stick,' noted Connor, taking a gulp of coffee.

'Easy to see why,' said Klay, drily.

'You should get a job with the Samaritans.'

'How's it going on the woman front by the way?'

asked Klay.

'As you can see, swimmingly!'

'Maybe you should try men.'

'No thanks, but nice of you to offer,' said Connor, edging away along the log from his friend.

'Very funny. I told you I've met a Brazilian beauty,' said Klay.

'Ayrton Senna?'

'Claudia.'

'Men not my scene,' continued Connor. 'Touching some hairy-arsed, flatulent, half-wit, no thanks.'

'You mean someone like you?'

'Exactly. It would almost be like masturbating.'

'Better get used to it,' shouted the female punk rocker, reappearing from behind the shattered wall.

Both raised their metal mugs in her direction.

'Her name is Sasha by the way,' said Klay. 'Just turned eighteen yesterday, she told me last night.'

'Well at least she's legal to drive that rig now,' Connor said as he nodded towards the menacing-looking articulated vehicle. 'No, wait, I remember now. We were dancing together last night?'

'Yep. The guy, Rat, wasn't happy.'

'Why, are they together? I wasn't after her by the way, as I'm at least ten years older.'

'Fifteen! Anyway, I don't think it was that. More likely, he was pissed off when his drink went flying; both of you were on the table at the time.'

Connor laughed. 'Yes, I remember now.' He turned to his friend. 'You're serious about Claude, aren't you?'

'Claudia,' he said, looking up at the sky. 'Come to South America. I'd like you to meet her; then you'll understand why.'

'I'll start writing my best man's speech.'

'You do that.'

'Really?'

Klay nodded and smiled. 'Yep. She's the one; that's if she'll have me.'

Connor slapped his friend on the back. 'Of course she will, but you do know it's illegal to marry someone in a coma.'

Chapter 7: Suffer the Children

10.20am, 12 July 1990, Bucharest, Romania

'I drink hard, because life is shit.' There was no anger in Connor's voice, only acceptance.

He watched Lenka, who was sitting on the bed opposite, wiping tears from her cheeks as she cradled an immobile but awake four-year girl. Sixty or more children were rocking back and forward around them. The children's ward was one of ten within the grey walls of Orillia orphanage, all packed with anguished children. They were cared for by a few staff whose spirits were broken by the pain and death around them and the apathy of officials beyond its walls.

The boy on Connor's lap was seven, maybe eight years old. Nobody knew, as he had been left in front of the orphanage that morning without any message or any form of identification. The boy was wrapped in a large, clean, white towel having been bathed by Carlotta and Martina, who had tagged along with the Rogues. They had travelled to Romania purely with the aim of helping someone, somehow. Once they reached the outskirts of the city, Turkey Shoot and the other vehicles had dispersed towards other orphanages.

The boy began to defecate into the new nappy, as he continued to tear at the sores that covered his body. Connor, with Lenka's help, quickly cleaned him and changed him. Within minutes, the boy was quietly rocking on Connor's lap again in the middle of the crowded room.

Lenka turned to look at Klay who was helping to change the mattresses on the beds for new ones. Carlotta, Martina and some of the local nurses and orderlies were washing the walls and floors.

'You've seen this kind of thing before, Connor?' Lenka asked.

The man nodded. 'I've delivered medicine to many hospitals around the country in the last six months, and trust me, this is far from the worst.'

Lenka looked down at the girl and knew that at least here she had a better future.

'The nurse that let us in, Carol, said this was a children's orphanage, but it isn't,' said Connor.

'What do you mean?'

'It's a children's hospice in all but name.'

'I still don't understand.'

'I would say that most of the children here have been inoculated or injected with something to cure a particular aliment during their time here. Until Carol and Anita arrived, it was a death sentence. Not in a deliberate way. AIDS is a new phenomenon. With no fresh syringes or needles, AIDs has been spread to epidemic proportions throughout institutions such as this in Romania and Albania.'

Connor looked around the ward and finally down at the boy and feigned a smile. 'AIDS will kill many here.'

Lenka looked around the room, with a mixture of bewilderment, sadness and anger.

Over in the far corner, Klay had amassed an audience of inquisitive eyes, as he stripped beds and replaced them with clean sheets from his truck. He had been the subject of similar looks before on aid missions to Eastern Europe. *Were their looks of wonder due to his size or that he was the first black man they had ever seen?* He met each tentative look with a smile.

The little girl in Lenka's arms clung onto her orange cardigan tightly with both hands. When she had first lifted the girl up on to her lap, she had asked Anita, a nurse from Naples, her name. The nurse had given her the name Helen, but like most of the children in the hospital, no one knew their real names or ages.

Simon appeared in the doorway. He spotted Lenka and walked over to her. 'Do you think you should be holding the child? One of the nurses has just told me that AIDs is rife here. A bite or scratch might infect you.'

She said nothing and continued to cradle the child in her arms.

The British officer sat down beside her and lifted the little girl into his arms. 'Let me hold her. I was only thinking of you and that you need to make sure that you don't spread disease to the children back in the orphanage in Ireland.' He took Lenka's hand. 'Perhaps you should go and talk to Carol and make a list of what else this facility requires before we leave?'

Anita appeared. 'Helen barely moves, she won't bite or scratch you, Lenka, but we would be grateful if you could make a list of what we need for the future.'

Lenka nodded, squeezed the man's hand, before kissing the child on the head and heading over to the office.

Connor and Simon, each with a child rocking in their arms, glared at each other.

'How kind of you to finally descend to earth and join humanity; unless of course your little gesture was purely to impress the lady,' said Connor.

'You see the worst in everything I do, Irishman.'

'Perhaps, but you had better relax your grip on the back of the girl's neck before I do it for you.'

'Do all the children have HIV or full-blown AIDS?' asked Lenka.

Carol, who was sitting opposite her, behind a rickety desk, was in charge of the eight nurses who had arrived in Bucharest in April. They were all volunteers who worked for the international charity, Nurses Abroad, who supported staff in orphanages across the globe.

'Anita and I arrived with a large consignment of syringes and needles so recent arrivals should be fine, unless they have come from another orphanage. I thought we had enough for six months, but conditions are far worse than we were led to believe. We have only enough for two weeks at most, but you have 5000 in boxes in your van, you say.'

'I'll unload them next.'

'With more on the way next month, we have a real chance to stop HIV and hepatitis spreading.'

'Can you compile a list of what else you need here?'

'I will, straight after I put together your paperwork.'

'Thank you. What else can we do to help whilst we're here?'

'I need the Rogues to get the basics up and running. Connor's got the lights working again in the kitchen, but the heating system is knackered – in fact I'm not sure it ever worked as the boiler looks completely rusted up to me.'

'Then?'

'Renovate the building your Irish friend Estelle . . . sorry, what's her surname?'

'Rudger, she's German.'

'Has bought in the gypsy quarter so that we can transfer some of the children there. Then we can start turning this place into a preparatory centre. We can feed, clean and make a proper diagnosis of their mental and physical heath, before sending them to facilities like Estelle's and others that can offer the appropriate care.'

Lenka nodded. 'We'll keep the aid coming.'

Carol smiled. 'We'll need it. Since we arrived, we have been inundated with the most severe cases of trauma from other orphanages. Nurses Abroad, UNICEF, Save the Children, Oxfam and others' aim is to turn these,' as she looked at the walls with disgust, 'storage boxes to hide children, into proper homes. Then the children can finally laugh, play and breathe clean air.' She stopped herself from adding 'again'.

'We have also brought boxes of antiseptic, bandages and nappies, which we'll unload before we go. Klay has four baby incubators on his truck. We also have two industrial dishwashers in our vehicle. Simon, Klay and Connor will bring one in once the children are asleep.

'Klay could do it by himself. I must thank him for the new bed frames and mattresses. Did your friend Estelle purchase all these?'

'Klay has connections with several large charities, and his supplies, as well as the truck, were surplus from a recent relief mission organised by the Red Cross in the Philippines.'

'And Connor's brought the heavy lifting gear. He told me he has friends in the building business who also donated the truck he's driving. New beds, fresh bedding, proper medicine, cleaning gear, sterilising equipment and a little love make all the difference here, but it's going to take a long time to mend the emotional scars these children are carrying.' She looked out into the ward. 'You noticed the rocking?'

Lenka nodded sadly.

'No doubt, you've seen it in animals at the zoo. A symptom of the stress and anguish caused by captivity,' added the nurse, rubbing her troubled brow.

'You know the Rogues?' asked Lenka.

The furrows on the nurse's forehead disappeared.

'God, yes. There have been times when I have found myself in the middle of hell, with absolutely nothing to help the children around me. Thankfully, Connor, Klay or the other benevolent mavericks we call Rogues, would often appear out of nowhere and get to work.' She tilted her head back and laughed. 'It's not just the aid that's needed. They bring hope and raise the spirits of relief workers like myself, despite the shit they find us in.'

Lenka peered out at Connor. 'Klay said it's never dull with a Rogue around.'

Carol dropped her head and sighed. 'Many years ago, when I first volunteered for relief work, I was in a medical tent in Somalia. I was on the verge of throwing the towel in. I felt so helpless. Children were pleading for milk I did not have and were dying in my arms because of it. Suddenly, our friend Holey Mary appeared with a wheelbarrow loaded with bags of powdered milk and sachets of water purification tablets.'

The nurse leaned forward and rested her hands on the table. 'Today it's Romania. This place is falling in.

Connor's doing a fantastic job, as there's nothing he can't get up and running. But we urgently need building supplies. Thankfully, a building firm in Doncaster, my hometown, have offered to send over some of their bricklayers, plumbers and electricians next month. People have been extraordinarily generous. It does restore your faith in humanity.'

Lenka turned around to peer at the children through the glass panels of the office. 'Where was the humanity here?'

'It was in the staff that work here, Mihai, Andreea, Alina, but no one beyond these walls helped until they hung the president, Ceaușescu. The bastard got off lightly,' continued Carol, with venom. 'Ceaușescu and his cronies wanted Romania to become a great economic power, but they didn't have the industrial might of the Russians. They thought they could do it the Chinese way, by creating a massive labour force. Families were forced to have more children to create an army of workers, but most families were already struggling to feed the children they had. The fruits of the labours of their communist masters is what you see around you.'

Carol leaned forward and began writing again. 'Anyway, I'm a nurse not an economist, all I know is that the children became an embarrassment when the cameras turned up . . . Actually, the children still are. Many in the new government want them to simply disappear. I'm surprised they don't send in the equivalent of . . .' She stopped. 'Damn! This one isn't signed.' Carol lifted the *Collins* English/Romanian dictionary from the table and flipped through the pages. 'Good! No one is going to look too closely at this, as it's for the toilet cisterns.' She began to trace the signature from another document into the blank space above the word *semnătură*.

'Crossing the borders was a nightmare,' said Lenka as she saw Anita comforting a little brown-haired girl who had just head-butted the wall.

Carol returned to the task of adding the official papers she had secured from the Ministry of Internal Affairs to Lenka's file of official documents. After a while, she smiled and looked up.

'Lucky you.'

'Lucky?'

'Your captain out there; he's gorgeous. He's got the body of a swimmer,' grinned Carol.

'He's not my captain,' replied Lenka, as she looked across at her co-driver who was sitting silently with the little girl asleep in his arms.

Carol plonked her elbow onto the desk and rested her head on her hand. 'Ah, I'm a happily married frumpy thirty-nine-year old, with two teenage boys, but I can daydream about a jump in the hay with him.'

Lenka wondered at the lack of emotion in Simon's face. *I know little about him, but I know he has not experienced much warmth in his life.*

'I'm only joking, Lenka, please don't say anything.' Then she sat up. 'Oh, you're not a lesbian, are you? Sorry, I didn't mean that to sound derogatory.'

Lenka continued to stare at Simon who caught her look and smiled. 'No, I don't think I am.'

'Mary's one of my best friends,' continued Carol, clearly flustered.

'It's okay. I know what you meant.'

Carol carried on checking the files and inserting

signed official papers inside them.

'Anita has a soft spot for Connor,' said Carol. 'We heard that he was delivering insulin recently, but we were not on his itinerary. I met him briefly when I was working for Médecins Sans Frontières in the Sudan during the famine, three years ago. He turned up with pumping equipment and worked around the clock. Within two days, he had dug a well and we finally had water. When he'd finished and learnt we had no alcohol, he produced a litre bottle of Smirnoff Blue Label vodka from a secret compartment in the roof of his truck and launched an impromptu party. In the morning, he was gone.'

'He's surprisingly resourceful, behind his hedonistic façade,' added Lenka.

'Anita knows him better than I do. She first met him in Albania two years ago. She had just arrived in Tirana and he was on his way to deliver medical supplies to a number of hospitals. He offered her a lift to the orphanage where she was going to work. When they arrived, she said he nearly ripped down the Iron Curtain when he saw the appalling conditions in the orphanages. After he delivered his supplies across the capital city he returned and helped her get the basics, light, heat etc. back up.' She smiled as she shook her head. 'Incredible, really, that he managed to get food and medicine into a country that is less accessible than North Korea – God does love a Rogue!'

Carol stood up when she saw a stout, middle-aged woman entering the ward carrying a box of toys. 'Mary, brilliant!'

'When did you last see her?' asked Lenka.

'A few years ago, I worked in a favela in Rio. Mary delivered some food aid. God that woman could drink even a northern lass like me under the table. She's got bigger balls than any man I've ever met.' As Carol went to greet her old friend, she stopped. 'How strange; before I noticed that the signature on the paper was missing, I was about to say "the death squads in Brazil".'

'Sorry, Carol, you've lost me.'

'A few minutes ago, I said the authorities simply want these children to go away. In Brazil, a few years ago, there were death squads who hunted down and murdered street children.'

'I've heard of this. Is it true?'

'Sadly, yes. Just ask Mary, she was there when the killing was at its height.'

Lenka stared out of the office window. *Man's inhumanity to man, the saying goes. But look what they do to the children.*

'Thanks for all your help again here, and with the new orphanage,' said Carol. 'Sorry for going on. We're so busy, we just never get a chance to have a natter.'

Lenka forced a smile. 'No problem, and at least there are no death squads here.'

'No, but there are always the Wolves,' said the nurse before leaving the office to embrace her old friend.

Lenka leaned forward as she lifted her hands up and joined them as if in prayer and placed them over her mouth and nose. She turned to look through the glass panel at Carol and Mary laughing, then at Klay and finally Connor. *They were few, but the Rogues had been involved, one way or another, in aid missions across the globe. And that word Wolves again. Had the Rogues heard of them?*

Her eyes fell on Simon once more. *The Wolves that he had asked Foxy about, really did exist. But who were they? Where were they?* She began to bite on her lip. *Rogues! Wolves! Grandmother's diary! The further I travel from home, the more the past ensnares me.*

'I have never seen faces looking at you in awe before, so don't open your mouth and spoil it,' said Connor, still holding the boy asleep in his arms.

'I always miss your humour when we go our separate ways – visual humour of course,' replied Klay.

The children around them could not take their eyes off Klay.

'I was thinking that maybe they've never seen a black man before,' said Klay, as Anita appeared beside them.

The Italian nurse smiled. 'I heard a little girl say *gigant robot.*'

'So, big man, you've already opened your gob,' said Connor, smiling at the nurse.

'And how are you, Connor? You just dashed in and started working on the generator, before I had a chance to say hello,' said Anita.

Klay turned towards his friend, away from the nurse and mouthed silently: 'She loves you.'

Connor turned to the nurse. 'Sadly, my life is my work. If only I could find someone to share it with.' He jutted out his bottom lip and peered down pathetically. 'Fancy a drink later?' he asked gleefully, retracting his bottom lip.

'No.'

'Ah,' said Connor, as he turned his head away from Anita and mouthed to his friend silently, 'You know shit about women.'

'Seriously,' said Connor turning back. 'It's great to see you again, Anita. Whenever there are children who need help, you and Carol can be found in the thick of it.'

'That's our job. We've been here two months, supporting the staff who were doing their best with absolutely no help whatsoever from the authorities. We were about to run out of the essentials until you all arrived this morning. We've had to wash the children in cold water, as the boiler is broken.'

'I have two in my truck; I'll fit one now. The other

is for the new orphanage,' said Connor. 'With all the expertise around us, we will soon have the other orphanage up and running.' He bent his head to look into Anita's blue eyes, and said softly, 'I'm sorry for hitting on you. Very unprofessional. Do you forgive me?'

'Dinner would be nice. It's just if we go drinking, you'll make a complete idiot of yourself, jump on the table and start singing, "*I'm Still Standing*" before falling off.'

'November 1988, the Tirana International. I bumped into you both there,' said Klay, before laughing loudly.

Connor looked genuinely puzzled. 'You were both there?'

Anita shook her head, while Klay laughed even louder. The children leaned forward in their cots, as they had never heard robot laughter before.

'And in Mogadishu, last July,' added Anita, raising her eyebrows.

Connor noted her dubious look. 'I'll have you know that I am not the same man.'

'True, he's singing *Centerfold* these days,' added Klay.

'Oh, thanks for pointing that out,' said Connor, raising his eyes.

Carol wrapped her arms around Klay from behind and pressed her face against his broad back. 'Good to see you, big man.'

He turned, bent down to embrace her and kissed her on top of her head. The children's eyes widened.

'You too, you lunatic,' Carol said as she turned to embrace Connor. 'Mary says it's the first time she has ever met you. How can that be, you can be heard from the moon.'

'She must have gone underground these last few years, after her personal stylist committed suicide.'

'Still a prick!' said Mary, stepping into the circle of Rogues. 'After we find the hospital that Lenka is hoping to renovate and unload the medicine and supplies, I suggest that we all head to the International to celebrate this unique reunion of Rogues.'

'Then dinner,' added Anita, glancing at Connor.

'For once I don't feel a song coming on,' said the Irishman, returning her look.

As they made their way back to their various tasks on the ward, Anita whispered to Mary, 'Wonderful to see you again, but I still don't understand English humour.'

'That's because you're a grown-up,' said Mary.

Behind them, Klay began to take sharp, jutting steps, rotating his head and body as his arms moved up and down sharply. One child turned to a smaller boy, nodded and whispered, '*Prietenos*' (friendly) '*robot.*'

Three hours later, with Klay's help, Connor had installed a new boiler and hot water was finally flowing through the taps.

Lenka took one last look at Carol and Anita and the Romanian staff as they continued to care for the children. Children, who were rocking, pulling at healing scabs, theirs and others, and looking blankly at nothing.

Simon joined her outside as the others prepared the trucks to move on to the building three miles away that Estelle, with Foxy's help, had purchased. Lenka watched each Rogue, as they reloaded the essential building supplies for Estelle's orphanage, conversing and sharing jokes. *They looked unaffected by the plight they had witnessed. Others might think that they had seen so much suffering that they were immune to it, but Connor's confession on why he drank had exposed the price they paid for the help they brought.*

Lenka continued to stare at the building, as Simon turned the key and angrily woke the engine of her truck. She thought of the children back in Marisa's Arms. Her tears ran freely as she thought of their knowing winks, scrubbed rosy cheeks and mischievous smiles.

Chapter 8: Righting All the Wrongs in the World

5.20pm, 12 July 1990, Bucharest

It took little over an hour to unload the contents from the two trucks and the van, and carry them into various rooms in the crumbling building being renovated on Strada Zabrautului. After WWII, the area was renamed Sector 5 by the country's new communist rulers, who divided the city as if in accordance with an Orwellian nightmare.

If it were not for the assistance of the security guard and eight local builders that Estelle had employed through Foxy's contacts, they would have been working into the night. Connor offered bottles of beer to the others from a crate in his truck. Simon ignored the offer, Klay smothered a beer in his hand and Mary removed the lid of hers with her teeth. Lenka nodded politely but squirmed as the other woman spat the lid out along with a fragment of tooth, before taking a swig from her bottle. The Romanians broke into raucous laughter before raising their *Keos* in a toast to Mary. Carol, Anita and the security guard declined Connor's offer of a drink, but the Italian nurse whispered, 'I have to help put the children to bed, so I'll see you in the restaurant of the Intercontinental around 10 tonight.'

The nurses were given a lift back to the Orillia orphanage by the security guard, and as it was nearly dusk, the local labourers began to drift home in various directions.

The Rogues completed the final security checks of their vehicles and, as always, removed the distributor caps to ensure they were completely immobilised.

A matt-black Chevrolet wobbled towards them along the unlit pot-holed road, lined by other run-down residential blocks. It came to a halt in front of Lenka and the others. The driver jumped out and opened the back door. A short, overly developed muscular man, seemingly without a neck, wearing a black, leather jacket that had ridden up over his ample stomach, emerged from the vehicle. He opened his arms wide. 'I come to secure building. Secure contents,' he said in staccato English.

Klay straightened up, but unsurprisingly, Connor spoke first. 'That's very kind of you, but we could not take up your offer without offering free tea and biscuits in return for your generosity.' He turned his ear towards the man. 'Sorry, I didn't get your name.'

'Bulla. I rephrase offer. You will pay 1000 deutschmarks now,' he said as he directed the men who exited the car to pan out. He shrugged his shoulders, 'or contents disappear.'

Through the open door of the car, Lenka noticed a tearful, young girl sitting in the back seat, whose wrist was secured to an armrest by a belt.

Simon strode up to Bulla. 'Of course we need security as the building is unoccupied, but we were going to come to an arrangement with the police.'

Lenka looked up in surprise at her co-driver, but said nothing.

Klay and Connor each selected one of Bulla's men to square up to, while Mary removed a spanner from the toolbox on her truck and walked towards the remaining gangster.

'Now give you security demonstration,' turning to

his men, who immediately lifted their jackets to expose automatic pistols wedged into their overly tightened belts.

'Is the girl in your car your daughter?' demanded Lenka, taking one pace ahead of Simon.

'I have three. Why I need more?'

'Then who is she?' demanded Lenka, as Simon stepped behind her.

'Lenka, this is not our business,' whispered the Englishman, as the Rogues edged towards the vehicle while keeping the henchmen in their sights.

Lenka tried to calm the rage in her voice. 'Who is she?'

'*Mis*,' said Bulla, shaking his head. 'You think I have relations?' He turned and smiled, which triggered laughter from his men, exposing three sets of tobacco-stained, chipped teeth. Bulla turned back and looked coldly at the blonde-haired Irishwoman. He splayed his arms out wide. 'I trader. No mix business and pleasure. Unless whore your age.'

Lenka's mouth opened as she turned towards the car, 'Trad . . . er!' She spun around and lifted her arm, but Simon seized her wrist. 'Lenka, he has his hand on a knife in his pocket.'

'Good, Englishman!' said Bulla, lifting his hand from his pocket, exposing the flick knife cradled inside it.

Lenka spun around. 'He's trading in young girls!'

'Let's not discuss this now,' said Simon softly. 'Our prime objective is to secure the building and our aid.'

Bulla turned around and eased himself into the car next to the young girl. 'Too much emotion. Caru' cu Bere club tonight. Bring 1000 deutschmarks. We agree security,' he said as he signalled his men to return to the car.

Simon released Lenka's arm. She ran towards the Chevrolet as its wheels spun, and its driver swung it around. Once again, it rocked along the pockmarked road, heading back to the wealthiest part of the city.

An hour later, in the back room of the building, Lenka appeared in the doorway of the room where Simon was rolling out his sleeping bag on the bare floor. 'I don't understand you!'

'There's nothing complex about me,' said Simon,

quietly. 'I am what you see,' said the man as he walked towards her.

'You did nothing to help us free the girl!'

'Bulla's men did not carry guns simply for show. If you and your friends had tried to seize the girl a gunfight would have broken out, and the girl would have been caught in the middle of it.'

'Is that really it?'

'Yes.'

'I so want to believe you.'

'Why?'

'Because, I don't want to fall for someone without a heart.'

The man looked at her and raised his arms to gently take her hands. 'I do have a heart, it's just that I'm not very good at showing emotions.' He squeezed her hands. 'Teach me, Lenka. This is all new to me. Help me.'

Lenka looked up into his pained face. 'Simon, we must help that girl.'

'My first concern is your safety; if we start a war here with Bulla, you may get hurt.' *He looks genuinely frightened, but is his fear for me or for himself?*

Lenka pulled away from his arms. 'Let's talk tomorrow. It's been a long day and I'm tired. I'm going to bed.'

'Okay. It's sunset, but we're all shattered.'

'Night Simon,' as she shut the door behind her.

Lenka heard the metallic sound of something being assembled in the room opposite hers.

'Are you mad?' said Lenka as she peered into the room and saw Klay cleaning the barrel of a snub-nosed .38 special colt 'Fitz special' with a pencil wrapped in a linen handkerchief, dipped in linseed oil.

'Yes, ask anyone who knows us,' answered Connor, as he flicked Bulla's extended switchblade into the air and caught it by the handle with his other hand.

'But . . . a gun!' spluttered Lenka, incredulously.

'I keep the pieces in a sealed plastic bag, which is just small enough to squeeze through the cap of the fuel tank of my vehicle. Insurance is hard to come by in this line of work,' replied Klay, as he continued to clean the mechanism around the hammer spur.

'We're freeing the girl so arm up, or tuck yourself

into bed, your choice,' said Mary.

'It's none of our business,' said Lenka, stepping into the room.

'You've changed your tune. Five minutes ago, you wanted to free her. Why the change?' asked Mary.

'The girl is a prisoner, we can't ignore it,' added Klay, as he screwed the wooden side plates onto the butt.

'Look,' said Lenka, firmly. 'We can't right all the wrongs in the world.'

'You sound like Major Calamity next door. Are we playing a game of "Simon says" now?' mocked Connor.

'Well, he's right. If a firefight had erupted outside, the girl would have been caught in the middle. And you know as well as I do, this place, and probably Carol's orphanage, would have been burnt to the ground.'

Mary straightened up. 'So we just leave the girl with those bastards?'

'Sacrifice the girl, so we can build this place,' said Connor, tapping his chin with his fingertips as if in thought. 'Bollocks! Not a firm foundation, if you ask me,' said Connor, launching the blade and embedding it dead centre into the cross panel of a door. 'Maybe we can name the orphanage after the poor girl, to make ourselves feel better.'

'It's for the greater . . .' began Lenka.

'Spare me,' snarled Connor. 'For the greater good, always means sacrificing the innocent. What's got into you? We thought you were one of us.' He eyed Mary as she dropped down and began to wrench something out of her rucksack. 'A baseball bat?'

Mary patted the bat in her hand. 'We may need stealth to neutralise the first ones.'

Connor smiled. 'Ah, my little sweet pea, I was right to love you all those *days* ago.'

Mary laughed, as she wrapped her scarlet bandana around the grip. 'I'm starting to like you, Irishman. If only you had tits.'

'I don't work out much so be patient, I'm sure I'll develop a pair in a couple of years.'

Klay smiled at his friend's irony, as Connor, when he was sober, would often train through the night.

Lenka shut the door behind her. 'It's all one big joke; one big adventure,' she spat. 'Is this what it's like to be a Rogue?' Lenka stepped into the semi-circle of Rogues. 'You may be the experts when it comes to transporting aid and crossing shadow borders, but when children are involved, violence is *never* the solution.'

'Okay,' said Klay, slipping the gun easily into the coat pocket of his British army combat jacket. 'The least we can do is hear you out.'

Lenka scanned their faces as she spoke. 'Bulla described himself as a trader and said he was not going to touch her. I believe him.'

'You believe him, because he's a morally upright citizen?' said Mary, ironically.

'No, it's because he views her as saleable goods. It was clear that he is a businessman, first and foremost. She is simply an asset and he will therefore do nothing to depreciate her value.'

'Oh, that's all sorted then,' said Connor. 'I'll start painting the toilets in the morning – something light, maybe a pastel shade.'

Lenka refused to be silenced and turned to Klay. 'I will contact Foxy. You know him. He can achieve the impossible and, if anyone can free the girl, he has the influence to do so.'

Klay turned to the others. 'It makes sense.' Mary and Connor folded their arms, exchanging looks as they leaned against the unplastered walls. 'Okay, Lenka,' nodded Klay. 'Foxy has one day to free her. If by this time tomorrow she is still Bulla's prisoner, I'm going in.'

'And I am going to batter the fucking lot of them,' added Connor.

'You won't be alone,' added Mary, swinging the bat as if warming up.

'Okay! One day,' said Lenka. 'And that means we all stay here, that no money will be paid to Bulla and that no one goes to the Caru' cu Bere tonight.'

Three hours later, Klay entered the Caru' cu Bere, the gothic-designed bar on Stavropoleos Street. The oldest bar in Bucharest, with its époque décor and brilliantly bright stained-glass windows, had been the arena for many passionate and violent encounters. Tonight it

155

was packed with wealthy customers, served by officious waitresses, briskly manoeuvring around oak tables dressed in peasant girl garb.

'I can handle this myself, stay out of this,' said Lenka, firmly, as Klay approached the table where she and Bulla were sitting.

'Yes, I can see that,' said Klay. 'You two look like you are about to conclude your negotiations,' as he sat down on a chair at their table.

Klay stared at the crime boss who had the woman's wrist gripped in his tobacco-stained fingers and a large roll of deutschmarks in the other. Lenka was holding Klay's revolver in her other hand beneath the tabletop.

'How did you know I was here?'

'You're a great liar: you had me convinced that the last thing you wanted to do was come here. But you'd make a terrible burglar, as you crashed about my room when you took my travelling companion from the drawer.' He leaned back to peer down at his gun in her hand. 'As an advocate of non-violence in these situations, why bring that to the party?'

'Insurance,' said Lenka, curling her lip.

A body bounced down the steps of the stairwell. Klay watched as the unconscious man landed at the base of the stairs. 'I didn't say anything to Connor, but I guess he worked it out for himself.'

Connor bent his head under the beam as he descended the steps into the bar and waved at everyone. 'Evening all! Sorry I'm late for the party, but I didn't have any ID on me.'

He was followed by several pairs of dead eyes seated in a dark alcove in the far corner of the bar, as he strode towards the others.

'Oh Christ. I just want to get the girl out, not start World War III,' sighed Lenka.

'Too late,' said Connor as he pulled the thickset henchman up from the seat next to his boss by the collar of his black duffle coat. He shook his head as his grey-green eyes looked questioningly at the woman. 'Ye of little faith. You think I'm a total lunatic; give me some credit. World War III, indeed!' He sat down and beamed broadly at Bulla. 'Hello Fucko!' he said as he grabbed a steak knife from the table and prodded him in the side with it. It was enough to pierce his thick, brown leather coat but not enough to cut the skin. He curled Bulla's finger and lifted Lenka's money from his hand. 'You can have your thousand deutschmarks back,' glancing at the knife, 'but it will mean I will stuff it up your arse with this.'

'Klay told you I was here?' asked Lenka, deflatedly.

'Nope, I knew you were up to something when after being prepared to pull the girl from the car, a few hours later you announced it was none of our business – only politicians do U-turns that quickly.'

'Don't ever think you know me,' snapped Lenka.

'So, what are you doing here, anyway?' continued Connor, staring at her. 'Didn't we all agree that we wouldn't come here, tonight?' He did not wait for the woman to answer. 'Your problem, Lenka, is that you think you know best and just go off and do your own thing.' He prodded Bulla with the knife, as he smiled at Klay. 'She's definitely Rogue material.'

'Told you!' replied Klay. 'The woman has steel, and now we know she has cloth ears; a perfect Rogue.'

Lenka gritted her teeth. 'This is all some delightful game to you two, but I am here to make a deal and buy the girl back.'

'Weren't you the one who said she would not offer bribes, yet now you want to make a deal with a black marketeer?' said Connor, wryly.

'You've corrupted me,' said Lenka. 'Anyway, it's the money you stole from the shadow post.'

'Which you then stole from us. That's the problem with the youth of today, no morals, and they just fritter money away.'

'And what were you going to do with it?' asked Lenka.

'Invest it in various bars on the way home. Anyway, welcome to the real world, Lenka' said Connor. 'Well, you certainly managed to fool this big lump, but,' he said, handing her the blue notes, 'negotiating does not mean giving the other side everything and getting nothing in return.' Lenka ground her teeth. 'And what of your friend Foxy? I thought you were going to ask him to sort this out?'

'I called him on the way here.'

'Ah, on the way here,' said Connor, giving her a knowing smile. 'I guess you knew that even your friend, with all his influence, wouldn't be able to pull enough strings over the telephone to free the girl overnight.'

'Do not underestimate Foxy,' glowered Lenka.

Connor huffed. 'And you never believed that the girl was safe as long as Bulla has her, did you? Even for one night,' said Connor.

Lenka said nothing.

'You all mad,' said Bulla, coldly, staring unimpressed down at the blade sticking into his side. His eyes turned towards the dimly lit alcove where his men were drinking. ''You surrounded. Think again, idiots!'

Connor grinned as he leaned into the man. 'I'll think about it. I thought about it. Bollocks!' and pressed the sharp blade further into the leather jacket. It nicked the surface of the man's fleshy waistline.

Bulla grinned, as he looked down at the slowly growing map of crimson that appeared on his thick grey woollen jumper. 'I wait until new children's home packed with bastards.'

Klay leaned forward.

Lenka reached out, staying his arm.

'When you leave. Poof!' Spreading his arms out wide. 'Big explosion . . .' the crime lord stopped suddenly, when he saw Connor's now glacial-blue eyes locked on him.

'Devil! Your eyes change . . .'

Connor lifted Bulla's flick knife from his pocket, 'You have just made an excellent case for why it would not be a good idea for you to still be breathing when we leave here.'

In one sweeping movement, Connor flipped the blade from the handle, and pressed the razor-sharp stainless-steel blade against the side of the man's throat. Seeing the blade, several men in the dark alcove leapt up, but their leader's darting eyes brought them to a halt.

'When we've gone you'd better make sure that not a brick is disturbed in any orphanage in this city, or a child goes missing – not even for a minute,' whispered Connor into the man's cauliflower ear.

Lenka stared into Connor's eyes, unable to speak.

'If you fail in your responsibilities I will come back

and carve you up, you bloated pig, and feed you to your henchmen,' continued Connor.

As blood streamed from Bulla's throat and began to spread across the collar of his cream linen shirt, the crime boss' eyes flicked rapidly as if in agreement.

'Nod,' demanded Connor.

Bulla did, grimacing as a few millimetres of steel disappeared into the cushion of blubber that encircled his throat.

'We're taking the girl,' said Lenka, in an icily cold voice that surprised her.

'Girl, not far from here. I no fuck. Only buy her,' stammered Bulla.

'You bought her?' said Connor. 'From whom?' pressing the blade closer towards Bulla's windpipe.

'Super . . . intendent.'

'Of what?' continued Connor.

'Lupa orphanage.'

The men standing in the dimly lit alcove suddenly raced forward.

Klay swung his arm across the table behind him sweeping all the glasses towards them. He followed up by launching the table at them, and gathering two bottles from another table by the necks before smashing the bases off on the edge of the table.

The army of duffle-coated thugs halted their advance.

'Now, where were we?' continued Connor, twisting the blade. 'Oh, yes!'

'Stop it, please,' pleaded Lenka, as the crime lord looked on the verge of collapse with the unwavering blade under his chin.

A woman in a thick black leather jacket, who had been sitting at a table to their right with her back to them, turned and placed her hand on Connor's arm. 'This is now a police matter.' She flashed a warrant card. 'I am Sergeant Elenuta Dimetre.'

Connor looked across at the peroxided-straw-haired woman. Her manner, movement and eyes were that of someone in their thirties. But her grey skin, scored by broken blood vessels forced to the surface by tobacco and alcohol, was that of someone in their late fifties. She also had the look of someone who had witnessed and suffered much pain.

'I will ensure that Bulla upholds the agreement you two have *cordially* reached.'

'Elenuta!' scowled Bulla, glaring at the police officer. 'You sat and watched, and did nothing,' he growled in Romanian. The woman bent down and responded in their native language. 'I am here because my superiors are agitated. The British Government have made numerous calls tonight, expressing outrage that child traffickers are operating freely in the city. It accuses my superiors of turning a blind eye. Unless we smash your – and you were named – operation, future foreign investment will be stopped.'

'Go fuck . . .' yelled Bulla, only to release blood from his lips as Connor jerked the blade forward.

The police officer continued. 'I would say, Bulla, that the superintendent of Lupa orphanage failed to tell you that the girl is not an orphan and that she is from a gypsy family who trade in the Piaţa Unirii market. It is a twenty-three-minute walk from your home. I timed it – though I think they will be running. If they were to learn what you have done they will exact their own form of vengeance. That is unless I intervene on your behalf.'

The crime lord's hands clasped the edge of the table, as he turned to the man with the knife in his throat. 'This first child. Superintendent sold girl this morning; not know she gypsy. Oath!'

Elenuta nodded. 'We will return her to her family, but they will take the view that you may come after more of their children.'

The crime lord's body started to judder, through a combination of the loss of blood, and fear. Lenka was about to intervene. This time Klay placed his hand on her shoulder, while looking sternly at the man on the verge of collapse.

The police sergeant placed her hand on Connor's and twisted the blade. 'So what will I tell the girl's family, Marcos Bucatinia of the blue house on Boulevard Gheorghiu-Dej?'

'I no more buy children. Swear on wife and children's hearts,' replied the man whose trousers were soaked in urine.

Connor spoke: 'Not good enough. We need you to swear on something that means something to you.'

The man began to choke, 'I promise . . . on . . . my life.'

'Excellent,' said Connor. 'Now let's take the girl out of here, and I can finally go to dinner,' he said as he pressed the silver button on the handle and returned the bloody steel blade back inside the handle. He leaned towards Bulla, who had thrown his hand over his wound, while grabbing the table with the other. As he began to slip to the floor holding the tablecloth, he launched mixed sausage, bread and cutlery across the room, before passing out.

Connor bent down to look at the unconscious man lying on broken crockery, and clasped his hands. 'A captive audience, good. Now, I've got a date tonight. I've known the lady for a while and . . . no, wrong time, you've got a lot on your plates,' he slapped his hands on his knees, before rising.

Klay strode over to the largest of the startled henchman and lifted him up by his collar on to his toes. 'Best you go with the police now and free the girl or I'm coming to find you.' Elenuta walked over and translated the threat, before passing her outstretched hand across her throat.

Lenka remained seated and watched in amazement as Connor's eyes had reverted to their natural grey-green colour.

The sergeant scanned the faces of Bulla's men as if she were compiling a register. They bent down around Bulla and staggered as they lifted him off the floor, and carried him up the staircase. The other customers returned to their conversations.

'They are scared of you,' said Lenka, as she offered her hand to the police officer who lowered herself into what had been Bulla's chair. Elenuta shook it, firmly.

'I police the gypsy area where you are building the new home. I keep the peace between the local residents, crime bosses like Bulla and the gypsies. To do so, I bend the law a little to ensure that they don't kill each other. I believe that during my time here I have secured respect or fear, on all sides. I can and have secured the support of one against the other.'

'The gypsy threat was real, then?' said Lenka.

'Yes. The girl, Rosanne, is a gypsy and her father is as brutal as Bulla.'

'At last the poor girl has a name,' sighed Connor.

The policewoman continued. 'If I fail to placate Rosanne's family, I have no doubt that Bulla will be captured and tortured for days – no, hours as his heart would explode. Then there will be a war of . . .' she fumbled to find the word.

'Of succession,' added Lenka.

'Yes,' continued the police officer.

'How will you placate Rosanne's family?' asked Lenka.

'By telling them the truth. That Bulla did not know that she was their daughter, or that she was a gypsy. Retribution will be required. He will be caught and punished, but I believe he will not be killed – maybe lose a few toes, maybe a hand or testicle but no more. After that, he will not attempt to traffic in children again and the Pink Floyd . . . will be . . . no, what is the name of the rock band?'

'Status Quo,' added Connor.

'Yes, them . . . will be maintained,' continued Elenuta.

'Will you tell them of this superintendent?' asked

Lenka.

The policewoman pondered. 'Let's just say, that man is connected. I would only be putting Rosanne's family in danger if they sought reprisals against him.'

'If you knew about the girl, why only act now?' asked Klay.

'I only just heard. The telephone calls from the British this evening were a surprise to everyone, even me. Bulla specialises in extortion, prostitution, smuggling, the occasional gang murder, but not child trafficking until today; at least not to my knowledge. It does go on. Unfortunately, since the world has learnt of the tragedy of our orphanages, there are always those who will exploit such situations.' She reached for the wine, removing the exposed cork with her teeth.

Elenuta reclined. 'The trafficking of children has happened virtually overnight. A number of people in the United States and the rest of Europe have, as you have done, rushed to help the children with donations and medicines. However, criminal activity has followed at an exponential rate.' She sighed. 'Please don't think we are ungrateful, but as I say, where there is an influx of wealth the criminals follow.'

'Black marketeers we get, but children?' asked Lenka.

'Adoption. Children have suddenly become commodities.'

'How?' asked Mary, who appeared behind them along with Simon, who pulled two chairs over to the table.

'And how did you know I was here?' asked Lenka, dejectedly.

Mary helped herself to a glass of tzuica, local plum spirit, from another table, before slamming her baseball bat on the table. 'I didn't. I came to get the girl back.'

Connor placed his hands over his heart. 'How can any woman hope to replace you?'

'The Captain here followed me,' continued Mary.

Simon stared at Lenka and shook his head.

The police officer continued. 'Rich couples in the West wish to adopt children in the hope of freeing them and giving them a new life. But unscrupulous officials have seized the opportunity to make themselves rich. Lucrative bribes are extracted to fast-track adoptions.'

'But we know the girl is not an orphan,' said Lenka.

'She was from Lupa Orphanage,' continued Elenuta. 'Her mother is sick following the birth of her tenth child, and her father was in jail until last night. No doubt after bribes were exchanged, she was transferred to the orphanage run by a man called Demetri Hava. It was he who sold her to Bulla.'

'Why, there's no shortage of orphans?' said Klay.

'A healthy child is highly prized, and they are in short supply in the institutions.'

'If a child from an impoverished family finds a home with a wealthy family in the West, why care if someone makes a profit?' said Simon.

Connor scowled at the Englishman. 'I couldn't put my finger on why I disliked you, maybe it was because I was spoilt for choice. But now I know why; it's because you're a heartless, brainless robot. I think Rosanne's family might object to having their child kidnapped, and ripping a kid apart from her world and plunging her into a completely alien one would screw her up for life.'

The others were surprised at the anger in Connor's voice, and wondered if something similar had happened to him.

'When this is over, I promise to teach you a lesson you will never forget,' said Simon, coldly.

'Why wait?' snapped Connor spreading out his arms, inviting the other man to throw a punch.

'Stop it. This is ridiculous,' said Lenka, raising her hand up to the faces of the two men. 'We may have saved Rosanne, but what of the other children in Lupa Orphanage? We need to confront its superintendent now!'

'I'll go,' said Connor and Klay in unison, before looking at each other in surprise.

'No, I'm going in the morning,' said Lenka, firmly. 'You lot blow up too easily,' she said, before rolling the baseball bat back across the table towards Mary.

'Shame, I wanted to get some practice in,' said Mary, grimly.

'Then I'm going with you,' said Simon.

Lenka looked at the Englishman. She paused before

finally saying, 'Thank you, Simon.'

Outside, Lenka grabbed Connor's arm and spun him around. 'Who are you?'

'An arrogant Londoner. There's only one type, why?'

'Your eyes?'

'Oh that!' interrupted Klay. 'That happens whenever someone pisses him off. Weird, eh! I think he's an alien.'

'Maybe that explains why I can't hold a tune,' said Connor.

'And that you use karaoke as a cover. Your wailing is you sending a message home to the mother planet,' laughed Klay. 'It all makes sense now.'

Elenuta nodded, turned and made her way towards the unmarked police car across the road.

'I have kept Anita waiting long enough. Time I bought dinner for the poor woman. Night!' shouted Connor, who was already half way across the road heading in the direction of the Intercontinental Hotel.

'And I need a drink,' said Klay. 'Anyone wish to join me?'

'Come on,' said Mary, heading towards a bar on the other side of the street.

As they walked along the wide, empty road towards Estelle's orphanage, Simon asked Lenka if she was okay, but she did not say a word.

Chapter 9: A Drop in the Ocean

9.55am, 13 July 1990, Bucharest

The sun scorched the flaky paint chips on the window frames of Lupa Orphanage. The bored-looking woman in a heavily stained white gown, who had led Lenka and Simon into the institute's hallway, had disappeared along with her cigarette. The blindingly white walls were wet, having been sprayed with overpowering industrial disinfectant

As they edged down the corridor, the screams and wailing from behind the doors grew louder. They opened a door and entered the first of the building's many hells.

Inside were sixty, maybe seventy children, ranging from terrified, screaming toddlers to fly-covered, vacant-looking teenagers, all covered in bruises, cuts and sores. They were rocking back and forward like those in Orillia orphanage. But they did so violently, straining at the ties that secured their ankles to the bars of their cots and beds. The smell was overwhelming.

The walls and lower back windows were caked in excrement, while pools of rancid urine covered the floors.

Lenka wretched into her hands. Expressionless, Simon used his linen handkerchief to try to clean her hands as best he could. There was no water in the room.

Lenka's legs buckled. She grabbed hold of the corner of an iron cage, as she stared at the horror. 'This is not care, nor is it treatment, this is incarceration,' she spluttered.

A small, trembling hand passed through the iron bars of a cot and gently cradled her finger.

Lenka bent down. The little girl's pained face, covered in scratches and filth, stared at her. She did not smile. Her hair was matted with excrement, her sheets and clothing were wet with urine, a mixture of hers and the four children squeezed in behind her.

'TU!' (You!) came a scream. The children leapt as far away from the cry as their caged cots and restraints would allow.

Lenka and Simon turned towards the doorway. A

tall man in a suit wearing a disposable medical mask continued to shout but did not enter the room. Instead, two heavy-set orderlies pounded towards Lenka and Simon.

Simon stood squarely in their way.

As the orderlies produced truncheons, the children began to scream and rock faster, while others cried and tried to bury themselves under the single sheets that covered the metal wire grate that was the base of their beds.

'The nurse who let you in said you're either American or English,' shouted the man in the mask. 'Do you wish to cause further discord to the children by starting a fight?'

Simon turned to Lenka, who was squeezing the girl's hand while wiping away her tears.

He slowly raised Lenka, then placed his arm around her and guided her towards the doorway. The tall, grey-haired man in his mid-fifties, wearing an immaculate, dark grey, pinstriped suit, stood back as they entered the corridor then ripped off his mask. 'It is best that we conduct our business in my office.'

The superintendent led Lenka and Simon down the hall, followed by the two orderlies.

Inside his plush office decorated with awards and photos of the superintendent shaking hands with various local dignities, the superintendent directed them to the chairs facing his desk. He sat in the tallest chair.

'You are not the American couple we were expecting,' said the superintendent, in an avuncular manner.

'How can you allow these children to live in such vile conditions?' said Lenka.

'I am the superintendent of this institute. Who are you?' demanded the man, quietly but firmly, facing Simon.

'We are here about Rosanne Badžo,' interjected Lenka.

'Who?'

'She was transferred here from a hospital last week.'

'I can't be expected to remember their names, and the surnames of many of the orphans are unknown. How much are you offering to pay for this . . .

Rosanne Bad . . . ?'

'We already have her,' continued Lenka.

'Then why seek her here?'

'You sold her to a criminal called Bulla.'

The superintendent's genial disposition was now a memory, as his overgrown, grey, bushy eyebrows closed together like theatre curtains at the end of an act. 'GET OUT!'

It was approaching midnight. Lenka lay in her sleeping bag in a large, bare room on the top floor of the renovated, four-storey building. Even though the windows had no panes of glass, the odour of fresh PVA plaster bond that she and Simon had applied to the interior walls, wrung tears from her eyes. Once again, she gave up on sleep and lifted her grandmother's diary from her rucksack and turned to the next page.

13th January 1965

I'm waiting for a ferry to England. Poor little ones are already throwing up around me at the thought of the cattle boat to Holyhead, and the waiting embrace of the bullying sea . . . 'Bullying sea', I like that, maybe I will write a novel if I survive my visit to England. But now your grandmother's thoughts are on love and sex.

Women not my scene, I always preferred a good grind with the inferior beast called man, but whatever makes you happy. One warning, love and heartbreak occupy the same territory, so prepare yourself.

Estelle had warned her, and now the same message from beyond the grave. Lenka stared through the polythene sheet covering the window at the crescent moon nesting in the black night. She wondered if Simon's sleep was as troubled as hers.

Men: I've had shedloads. A waste of a shed, at least until your grandad, Sean, turned up. For men, young men at least, everything revolves around sex, drinking (nothing wrong with that) and a ball of some description. But for a dangerous few, it's power. If you sleep with a man, do so because you want to; never feel obligated or bullied into it. It's your body, you control it. If a man forces himself on you, tell your parents. If I know my son Lock, he will put a considerable distance between them and their dick. If they are not around, you must tell someone, Estelle, Foxy, the police, scream it from the rooftops, scream it from the hills.

Silence allows abuse to continue. If it's not you, it will be someone else. It happened to me in the orphanage in Krakow, frequently, and no one listened. One night, I sorted it with gunpowder, a candle and a match. I drugged my abuser and waited

180

for his mouth to open when he snored. Then I blew his fucking head off.

I know I'm not a typical woman. We are all different. If you're too traumatised to tell anyone, for fuck sake never blame yourself. Men are, in general, physically stronger. And refuse to be silenced by all that 'She asked for it', bollocks!' Sean once said that the only ones who ask to be physically abused are members of parliament. I never got his humour, but he was right.

Your mother (Kirsten) *insisted on joining me on my trip to England, though she's not at all well. She is pregnant and carrying the first/eldest of you. Though she hasn't told me that she is, I'm a mother, I know these things. She is asleep now, with her head resting on my lap.*

10.25am, 14 July 1990, Bucharest

'You are not the type of person I expected to get involved in this,' Lenka said.

'You mean helping people?' said Connor before breaking into a laugh. 'It's surprising how many people ask me that though. Why do you think that is?'

'Forgive me for being blunt, but it's because that in every other respect you seem to care only about yourself.'

'You do know that there's a difference between

181

blunt and rude?'

'Why do you do it?'

'Maybe it's in my blood. Or it might be the adrenaline and the thirst for adventure.'

'Is that really why? You could have joined the army or been a racing driver.'

'I tried the army.' Connor looked uncomfortable, before adding softly, 'Perhaps like you, it's not only about us. What we do is just a drop in the ocean of misery, but maybe, sometimes, it's just enough to let one boat float so a family or two can climb in.'

Lenka nodded, but said nothing, as those labouring around them outside the renovated orphanage were loading and unloading the trucks.

'Why the interest in the motives of a drunken bum?' Connor asked, smiling.

'I need to ask you something.'

Connor opened his arms. 'Anything, I have no secrets, though recalling exact events can get a bit hazy when I'm drunk.'

'In the bar, when Bulla threatened to burn down the orphanages, the colour of your eyes . . .'

The matt-black Dacia 1300, marked POLITA, appeared from a side road and began to rock its way towards them.

When it pulled up in front of Klay, four police officers stepped gingerly out onto the crumbling tarmac.

Inspector Alexandru Petrescu flashed his identity card abruptly, having no interest in it being read. Behind him stood Sergeant Elenuta Dimetre, who briskly nodded. The inspector eyed up the Rogues, before addressing them in Romanian. When he finished, the sergeant translated.

'The superintendent of the children's hospital was found dead this morning,' said Elenuta.

'Oh dear; how sad; never mind,' said Connor, as he picked up a cardboard box containing tinned fruit and marched into the building.

Elenuta continued translating. 'He was found with his neck broken, having been thrown through his office window three floors up. He was about sixteen stone, so his killer would have had to have been very powerful.'

The inspector stood in front of Klay, looking up at him.

'Maybe he was drunk and just fell out of the window,' said Mary, as she stood beside Klay.

The sergeant shrugged. 'The pathologist on the scene said his neck was broken before he was propelled through the window.'

The Inspector continued, while Elenuta nodded and listened until he finished.

'Two of the orderlies,' continued Elenuta, walking towards Lenka and Simon, 'said, that the two of you broke into the building yesterday morning and they had to physically throw you out.'

'We didn't break in. We went there to confront the superintendent about Rosanne,' said Lenka.

'In light of the man's death, "confront" is an incriminating word,' said Elenuta, but she did not relay Lenka's response to the inspector. She stared at Simon. 'We checked with your government and you're a captain in the British Navy. But you don't have a ship?' Simon stared down at her, but said nothing. 'You're supposedly on vacation.' Elenuta threw a glance towards Lenka. 'Maybe it's a fishing holiday.' She shrugged. 'After that, your government officers refused to answer any more of our questions.'

Elenuta walked over to her inspector who was still staring up at Klay.

The inspector did not avert his eyes from the powerful man, as he passed a file to the sergeant instructing her to read it aloud.

'It says that you served a year in a military jail, having deserted from the British army.'

Klay shrugged. 'If that's what it says.'

'Apparently, during a covert operation in Saddam Hussein's Iraq you refused to abandon the Kurdish people and continued to fight when your squad was ordered to retreat.' Elenuta raised her head. 'Perhaps failing to obey orders would be more accurate.'

Connor returned carrying a ten-litre jerry can full of diesel. Elenuta blocked his path.

'And you, Mr Pierce, you served in the Irish Army, as part of several UN peacekeeping missions: Asia, South America, even Afghanistan. Though, I wasn't aware that the UN or the Irish had a presence there.

The woman I spoke to in the Irish Embassy got quite carried away with your exploits.'

The inspector spoke gruffly, which Elenuta translated to Klay and Connor. 'After your friends were thrown out, the two of you paid the Superintendent a call.'

'We went there with the same aim as Lenka and Simon,' replied Klay. 'To challenge him on the abduction of the girl, not to kill him.'

'I hate to talk ill of the dead, but he didn't even offer us a drink,' said Connor, stepping past Elenuta and lifting the fuel up onto the back of his truck. 'He showed us the door, but someone else showed him the window.'

The inspector issued more instructions then turned and marched back to the police car.

'None of you are to leave Bucharest,' said Elenuta. 'We have to return to the coroner who is completing a full autopsy, but we will come back this afternoon. We have more questions.'

'How is Rosanna?' asked Lenka.

'She is reunited with her family,' Elenuta said, and

smiled before joining her colleagues in the car.

As soon as the police vehicle began to drunkenly negotiate the unwelcoming road, Klay, Connor and Mary disappeared into the building. Within minutes, Klay and Connor had gathered the last of their belongings and had loaded them into their trucks.

'You're leaving us to face the music?' challenged Simon.

'They think Connor and I murdered the superintendent,' said Klay, before shaking Simon's hand. 'They'll be angry for sure, but they'll direct all their resources into tracking us down.'

'They'll track you down before you reach the border,' continued Simon.

'A full post-mortem takes between four and six hours. As the cadaver is someone of influence, I'd say we'll have six hours, maybe more,' said Klay.

Connor walked up to Lenka. 'The orderlies have confirmed that Klay and I were the last visitors, as they had already sent you and the automaton packing.'

'Do you have a place in London?' asked Lenka.

'Correspondence address?'

'No. I need to speak to you in person.'

'You're an attractive woman and all, but Anita and I are an,' he paused. 'Yes, we're an item, that's the term. And it may surprise you to learn, that I'm a one-woman guy.'

'Why do men think it's always about sex?' said Lenka, shaking her head.

Connor shrugged. 'It's because, well . . . we're men.' He took her hands. 'Not that it's any of my business, but you're too good for Action Man over there,' he said, winking at Simon who was now sitting in Lenka's van, fifty metres away and watching them intensely. 'Find someone who will let you breathe.'

Lenka squeezed his hands. 'You're right, it is none of your business. But, it would be nice to one day find someone who respects my choices for a change.'

'Ouch!' said Connor lifting his eyes to the sky. He lowered his head. 'Well, I hope that Anita doesn't start to respect my opinions, or I'll start questioning her sanity.' He released Lenka, jumped into the driver's seat and slammed the door. 'Leave a message for me with Teresa at the Twelve Pins in Finsbury Park. She's the manager and a good friend. I sometimes go there to find building work. Then I'll find you.'

He blew a kiss towards Lenka, as he lifted a finger in Simon's direction. 'Take care. Until the next time,' he said, turning the ignition and abruptly punching the engine into life.

Klay appeared beside Lenka as they watched the white, turbo-charged truck rock its way over the craters in the road.

'Where did you first meet Connor?' asked Lenka, staring ahead.

'In a bar in Beirut in '87. He was part of some covert exchange programme between the Irish, American, Australian, and various European, elite fighting forces. In the Lebanon, he was part of the first contingent of UN troops brought in to guard the leaders of the major parties trying to bring an end to decades of civil war.'

'And you?'

'I was there as part of a covert British reconnaissance force.'

'That's when you first talked of working on

humanitarian convoys together?'

'God no, we were so drunk that night I doubt we were even coherent. No, that was a few years later, when I bumped into him in another bar in Berlin. I had left the Army, and had completed a few convoys delivering medical aid into East Africa. Connor was drinking and screwing his way across Europe and getting involved in various fights. He was totally directionless. If I have done one good thing in my life, it's convincing him to drive aid trucks. He's bloody good at it, as I've said.'

Klay smiled at Lenka. 'Why? You don't fancy him, do you?' he asked softly, checking that Simon, who was standing over a local mechanic whilst he fitted a new carburettor on their truck, was out of earshot.

Lenka smiled. 'No, it's not that. It's the anomaly of his eyes changing colour. Have you ever read a Rogues comic?'

Klay laughed. 'Too busy for comics, but what's that got to do with it?'

Lenka smiled and shrugged. 'Oh nothing; another time perhaps.' Klay bent down as he placed his hands on her shoulders and kissed her on the cheek. He walked over to Simon and shook his hand. 'Look after her, she's some woman.'

Simon nodded, before Klay climbed into his truck.

'Take good care of yourself,' he shouted towards Lenka, before heading off down the road in the opposite direction to Connor's truck.

Mary strode out of the building carrying her rucksack on her back and a box of Pilsner cradled under her arm, heading towards the faded-grey 7.5 tonne box van.

'So, you're off too?' shouted Lenka. 'You've missed the others.'

'Rogues are not big on goodbyes, and we never hang around when the police turn up. We'll cross paths again in places where others fear to tread.'

Mary threw her baggage onto the passenger seat and slipped the case of beer beneath it.

Lenka raised herself up on the step of the truck and gave her a hug. 'I take it that like the others, you're not a fan of the police?'

'Surprisingly, a Rogue's past is full of grey areas,'

said Mary, as she raised herself into the truck and kicked the engine rudely into life. She reversed the truck alongside Simon but neither acknowledged each other before Mary winked and smiled at Lenka and headed down the alleyway opposite.

Chapter 10: *"If You're Irish Come into the Parlour"*

7.55am, 15 July 1990, Bucharest

Lenka and Simon turned into the road where the Orillia Orphanage stood, as they had promised Carol and Anita that they would have breakfast together each morning and update them on the progress of the new facility. As they pulled up at the entrance, a rotund, blotchy-cheeked man, wearing a matching Hawaiian shirt and shorts, was yelling at Carol in English.

'My wife and I drove all the way here from Cambridge to deliver aid to these children, and what reward do I get for it? I find one of these brats you sent to help us unload our van this morning, helping himself to my wife's jewellery from the glove compartment.' He was lifting a little boy, who was holding his screaming sister's hand, up on his toes by his ear.

Carol remained calm and continued apologising, while pressing the man to release the boy. But the man's anger only increased. His wife stood beside him with her arms folded, looking sourly at the nurse.

Lenka strode over. 'Look, it's none of my business but we have brought aid too and unfortunately, the children around you have nothing . . .'

The man's rhubarb face erupted. 'You're right young lady, it is none of your business! These ungrateful little bas . . .' He stopped when he saw Simon jump down from the truck. 'We want no violence, but we demand that the police are called,' he continued, as he twisted the struggling boy's ear.

Lenka squared up to the man and leaned in close to his ear and whispered, 'The children around here are from gypsy families. They have nothing. If I were that little boy and,' she said, looking down at the man's top-of-the-range Timex watch and then at the gold chain around his flabby neck, 'my brothers and sisters were living on scraps, I'd look to see what else you had.'

'There is no excuse. My wife and I have raised a lot of money through the local press and . . .'

'I'm sure your photo was on the front page.'

'How dare you, I'll . . .'

Lenka lowered her voice a little more, as she was nearly touching the man's red ear. 'Carol has repeatedly apologised. If you continue to use this as an excuse to browbeat her and hurt the boy, I'll go and find the boy's parents. Then you will find out who dishes out justice here. Best you leave your address on the dashboard, and I'll see that any internal organs the dogs leave behind are shipped back to England in a matchbox.'

The man lifted his head and scanned the troop of barking mongrels. He released the boy. The child immediately launched the tip of his shoe into the man's shin, before grinning at Lenka. The purple-faced man grabbed his protesting wife's hand, dragged her over to their van and manhandled her into the passenger seat without a word.

Lenka went to the back of the man's vehicle and started to unload the rest of the boxes, which were mainly crisps and other junk food past their sell-by date. Ten minutes later, the vehicle set off back along the road, leaving Lenka, Carol, Simon and a hoard of local children who were carrying the boxes and a toilet base without connections into the building.

Lenka bent down and smiled at a sweating six, maybe seven-year-old, little boy who had carried the toilet inside and gently placed her hand on his bruised cheek. She removed her watch and handed it to him. The boy lifted it from her hand uneasily, before running off, dragging his little sister laughing in his wake.

Carol appeared carrying a tray of steaming mugs of tea. 'Thanks for your help with Mr and Mrs Angry, earlier. You really are quite resourceful, Lenka.'

Lenka smiled. 'Nothing that you couldn't handle.'

'Anita and I have to tread carefully. We can't appear to be ungrateful, and often it's best to accept the aid even when it's worthless. I heard the police paid you a few visits yesterday. The Rogues are gone, I take it?'

'How did you know?'

'Connor called Anita last night. She's a bit down in the dumps today. Relationships in our line of work are never easy. I was lucky to find Tom. He's had to put up with a lot, but now our kids are grown up. He can come out and see me more often and help me with my work.'

'When the police came back yesterday afternoon, the inspector blew a fuse when he discovered that Mary, Klay and Connor had gone, but his sergeant . . .'

'Elenuta,' Carol said, and smiled.

'You know her?'

'Yes. She threw her protective cloak around us, when we arrived here,' she said, tilting her head towards the building.

'She appeared not the least surprised that the Rogues had gone. Her boss made quite a show though. Shouts, flapping his arms, stamping his feet. Elenuta translated, and told us that her boss promised that all the Rogues would be captured by nightfall.'

The women took a sip from their mugs, and smiled.

Ninety minutes later, in the central Post Office in Bucharest, Lenka's call to Marisa's orphanage was finally put through.

'Is that you Robert?' greeted Lenka. 'How is everything going? Are you and Margaret okay? How are the classes going?'

'We're all good. The children are a credit to you and Margaret. So far we only called on Marisa's services once.'

'Davy and Peter fighting?'

'Afraid so, but for some reason the boys said afterwards that they would never play cards again.' Lenka smiled but said nothing. 'Did you hear about my grandfather?'

'If he's buried the hatchet and taken up cards with my aunt, forget your inheritance,' said Lenka, laughing heartily.

'He was murdered the day after you left.'

'What!'

'He was shot in the back of the head at his desk.'

'Dear God! I'm so sorry, Robert.'

'Don't be.'

'Did they find out who did it?'

'No, but I heard the police questioned your guardian, Foxy.'

After checking on Marisa's health, and how the children's studies were progressing, twenty minutes later Lenka finally replaced the receiver. She turned to find Simon standing in the hall. 'You heard?'

Simon nodded. 'Your friend Foxy may have gone too far this time.'

Thirty minutes later, Lenka drew her truck to a halt outside Estelle's building.

'What the hell!' said Lenka, before she and Simon jumped out of the vehicle. The building now had four ladders scaling its walls, with two men on the flat roof applying what appeared to be asphalt, all accompanied by the incessant sound of hammering and drilling from inside. As they approached the entrance, a burly man with short, tightly curled hair, sprinkled with dabs of wet plaster, greeted them.

'I'm Brendan Cline. Pleased *ta* meet you both,' he said, as he grabbed their hands with his heavily calloused one. 'We're *Da* Boys from *Da* Hill.'

'Is that some secret society?' asked Simon.

'Ah, *yer* mean like *yer* Freemasons. *Sur*, I suppose it is. It's an elite fraternity where membership is offered to those who are barred from every other boozer in town.'

'A pub,' said Simon, huffily.

'It is,' said Brendan. 'And we've flown in from the centre of God's country to help *yer* finish *yer* little project.'

'You've flown in from Cork?' said Lenka.

'*Jasus*, not that *shitehole*. I was referring to Dublin, of course.'

'I'm from Cork,' retorted Lenka.

'A beautiful place,' added Brendan. 'I'm a huge fan of it, *meself*.'

'Who sent you?' said Simon.

'*Da* "Big I Am"; Joseph McNamara.'

'We just heard that McNamara is dead,' replied Lenka.

'*Sur* no worries,' continued Brendan. 'We've been paid in advance. I insisted, for he's – ah no, was – with the greatest of respect to *da* man, a tight old *fecker*. I'm very sorry to hear of his death. A tragic loss to us all.'

'Joseph McNamara is not known for his philanthropy,' said Simon.

'I didn't know he collected butterflies,' replied Brendan. 'Fair play to '*em!*'

'Simon is saying that McNamara is not known for

his generosity,' said Lenka. 'So why would he send you?'

'I don't know, but *da* boys and I welcome the change, and if it's to help *da* poor orphans we'll work from dawn till dusk.'

'When did McNamara ask you to come out here?' Lenka asked.

'About two weeks ago. *Da* afternoon of the *da* 4th July. *Sur*, I remember it well. Independence Day and *me* birthday. I got *fek* all.' He clapped his hands. 'Come in. A brew is on, and *ya* can meet *da* lads.'

'The day we left Cork,' said Simon.

Lenka did not move. *Foxy had promised he would pay McNamara a visit after they left and "beat some kindness" into him. I pray to God he didn't kill him.*

Inside, the throng of men on ladders and plastering the ceilings moved at an exhausting pace. Wheelbarrows, full of bags of cement, were manoeuvred around scurrying bodies at inclines that defied gravity; in weaker hands they would have toppled over. Towers of 10 litre tubs of Donoghue's white trade paint stood in every corner.

201

As the moon waited in the wings for the sun to leave the stage, Lenka smiled at the dazzling bright ceilings and walls, that either Duggie, Stevie, Tim or Joe had marked with their initials followed by a number. The first round of drinks in the evening was always on the one who covered the least square yardage during the day.

On the dinner table, composed of three wallpapering tables whose earlier collapse had been accompanied by a loud chorus of swearing, Brendan loaded piles of potatoes, swede and boiled bacon onto tin plates. 'Get it down *yer*, and stay out of trouble when *yer* in town tonight. And be working at seven in the morning, or this *feckin* ladle will find another use.'

'*Fat Eejet!*' muttered one of the young men, who was smart enough to ensure his lips did not move.

'*Da* smartarse who *feckin* said that will wake in the morning covered in piss – mine along with their own,' said Brendan, setting off a wave of laughter around the table.

Lenka smiled, for though the language was coarser and the little boys were bigger, it reminded her of the children's banter at table in Marisa's orphanage. She almost expected to see Hannah's knowing look.

It was ten o'clock at night when Brendan, who was a plumber by trade, returned to the makeshift table, having finished installing the dishwasher and fitting new taps and washers throughout the building. He placed bottles of *Harp* lager in front of Lenka and Simon who had just finished scrubbing the kitchen clean and putting up new shelves and cupboards.

'After your question earlier, I confess that I was surprised when McNamara called me and told me to get a crew together and fly out here for a week.'

'You knew him well?' asked Lenka.

'I did a number of jobs for him over the years. A *basturd* to work *fer*, he made John Paul Getty look like Mother Theresa. When it came to paying us after a job, he diddled us every time. He set some goons on me once; I spent a week in hospital. I swore I'd never work for the *basturd* again.'

'But here you are. Is that because he paid you in advance?' asked Simon, ignoring the beer in front of him.

'No. When I discovered that it was to help orphans, I was in. I'm an orphan *meself.*'

Lenka tapped Brendan's bottle with hers before taking a sip.

1am, 16 July 1990, Bucharest

'Up *da RA!*' yelled Ghillian, quoting the words printed on his tatty tee-shirt, as the drunken young man staggered through the door.

Lenka, Simon and Brendan sat at the makeshift table with three bottles of beer on it. Simon glowered at the drunken man.

'Ignore him, Captain,' said Brendan. 'He's only a kid. He has no idea what he's saying.'

Ghillian staggered over and collapsed face down on the bare wooden floor.

'Well, no ladder work for *yer* in the morning, lad,' said Brendan, who gathered up the unconscious man and threw him over his shoulder in a fireman's lift. He carried him off to the communal room where the others were sleeping.

Lenka tilted her head towards Simon. 'It's a song,

isn't it? I heard it once in a bar in Dublin.'

'It's a homage to the IRA,' snarled Simon.

Brendan returned and sat down at the table. Two more of Brendan's crew fell in the door, singing the same song.

'Not a good day *fer* brushing up the image of *da* country,' sighed Brendan.

The two young men slumped on the chairs at the table. '*Sur*, we mean no harm, Captain. It's just a song,' said Mickey.

Simon leaned forward. 'I've lost many a comrade to the IRA; it glorifies butchers.'

The other drunken man, Tom, nudged his friend. 'He's right, *sur* we are out of order,' he said before turning to the British officer. 'We meant no harm, sorry. Best we head to bed.'

'Away with *yer*,' added Brendan.

'Sorry, General,' said Mickey, raising himself. He started to slur another song. '"For Connor Pierce will die, and soon be food for flies. The *RA* will rise . . ."'

'Connor Pierce!' said Lenka abruptly. 'What do you know of Connor Pierce?'

Both men straightened up. '*Yer* know Connor Pierce?' asked Tom.

'Bloody hell, I've witnessed the quickest sobering up in history,' said Brendan. '*Feck* off *ta* bed *yer* pair of *wankers,* we've all a heavy day tomorrow and I'm running out of men who I can trust *ta* work with a ladder.'

Both men nodded and disappeared towards the room where the other ten were sleeping.

Brendan took a swig from a fresh bottle. '*Yer* know Connor Pierce, then?'

'He helped deliver the building materials you're working with,' said Lenka. 'You missed him by a day.'

Brendan whistled, and tapped the bottle. '*Jasus*, if he were still here, *yer* wouldn't have heard a dicky-bird out of my lads.'

'Why?' asked Simon. 'Is he a member of the IRA?'

'God no! Though for a few weeks he led the *RA* to believe he was one of them.'

'Explain,' pressed Lenka.

'In one night, Pierce caused more damage to *da RA* than Special Branch,' Brendan said, nodding at Simon.

'And *yer* British Army, did since *da* Troubles began.' He stared into the bottle wedged in his hands.

'Tell us, Brendan,' said Lenka, quietly.

Brendan rested his arms on the bare table. 'I have nothing *ta* do with *da* RA, but *da* story is common knowledge. And I love a good gangster thriller, particularly *da* Mafia; *The Godfather*, *Da French Connection*; lovely films.'

'Can we get on with it,' said Simon.

'I was just saying that I followed *da* tale more than most,' said Brendan. 'Pierce was in *da* Irish Army, though born in Belfast, he's *ma* being Irish was his way in. Irish Rangers, they say.'

'Do you know anything else about his mother?' asked Lenka.

'His *ma*, Lily, I *tink* she *wer* called, was a Catholic who lived in the Falls Road, a protestant stronghold. That's all I know.'

'Carry on,' said Simon, abruptly.

'When Pierce left the army, he returned to Belfast. The RA tried to recruit him, but each time they left with a '*Feck* off' in their ear.' Brendan took another sip from the bottle. 'But when they threatened his *ma*, Pierce said he would join up.'

'Bastard!' spat Simon. 'I knew he was a dirty Fenian.'

'Well, the *RA*'s chieftains thought so too,' said Brendan, nodding. 'But over *da* next few weeks, Pierce backed out of every bombing, every planned execution he was ordered to be part of by the *RA*. If the operation went ahead, *da* Brits were waiting. Then, so the rumours go, just as *da* chieftains, who were no fools, were about to put out a contract on Pierce, his mammy died of ovarian cancer. She was his only family. The belief is that he agreed to join *da RA*, until her illness took her. The night she died, Pierce tore *da* guts out of the *RA*.'

Brendan looked up at the studious expressions. 'Much of what I'm *ta* tell you, may be exaggerated – we're Irish, we know how *ta* spin a yarn – but every member of *da* hit team that threatened *ta* murder Lily Pierce was killed that night. Nine of them, including their leader, Tommy "Nightmare" O'Mara were found dead across Belfast. According to the papers, each one was "a professional kill".'

'I take it Connor Pierce left Ireland and was never seen again,' added Lenka, looking down at her half-empty bottle.'

'Oh no,' said Brendan. 'That is when *da* legend of *Da* Englander began.'

'The Englander!' spat Simon. 'But he's not English!'

'I know, but there is a character in the Rogues comics,' said Brendan, before pausing. 'Sorry, *yer* probably never heard of *'em.*'

'I have,' said Lenka without acknowledging that they were based on her family.

'Well, one of *da* original Rogues was an Irishman called Sean Ryan. He was also a member of one of *da* Twelve Apostles, Michael Collins' gang of assassins.' He peered over at Simon. 'But you Brits call them Murder Inc, I hear. I guess being a pagan country, *yer* don't know *yor* bible.' The British officer's eyes narrowed. 'Anyway, when Collins on behalf of *da* Irish government signed *da* Irish Treaty with *da* Brits, he and Ryan and many other fighters laid down their arms. This led *ta* civil war. The *RA* tried *ta* recruit

209

Ryan and, like Pierce, they were sent away, but with more than a "*feck* off" ringing in their ears.'

'Can we stick to the question. Why is he called The Englander?'

'Ah, sorry. I got carried away. It was because he had travelled around *da* world, and lost his Irish brogue. Having lost that beautiful lyrical voice, people must have *taut* he was English. That, and perhaps he was rude and didn't have a sense of humour,' said Brendan, smiling at the Englishman.

Simon did not return it.

'So that is how Connor Pierce got the name The Englander,' said Lenka, quietly, before taking a sip from the bottle.

'*Ta* be honest, it was probably more *dew* to the fact that when he wiped out O'Mara's whole unit, witnesses swore *dat* his eyes were the coldest blue.'

Lenka sat up. 'It's true! Connor's natural eye colour is grey-green and we saw them change in a bar here a few days ago.'

Simon glowered at her, though Lenka did not notice.

Brendan continued. 'In *da* Rogues comics, Ryan's eyes change colour when he *wer* threatened or when he killed. It is said that when *da* Englander's blue eyes fall on *yer*, *yer* are already dead. Course it may all be *shite* and blown up over a pint, but that's the legend of Connor Pierce. The only *ting* is that unlike other legends, he's still alive – at least *fer* now.'

'You said this was only the beginning?' said Lenka.

'*Jasus*, sorry! I wander about like a drunk after the Ballykelly Festival. Pierce's *ma* was buried a week later, but he refused *ta* leave Belfast until after *da* burial. That week, three *RA* assassination teams were dispatched to kill him, each bigger and *feckin* deadlier than the last.'

'And they all failed,' said Simon, grimly.

'Not just failed,' said Brendan, with a shake of his head. 'No one *feckin* returned. After that, *da* chieftains let it be known that *Da* Englander would no longer be a target, but if he ever returned to Ireland he'd be hunted down like a dog.' Brendan finished his bottle and placed it gently on the table. 'Well Pierce didn't *feckin* like *dat*. He told '*em* that if one *RA* man came after him, he would return and wipe out *da* chieftains.' Brendan drained the bottle. 'Time for bed; we'll finish *da* plastering tomorrow.' He smiled at the young couple as he straightened up. 'You're fortunate in having Pierce for a friend; no harm will ever come to *ya*.'

'He's no friend of mine,' replied Simon, acidly.

At first, the Irish contingent and the local tradesmen working on the renovation worked together uneasily. Each believed that their approach to the tasks was superior. When in doubt, the Irish ripped out everything and started afresh, whilst the Romanians built on what was already there. With the aid of the international language of football and beer, they began to learn from each other.

By the end of the week, the Irish and the local tradesmen organised a football match on the road outside the building; a building that all were now proud of. It was as solid as any of the new buildings reshaping the city's skyline, but more resilient. Incorporating the best quality materials from Ireland, held together with Romanian cement – adapted over the centuries so it blended quickly and solidly, yet would be flexible in the hottest of summers and coldest of winters. Before he left, Brendan told Lenka that he was bringing some bags of it back to Ireland.

'I've done a deal with a couple of *da* lads here, and I'm going *ta* open a little business back home selling it,' said Brendan, after posing for a group photo of all the tradesmen. 'I'm naming it in honour of *yerself*.'

'Lenka Cement?' she replied, incredulously.

'*Sur* no, "*Wogue* Cement", I'll be calling it, but I'd *luv ta* put a picture of *yer* gorgeous face on the bag.'

Lenka sighed, before forcing a smile. 'Of course, Brendan, my face plastered on a bag of cement, that's quite an honour. Would you mind if I offered to check the spelling before you print the bags?'

'Grand. If *yer'd* said no, though, I was going to put a picture of *meself* on *da* bag.' Behind him, the rest of The Boys from the Hill, were grinning and making obscene gestures about his size. Someone muttered, '*Sur* who'd *feckin* buy it; *yer'd* never lift it!'

Chapter 11: Boy meets Girl, Boy . . .

8.35am, 21 July 1990, Bucharest

Five days later, The Boys from the Hill reloaded their bags and tools into three transit vans to take them to Bucharest Airport. A throng of locals had gathered around the vehicles as young women presented some of the flush-faced youngest of the Irishmen with tulips. Andrew, at seventeen, went crimson when one young woman pecked him on the cheek. Four cases of Carling were handed over to the local tradesmen, as bottles of plum brandy passed in the other direction, followed by laughter and handshakes.

Anita appeared and approached Lenka. 'I talked to Connor on the telephone this morning. He wanted you to have this,' she said, as she handed her a Rolex watch.

'Why?' asked Lenka.

'He left it behind, and when I mentioned your clash with the Englishman at our orphanage and that you gave the little boy your watch, he said he wanted you to have it.'

'But it was only a cheap watch and . . .'

'Sorry,' said Anita. 'I've got to rush back. A number of staff have a virus and Carol is coping all on her own.'

Then the Italian nurse disappeared back into the crowd.

Brendan approached and threw his arms around Lenka. 'Keep in touch. We want to know how *da* kids get on. With the money I'll make from *Wogue Cement*, we'll be back like a shot if *yer* need us.'

Lenka leaned in and gave him a bigger squeeze followed by a kiss on his ruby cheek. He did not blush. 'I'll tell *da* wife when I get back of the beautiful Lenka, with the silky blonde-hair. She'll either take an interest in "a bit of how's *yer* father" again; if *yer* get me drift,' adding a wink, 'or stab me in *da feckin* heart.' He pondered. 'Ah *sah*, it will bollocks *me* new business, if I'm on a life support machine. Best I don't mention it at all.'

'You're a terrible man, Brendan,' said Lenka, before pulling away with blobs of dry plaster stuck to her

Arran jumper.

'*Sur* I am that, Lenka, but on *da* good side at least I'm consistent,' said Brendan, chuckling, before dragging himself into the passenger seat next to the driver of the lead vehicle. Brendan pointed ahead and the vehicles set off slowly, as parents hurried their excited children off the pockmarked road.

The humid air began to cool as the sun disappeared behind the skyline. Lenka and Simon had worked without a break since the departure of The Boys from the Hill, and residents from the surrounding, crumbling, grey blocks had dispersed back to their homes, carrying plastic cups of *Robinsons* lemon barley water.

The bright, pristine building seemed gigantic now that the only ones inside were Lenka and Simon.

Simon was scaling the ladder to fit a bulb into a ceiling light. He glanced over at Lenka who was no longer scrubbing the floor. She gradually began to slide forwards. Simon leapt off the ladder and raced towards her, as her head bounced off the bare stone floor.

Lenka's eyes flickered, until Anita's genial smile came into focus. 'You have a fever, Lenka, you need to rest.'

'My heart pills?'

Anita lifted Lenka's head and placed two small tablets in her mouth, before raising a glass of water up to her lips.

'What happened?' asked Lenka, after swallowing her pills.

'You passed out and Simon brought you straight to us. We summoned a doctor we know. He said that with your weak heart, fatigue has worn you down. But with rest you will be fine.'

'Thanks for looking after me. How long have I been here?'

'Twenty-four hours I'd say, but Simon has stayed here most of the time.' The Italian nurse smiled. 'Lucky you, what a catch. He looks like a film star.'

Lenka smiled. 'Carol said much the same, but we're not together.'

'Really,' replied Anita. 'You are far sicker than you appear,' she said, before grinning.

'You really are starting to understand English

humour. Connor's influence, no doubt.'

The Italian nurse laughed as she raised a spoonful of tomato soup from the pot, simmering on a Calor gas stove by the side of the bed. 'Come on, have some. Well, you may not be a couple, but he was fretting after you. He's quite *bitten*, I think is the English expression.'

Lenka smiled. 'Smitten.'

As Lenka lifted her head from the pillow, her clammy body began to shiver before she fell back into unconsciousness.

When Lenka opened her eyes again, the room was bathed in moonlight.

'How are you feeling?' asked Simon, as he sat up from the sleeping bag on the bare stone floor by her bed.

'Freezing,' though her temperature was still high. The man opened his sleeping bag and placed it on top of the four blankets covering her.

'You have no covering, climb in next to me. I could do with the warmth.'

Simon slipped in beside her and wrapped his arms

tightly around her, as her eyes closed.

Lenka's hazel eyes slowly began to open to be met by the light of dawn. Her body was no longer trembling or bathed in sweat; the fever had broken. Simon was asleep. She snuggled up to him. Slipping her hand between the buttons of his shirt, she rested her hand on his solid bare chest. The warming scent of his body and powerful physicality filled her senses. Lying beside him was so comforting, so natural, so right. He began to stir.

She whispered in his ear, 'Take your clothes off.'

Midday sunlight crept across their naked bodies. Lenka hesitated to lift her face up from Simon's chest. *Would his expression be one of elation, victory, indifference, or worst of all, regret? The look in his face, before I fell asleep, seemed distant, yet uneasy.*

She felt his breath on her hair, and to her relief, a gentle kiss followed.

11.10am, 28 July 1990, Bucharest

'With a lot of help from our friends and the locals,

we've done it,' said Lenka, standing outside the renovated orphanage, with her fists resting on her hips. 'In two weeks, it's been re-plastered, painted, the roof has been re-laid, the windows are in, the plumbing works and the lights are on.'

'A lot has happened, and,' as Simon inhaled deeply, 'much of this is completely new to me.'

Lenka looked up at him, and said drily, 'Please don't lie for my benefit and tell me that the other night was your first time.'

Simon smiled. 'But it was, in a way.'

Lenka frowned. 'I'm not an idiot, I haven't a clue, but you clearly . . .'

'I'm in love for the first time,' he said softly.

'With . . . who?'

'You have to ask?'

'Yes,' said Lenka. 'Because this world is completely new to me.'

He bent his head and kissed her hard on the lips, as she folded her arms around his hips.

Lenka threw her head back and laughed. She released him, skipped over to her truck and opened the glove compartment. She fumbled around until she found the cassette she wanted and slammed it into the tape recorder. Four notes on a piano introduced Phil Collins *A Groovy Kind of Love*.

'Come on, let's dance,' she said, jumping down and seizing Simon's hands.

'No . . . I can't dance,' said Simon.

'I am going to teach you,' she said, as she spun towards him and leaned into his arms before spinning back out.

As she quickened her pace and gyrated around him, Simon tried to follow. Each time he slipped, she caught him, only to reel away from him. Gradually, he managed to keep pace and they began to swirl around the truck. Simon's confidence grew, as Lenka's flight increased in speed and grace.

Lenka began to laugh and Simon began to join her. She realised that this was the first time she had ever heard him laugh. Simon lost his footing and began to tumble forwards. He tried to gain a hold on the passenger side mirror but missed. Lenka caught his waist, steadied him and turned him towards her.

Simon placed his hands once more on Lenka's hips and laughed. *I've never laughed like this; so easily, so freely.*

Lenka heard a dull crack and caught a flash and a small puff of smoke from a building to her left. Simon clutched her against his chest. She felt what she thought were droplets of water land on her head. It was raining, but nothing would spoil this moment. But the droplets quickly became streams flowing through her hair and down her cheeks. Simon gripped her tighter. He began to gasp, which became a seizure.

Lenka turned her face upwards. Blood fell into her eyes. Simon locked her arms in his frozen grip and dropped to his knees, dragging her down too. She began to scream.

Lenka's cries brought the new staff from the children's hospice into the sweltering courtyard. The nurses found the young couple locked together on their knees. It took four nurses to break the couple's hold on each other, as the love song coming from the truck ended.

It was not until she received an injection of morphine

that Lenka's screams finally fell silent. As her body relaxed, she softy said 'Simon,' before her eyes closed.

Chapter 12: Strange Bedfellows

Noon, 10 August 1990, London

'A first round kill, to the side of the head.'

'And the distance?'

'1300 metres. It was taken from the roof of a neighbouring building, so the marksman had to take into account the drop in trajectory. Not in itself an indication of a professional assassin, but a damn fine shot.'

'The weapon?'

The major shook his head.

'Shells?'

'One.'

'The marksman had plenty of time, so why a shot to the side of the head, rather than the frontal lobe?'

'A headshot nonetheless, so clearly the aim was to kill.'

'Of course.' Major Janus dropped his hands, though he was clearly perturbed.

In an office in a far corner of Admiralty Arch,

Janus continued to follow the order he had received from his superiors to answer Foxy's questions 'directly and no more'.

'And no sign of the killer, nor the rifle?' continued Foxy. The major shook his head.

'The Romanian police recorded one cartridge shell.' He picked up the file from his desk and flipped a page. 'I'm no expert, but the inspector . . .' He raised his eyebrows. 'No, Sergeant Elenuta Dimetre, clearly is though and writes that it's from a Mauser M98, adding a "deer hunters' rifle".'

'A bolt-action rifle, a robust weapon used on the battlefield in both world wars,' said Foxy. 'Have the Romanian police any suspects?'

'Numerous. It appears that a superintendent of a local orphanage was murdered two weeks earlier and his cronies, who are apparently linked to criminal organisations, believed that the aid workers were involved. They also crossed swords with one of the local gang lords, a man called . . .' The major re-examined the file. 'Bulla.'

'Anything else, Major?'

'For instance?'

'You continue to answer my questions, but no more.'

'I do as I'm told,' replied the major. 'Your influence in the corridors of Whitehall warrants this *open* discussion.'

'The only thing open in here is a decanter containing this excellent *Bowmore*,' interrupted Foxy, lifting a glass containing two fingers of single malt.

'Please help yourself to my finest whisky, why don't you,' grunted Major Janus.

Foxy was about to place the decanter back on the officer's desk but stopped. 'That's very kind of you,' he replied, before adding two more fingers to his crystal glass.

The major reclined in his chair while continuing to look sourly at the man opposite. 'I'll extend my remit; I don't like you, Foxy, I never have.'

'What a blow, as I always thought of you as that rare breed of officer who doesn't have a wasp up his arse.'

'Your dislike for authority is well-documented.'

'Sounds like a riveting read. Now, the truth. What was the story of Captain Syrianus?'

'An officer with an exemplary record. No tours of duty, a desk bod.'

'Still only obeying, Major. History has shown the contribution made by such soldiers,' said Foxy.

'Bait me all you like. Are we finished?'

'No. Tell me the names of his colleagues, his commanding officer, his . . .'

'I have no idea.'

'The Ministry of Defence Building is five minutes-walk, then eight floors in a lift to reach the top.'

'It's true. I never met him,' continued the major.

'According to his record, he was under your command for nine months,' snapped Foxy.

'Officially. He never reported to me, or my staff.'

'Ah!' nodded Foxy, rolling the crystal glass between his palms. 'A cuckoo's egg.'

'I didn't say that,' said the major, nodding.

'MI5 or MI6?'

The officer opened his hands and closed them.

'What do you know of the murder of Joseph

McNamara?' asked Foxy.

'Only what is in the newspapers. A bullet to the head. Nothing in the room was disturbed. A Webley revolver was found still inside McNamara's coat. A professional kill. The suspect was a man matching your description, but was not named. That's it.' Foxy refreshed his glass. 'How is your ward? I believe she has not returned to Ireland, yet.'

'She has stayed to help transport children to the new orphanage. I'm flying out to collect her tomorrow.'

'After what she went through, she is, indeed, an exceptional woman.'

'Why do you ask? Was it scribbled as a late comment by your superiors on your "remit" to show empathy at the end of our talk?'

'Don't be churlish. She has suffered terribly. The Romanian police reported that when Trevelyan's body was found, she was still clamped in his arms covered in blood, in a state of catatonic shock.'

'Churlish maybe, but I'm certainly angry,' snarled Foxy. His eyebrows drew closer. 'Are you asking, because you believe she is on the assassin's list?'

'If such a list exists, and she were on it, she would almost certainly be dead already.'

Foxy stared at the major. 'Is there anything else that I should know?'

Major Janus let his fingertips settle on his chin.

'I would suggest that your ward carries on her good works in the orphanage in Ireland and retires from voluntary work abroad.'

'Not good enough, Major,' spat Foxy. 'You know far more than you are prepared to tell.'

'My thoughts are based on instinct. I have no evidence to justify it.' Foxy scowled at the officer. 'I'm not a Dickensian character whose name reflects their nature.'

'Major Janus, I do not form judgements based on a person's name, but on their actions,' said Foxy.

The pulsing telephone shattered the tension in the room, like a bell ending the first round in a boxing bout. The major lifted the receiver and nodded a few times in response to the voice on the other end of the line. He placed the receiver back down. 'I have been summoned to an emergency meeting in Downing Street. You can find your own way out.'

'I will not let this lie, until I know Lenka is no longer in danger.'

As the major rose, he looked down at Foxy before pushing the decanter towards him. 'You know, following our talk, there is one thing that links the murder of Joseph McNamara, the superintendent at the orphanage and Captain Trevelyan.'

'What's that?

'Lenka Brett.'

7.30am, 13 August 1990, Cork

'Lenka,' said Estelle tapping on the door of the young woman's bedroom. 'Can I come in?'

'Of course, I'm just marking homework.'

Estelle sat down on the edge of the bed. She gently drew Lenka's head towards her and rested it on her shoulder. 'I got here as soon as I could. I'm so sorry,' said Estelle.

Lenka wrapped her arms around Estelle's waist and began to weep.

Twenty minutes later, Foxy bundled his way through the front door of Marisa's Arms, along with Cedric, both carrying fresh doughnuts from The Imperial Hotel's kitchen. The dam of cereal boxes in the dining room collapsed and a flood of children swamped the hall. Leaping hands grabbed frantically at the pastries.

'Away to the dining room', shouted Foxy. 'You demons in the guise of children.' The children screamed with laughter as the flood returned to gather around the upturned cardboard boxes.

Margaret began to untie the red ribbons around the array of doughnut boxes. 'How are we supposed to keep this lot in order, when you ply them with sugar first thing in the morning?' said the mousy-haired woman, whose abundance of freckles added to her genial demeanour.

'You are absolutely right, Margaret,' said Foxy. 'Of course, it could be worse.'

'How?' asked Robert, who had arrived an hour earlier to help Margaret set the table for breakfast for thirty, waiting for a playful response.

'Well, it could be *my* problem,' said Foxy, followed

with a grin.

Margaret and Robert exchanged knowing smiles, and the children laughed, with the boys the loudest.

'You are incorrigible, Foxy,' noted Estelle entering the packed dining room. Lenka, beside her, broke off to straighten Hannah's wheelchair so it was nearer her bowl of Kellogg's Cornflakes.

'No pastries until you've finished your cereal, milk and apple,' announced Lenka.

'Yes Miss,' came the chorus as milk and splashes of apple juice began to erupt.

Foxy walked over to Lenka. 'How are we this morning?'

'"We" are fine, though I fear for your health if you ever start the day with doughnuts again.'

Foxy bowed. 'I am suitably admonished.'

After breakfast, the mass of children split into three groups. The eldest children broke off with Margaret to exercise in the backyard, while Robert and Lenka divided the others into two classes.

Cedric placed cups of tea on the table in front of Estelle and Foxy, before setting off to fuel the Bentley.

'When did she get home?' asked Estelle.

'Two days ago. An RAF transporter collected her from Bucharest,' said Foxy.

'With you on it?'

Foxy nodded.

'I can't remember the last time I heard her cry,' said Estelle, quietly.

'She's putting on an amazing front for the children. When they greeted her in the hall, she hugged every single one of them and never shed a tear.'

'Do they know?'

'The girls ask for the handsome captain, but Lenka smiles and says he's gone away.'

'Has she talked to you?'

'Mostly tears, but she told me that she and Simon were lovers,' said Foxy.

'When you called me in San Francisco you said he was killed in her arms.'

Foxy shook his head solemnly. 'Yes. But fortunately, no injuries. The only physical evidence of that terrible moment is the cracked face of her Rolex, which was damaged when they fell to the ground.'

Estelle rested her face in her hands. 'My God!' After a few moments, she lifted her head. 'And her heart?'

'Dr Cassidy has examined her. It beats infrequently but that's because she hadn't been taking her pills.'

Estelle's eyes widened as she dropped her hands.

'It's okay. She forgot to take them, and she was in a morphine-induced coma for a day or so. She's fine now.'

Estelle slumped back in the chair. 'Is she fine?' Foxy shook his head. 'She cried her heart out upstairs.'

Foxy peered up from beneath his heavy eyebrows. 'Marisa says she cries in her room when she thinks no one can hear her.'

Chapter 13: Emptiness

5.30pm, 13 February 1992, Cork

Davy, who was nine, was always the first to answer a knock at the front door of Marisa's Arms. 'You're black,' said the little boy, when he saw the huge man.

Klay threw his hands out and looked down. 'Good God, you're right!'

'I've seen *Roots* on *da* telly, and I once saw a black man on the street when we all went on a day trip to the museum in Dublin. He wasn't in chains or in a cage, or anything like that, though.'

'I'm relieved to hear it,' responded Klay, with a smile. 'You must be the man of the house?'

'Well, Foxy and his chauffeur Cedric pop in occasionally, as does Father Kent, but I live here and I'm the one opening the door, so I guess I am.'

'Pleased to meet you,' said the man, holding out his hand. 'I'm Kenneth Clayton, but you can call me Klay.'

The boy smiled proudly as he shook his hand. 'I'm David O'Toole, my best friend Peter calls me "big tool", but you can call me Davy.'

'A pleasure to make your acquaintance, Davy. Now, I've come to see Miss Lenka Brett. Is she here?'

'Yes, she's teaching the little 'uns. I'll stick you . . . ,' then he paused. 'No, I'll *take* you to the kitchen and then I'll fetch her.'

Ten minutes later, Lenka and Klay were sitting at the kitchen table with a pot of tea and two china cups in front of them. 'It's been 18 months, Klay. What adventures have you been up to?'

'The biggest of all. I married a wonderful lady and we have a son and another child on the way.'

'Wow! You don't mess around when you put your mind to something.'

'Neither do you. That's why I'm here.'

Margaret walked in and stopped immediately, as Klay stood up.

'Hi, I'm Klay, a friend of Lenka's.'

Margaret struggled for words. 'I've never met a . . .'

'Such a tall, good-looking man before.'

Margaret burst out laughing. 'Oh, if only that was what I was thinking. I'm very sorry, it's just that I've . .

. I'm Margaret, it's a pleasure to meet you,' she said, as her hand disappeared in his. 'Lenka has mentioned you many times.' She collected her notepad from the table. 'I hope you'll be joining us for dinner, the class will blow up with excitement when they see a . . . our guest.'

She went out the back door and joined some of the children playing out the back.

'Margaret meant no harm,' said Lenka.

'No offence taken,' said Klay as he poured the tea.

'Tell me about your wife. Is this the Brazilian lady?'

'Yes, Claudia. She has taken on the challenge of loving this child in a man's body.'

Lenka stood up and embraced the powerful man, who was still sitting. 'I'm really happy that you found someone.'

Klay hesitated, but decided not to offer any platitudes, before placing his hand on her blonde hair and pressing her head lightly against his shoulder.

Lenka straightened up and said quietly, 'And thanks for not saying that I too will find someone soon.'

She took a sip of *PG Tips* tea. 'Right, hit me with it.

Rogues don't do social calls.'

Klay stretched his arms out across the checked tablecloth. 'I need your help. I have to drive a truck into Bosnia, and I need someone with your skills.'

'You drive HGVs, and I have an ordinary driving licence. You need a co-driver.'

'You've driven my rig. Lenka, I trust you and when I sleep, I need someone to rely on.'

'Buy a dog.'

'Lenka, you have an aptitude for this kind of work. Despite everything that happened in Romania, you were never diverted from what needed to be done.'

'You didn't see me at the end in Bucharest. I was a wreck. I had to be stretchered on to the plane.'

'You took on Bulla and his men by yourself. I heard about the fat Englishman and his watch, and even . . .' he hesitated, 'after Simon was killed, you went back to Estelle's new orphanage to ensure everything was finished. That takes considerable strength, in mind and in body. I'm entering a war zone and I need someone who has the resilience to survive whatever is thrown at them. That is more important than a licence to drive a truck.'

'I'm broken,' said Lenka, peering blankly into her cup. 'I'm not the Lenka you knew. I pretend to everyone that I am.' She peered up at Klay. 'I'm a joke; what people see is a façade; I'm a fraud, a hypocrite.' Klay tried to interrupt, but her piercing look stopped him. 'I'm no good to anyone, and when I am discovered, I will leave and Margaret and Robert can *officially* take over.'

'Look, to say that you've been though a terrible time would be an understatement, but deep down lies the Lenka that I knew. You can never change who you *really* are.'

Lenka appeared not to hear him as her head dropped. 'I fool the adults because they see what they want to see. But the children know I'm not the same; children see right through you.'

'Where's Connor when I need him?' said Klay, gruffly.

'Why?' said Lenka as she stood up and walked over to the window to watch the children play.

'Because he would say "Bollocks!"'

Lenka laughed. 'No he wouldn't, he would have added an F-word or two. Where is he tumbling off stages these days?'

'Last I heard of him, he was in Angola building an irrigation dam.'

'And Mary?'

'Again, the last I heard, Holey Mary was going back and forward with medicine between favelas in Rio de Janeiro. But I have sent messages to both of them, asking for their help on this venture. This is big!'

'I've seen the headlines. The Serbian and Croatian governments intend to carve up Yugoslavia between them.'

'And now Kosovo has proclaimed independence, and the Germans have recognised them. I don't give a damn about nationalism, but families are fleeing their homes, and hospitals and orphanages are under siege and starved of medicine and food.'

Lenka looked down at her fidgety hands. 'You know I have a weak heart. Even if I said I would help you, I would soon become a liability.'

'We'll look after each other.'

'I'd need a licence, and that would take time.'

'That can be sorted out tomorrow.'

'To do that, you must have a powerful friend,' said Lenka straightening up. 'Foxy has put you up to this.'

Foxy bounded into the kitchen and flumped into the leather armchair. 'My ears were on the verge of spontaneous combustion, so I guess I have been mentioned in dispatches.'

Lenka turned from the window. Her eyes narrowed on Foxy. 'We were just discussing what sentence I will receive when I murder you in your sleep.'

'Oh!' muttered Foxy, sinking into the chair.

'You appear to consider a war and the terrible plight of those under fire, as some kind of amateur therapy session for me,' said Lenka.

Foxy inhaled deeply. 'True, I think that it would help you. But when Klay called me and asked for help, even with all my contacts, you were at the top of the list because I know you can help.'

'You are the master of manipulation, so please don't patronise me,' said Lenka, turning back towards the window.

'I understand why you're angry,' said Foxy. 'It was a bad idea. I'm sorry.'

'I'm not giving up,' interjected Klay. 'I need someone I can trust. I'm entering a war zone and there are families who will live or die depending on whether our aid reaches them.'

'Klay, I told you that I'm . . .'

'Yes, I know, but you have proven that you have resilience and will battle on until the job is done.'

Lenka watched as some of the children started to play hurly in the yard. 'And what of the children here?'

Foxy spoke quietly. 'They, and indeed all of us are worried about you. Dr Cassidy says that the palpations of your heart are increasing and . . .'

'And?' said Lenka softly.

'He thinks that you're giving up.'

'So much for doctor–patient confidentiality,' said Lenka.

'He's partial to a single malt,' added Foxy. 'But he's worried about you, too.' He leant forward and clasped his hands. 'I know the little girl that I helped raise. You need purpose; it will ignite the fire inside you again.'

'I have the children,' said Lenka, smiling, as Ellen robbed the ball from Patrick's hurler just as he was about to score.

'It's the old Lenka they really want,' said Foxy. 'The girls look up to you. You were the strong, independent-minded woman they wanted to be. The boys respect you and in turn have learnt to respect women as equals.'

'So in my current state, I'm useless,' said Lenka with a shrug, as Christine claimed back the ball from Ellen with a side tackle.

'No. You are an excellent teacher, but the spark that brought so much light, is dimmed.'

'It's extinguished,' said Lenka, quietly. 'I'm empty.'

Klay looked over at Foxy. The Englishman reclined in the chair, leaving his crystal glass of Remy Martin untouched.

Lenka smiled briefly at Klay. 'You've come all this way for nothing. I'm no good to man nor beast; nor child or Rogue.'

'Tell us more about this endeavour of yours,' said Foxy, with a short nod, in the hope that the conversation would engage Lenka.

Klay returned the gesture. 'My transporter has undergone an upgrade. I've changed the blood-red livery, as it's a bit conspicuous in a war. The body has been refitted and behind the cabin is a refrigerated container to carry medicine, mainly insulin and penicillin. Nurses Abroad have raised the funding. The rest of the vehicle is packed with four baby incubators, oxygen cylinders, saline drips, transfusion kits, pacemakers, artificial limbs; you name it, it's on it.'

Lenka breathed in hard. 'And the route?'

'We collect my truck in Paris and drive through Luxemburg, Germany, Austria, Slovenia, down through Croatia, and along the Dalmatian Coast. Then before we reach Dubrovnik, we turn north towards the town of Split. After that we will finally cross into Bosnia, past Mostar and up towards Tuzla, where we will distribute the aid to the town's hospitals and orphanages.'

'Mostar is under constant bombardment,' said Foxy.

'How long will it take to reach Tuzla?' continued

Lenka.

'In peace time, two weeks, but the documents required for each border post change by the day, border posts appear overnight, bridges are regularly blown up and blockades are thrown up whenever one side advances.' Klay rested his arms on his knees and clasped his hands. 'Then of course, there will be those who will try to seize our trucks and our aid, or at the very least expect to take half of whatever aid we are carrying as a toll, or as we call it, a bribe.'

'So a month, maybe two,' said Lenka.

Klay nodded once.

'Anything else?' asked Foxy.

'As we did in Romania,' Klay said, looking at Lenka, 'we work as a team, we agree the way forward together, though if changing circumstances dictate, we just get on with it. Also, no photographs once we enter Croatia. It's a war zone, even though you won't see evidence of it until we cross into Bosnia. Keep plenty of sweets, as kids will beg you for them wherever you go. Biros are good too – drawing helps the children create a world away from the bombs. Never expect a vehicle to give way for you, whether it's the UN truck or otherwise. You'll be driven into a ditch. I've been to Bosnia twice in the last year; everyone is in a state of panic – apart from the mercenaries.' Klay nodded. 'To say it will not be easy would be an understatement.'

Foxy's right hand disappeared into his hair, as he mumbled, 'If Estelle or Marisa tried to kill me, I wouldn't blame them.'

'Cover your ears, Foxy,' continued Klay. 'No alcohol and never get drunk.'

Lenka huffed. 'You're intending to deliver the same speech to Connor and Mary if they join us?'

'I'll go through the motions, but they never saw a rule that wasn't worth breaking,' Klay said, and smiled. 'It was standard practice to say this when I was in the Paras, but I never met an army of teetotallers.'

Lenka nodded. 'You were right in Vienna.'

'Was I?' said Klay.

'When you said that Connor was a professional when it came to getting the job done. He was smashed at the time and though he liked a beer, he was never drunk on the road. Mary's the same. They would drink the legs off a piano in a stop-over, but never on the road.'

'Fine, upstanding people,' said Foxy. 'You could set your watch by them. I look forward to meeting them one day.'

Lenka laughed. 'In Romania I imagined what it would be like if the Rogues came here one day and finally met you and the children – we might need to move to a bigger island.' Foxy and Klay exchanged nods and smiled. 'Thanks for raising my spirits, guys. But you need to adopt a more secret code, as the nodding is a bit wearing: I'm here, you know.'

Lenka pulled her cardigan together and folded her arms, as Davy wrestled the ball from Christine and passed it to Philomena. She ran towards the goal and walloped it into the back of the net, much to Hannah's delight, who was sitting in the porch in her wheelchair. 'Where are you staying, Klay?'

'I have a room in Kennedy's; it's a bar in town.'

'I'm in The Imperial,' said Foxy. 'We'll drop you off along the way.'

'I need to talk to Estelle and Marisa,' said Lenka.

'I'll let you know what I decide before the morning.'

The stern face on the grandfather clock in the hall of Marisa's Arms, struck 7 o'clock.

'Right, time for a stiff drink,' said Foxy, hurrying Klay out of the kitchen, and grabbing Robert as he came in the front door. 'Come on! Marisa's study. When the authorities came to serve notice on this place, she used to ply them with some stain on the reputation of the whiskey industry, in the hope that they would forget why they came.'

'I'm not really a drinker,' said Robert.

'One should never boast about one's weaknesses,' said Foxy, as he opened the door to Marisa's former study to let Robert enter at his own pace.

'Why the cane, Foxy?' asked Klay, looking down. 'You don't seem to need it.'

'It was given to me by the renowned international singer and dancer, Josephine Baker. Its former owner was Samuel Clark, a veteran of the Great War and a good friend.'

'It has sentimental value?' said Klay.

Foxy pressed the silver button on the handle

releasing the steel tongue from the tip. 'And you could say a medicinal one, as it has extended my life on more than one occasion. Ah, found it', said Foxy as he lifted a half-empty bottle from a drawer. But when he read the label, *Murphy's Ruin*, it was clear from his expression that he wished he had not. He produced three crystal glasses from another drawer and filled them with the enthusiasm of a man about to tuck into his final meal before being hung.

Foxy smiled, as he lifted a frame from the desk. It contained a photo of Estelle, Marisa and a young Lenka laughing and covered in baking flour.

'My truck is fully laden with medical supplies and is in a compound by Charles de Gaulle Airport,' said Klay, grimacing after taking a sip of the scotch. 'I thought this stuff improves with age.'

'Usually,' said Foxy taking a sip of his drink. He gasped. 'But this is clearly some sort of fuel, so any improvement would be down to a rapid depreciation in taste buds.' Foxy handed an envelope to Klay. 'Travel documents, including a rush job covering Lenka.'

'You believe she will go?' said Robert before taking a sip of the whiskey and coughing profusely.

Foxy nodded. 'Lenka has never refused a challenge.' He lobbed a thick, brown envelope towards Klay. 'Here is additional currency in the relevant denominations to help cover the next few weeks.'

'Thank you,' said Klay, as he placed the packets inside his waxed green, Barbour jacket without checking the contents.

Foxy took the men's glasses along with his own and emptied them into a flowerpot containing a geranium. 'Never let it be said that I'm too much of a snob to sample the local hooch.' Foxy poured two fingers of Glenmorangie single malt whisky from his hip flask into each of the three glasses.

He flopped into the black leather armchair and turned to Klay, as each man sat on a chair by the desk. 'A Russian woman, Katalina Bulgakov, had her throat slit in the very chair you are sitting in,' said Foxy, studying the man carefully for his reaction. Klay appeared unmoved. 'You're not easily unsettled, are you?'

'You should have seen me the night Alberto, my son, was born. When they placed him in my arms, I cried more than he did.'

'Our previous encounters brought us to the epicentre of some of the world's bloodiest conflicts,' Foxy said, then paused.

'What is it?' asked Klay.

'When you were in the Paras or on your aid missions, did you ever encounter a group of mercenaries known as the Wolves?' Foxy continued, without removing his eyes from the glass.

'I've heard of them. Lethal killers who have banded together and operate wherever the financial rewards are highest. But I've never encountered them. Why do you ask?'

'When I first met the late Captain Trevelyan he asked about them, but as I knew nothing about them I paid no heed at the time. He also asked about Lenka's parents and their Nazi nemesis, The Alpha Wolves. It was only after his death that I began to wonder why he was so interested. Well, I made some checks and picked up mention of them in foreign dispatches, nothing more than that. A file had been opened on them two years ago, but was closed shortly afterwards.'

'So, Simon was simply snooping,' said Robert.

Klay eyed Foxy. 'Unusual for an investigation to be opened only to be closed so quickly without resolution.'

Foxy's Bentley drew up outside.

'Will your driver not join us?' asked Robert.

'No, Cedric has come to drive me back to the Imperial tonight.'

Robert nodded. Even though there was always a spare room made up for Foxy, he understood why he never used it.

'How do you think it's going upstairs?' asked Klay.

Foxy sighed. 'A decision will be reached in that room for sure. I talk the most and prance around like a peacock, but it's the women who make the decisions under this roof.' He shrugged and smiled before looking sadly at Klay. 'So, you're staying in a room above Kennedy's Bar.'

'Yes, not as grand as The Imperial, I expect.'

Foxy pondered. 'Kennedy's Bar used to be run by

an old friend of mine and Lenka's father. A good man.'

'Seamus O'Shaughnessy, the Quiet Mountain of Driscoll, as he was called in the Rogues comics,' said Robert. 'Have you read them, Mr Clayton?'

'Please call me Klay. No, I haven't. I've seen them on shelves in airports, but there's enough blood and gore in my life, already. Give me a good Harold Robbins any day.'

Foxy's eyebrows drew together quizzically as if to eavesdrop. 'You've read them, Robert?'

'Who hasn't, Sir?' Robert replied, smiling.

'Decent, God-fearing citizens, like Mr Clayton, here!' roared Foxy, mimicking Canon Moore's fire and brimstone voice, used regularly to scold his congregation.

Foxy's face grew solemn again, as he thought of his late friends.

'I've never read them,' said Klay, smiling at his troubled friend. 'Should I?'

'Oh, you should. They're not for the faint-hearted thou. . .' began Robert.

'Certainly not, they're testosterone-fueled Boy's-Own escapism. Then he added gruffly, 'And they make me look like a buffoon'.

The other two men glanced at each other and back at the rotund, rhubarb-cheeked man, wearing a canary-yellow waistcoat and bright red-tweed trousers, cradling an empty glass.

Foxy nodded at Robert, who continued: 'They used to be edited by Lenka's grandmother. When she died, Estelle took over the editing, until Lochran, Sean's son and our Lenka's father, story was told.'

Foxy smiled as he lifted his glass. 'Who knows, maybe one day, Lenka will have tales to tell.' He smiled and drained his glass. 'I hope I'm portrayed in a more mature, avuncular manner and less like an excitable, childish arsehole, this time.' Frowning, he looked up at the men. 'I refused to acknowledge that Estelle was in the room for over a month, after the last one came out.'

Robert leaned forward towards Foxy and said quietly, 'The Captain's interest in the comics could simply be that he was a fan of the stories.'

'I do not believe that the late captain was the type to let his imagination run riot,' said Foxy. He looked quizzically at Klay. 'What do you think?'

Klay shook his head. 'My friend Connor described him as an automaton.'

'Ah, Connor Pierce,' said Foxy. 'Lenka mentions him, but not in an animated way, as she does you, or this other lady, Mary.'

'Lenka and Connor have some connection, but I couldn't work it out,' said Klay. 'Neither can they I think.'

Robert tried not to make eye contact.

'Well, perhaps Lenka needs a new love in her life. She's a young woman and maybe it will bring her out of herself,' said Foxy. Robert's head dropped. 'If so, I hope this Connor does not treat her unnecessarily cruelly.'

'Unnecessarily is a strange word to use,' said Robert.

'All relationships have an element of cruelty, based on either possessiveness, jealousy or overfamiliarity, as I have learnt.'

'Were you married?' asked Klay.

'Married!' Foxy bellowed laughter. 'The world is not yet ready for such an event.'

The men finished their drinks and made their way to the kitchen. Foxy stretched his arm up to place his hand on Klay's shoulder. 'It's good to see you again.'

'We've only met in hotspots before, so it's a relief to have a drink in less dangerous surroundings,' Klay said, smiling.

'The danger has not passed and you will need every ounce of guile to survive your next encounter, my friend.'

'How so?' said Klay.

'You are about to undergo vigorous screening,' said Foxy. 'Marisa, Lenka's great-aunt wants to meet you.'

'Why?'

'Because the rest of us completely ballsed up the vetting of the last co-driver.'

'You mean Simon. Why?' asked Klay.

Foxy huffed, as he shook his head, 'Unfortunately, I believe Captain Syrianus Trevelyan's CV would have done Baron Munchausen proud.'

Upstairs in Marisa's bedroom, the three women were gathered around a tray containing a teapot and three china cups.

'I have to take up Klay's offer and join the convoy,' began Lenka.

'I understand,' replied Marisa.

'I don't,' said Estelle. 'You are entering a war. Romania was different.

'I just can't function any more. Without Margaret and Robert agreeing to stay on and help, the orphanage would have collapsed.'

'Now, that's rubbish,' said Marisa. 'They are both a godsend, but if anything were to happen to the orphanage you would pull us through. You need a challenge. For you, a challenge is to take on the impossible.'

Estelle shook her head. '*Mother*, you support this mad escapade?'

'Yes, because it's also the right thing to do. I've read the papers. Families are being forced from their homes, and women and children are the targets of gunmen. My brother Sean stood up for families in the last war and now his granddaughter wants to do the same.' She reached out to take Lenka's hand. 'I'd be surprised if you didn't volunteer.'

Lenka and Estelle exchanged looks of surprise. Never before had their *Mother* spoken with such passion on a subject that did not concern the orphanage or the Church.

Estelle had never challenged her mother or her ward until now. 'Lenka, please don't go.'

'I must. I have moped about here for two years, forcing the children to look at my pitiful face.'

'The children here need you.'

'Estelle, there are other children who need me more.'

'Lenka, you're in pain. You're trying to grab something, something of substance, but thinking that entering a war zone is the answer is madness.' She walked over to the bed and sat just on the edge. 'We cannot lose Lenka again. You must know that, *Mother*. Please don't support her in this. We raised her, and together we always swore to protect her.'

Marisa's frail hand fumbled to find Estelle's. 'I

never wanted to cause you pain, but Lenka must spread her wings. It is not for us to clip them.'

The elderly woman rested her head back against the pillow, the strain of keeping her head up having drained her.

Estelle wiped the tears from Marisa's cheeks and then her own. 'And if, like Icarus, she soars towards the sun, we stand back and simply watch?'

'A terrible waste to leave liquorice out in the sun, I prefer to eat it *meself*.' Marisa tried to reach the drawer. 'I think I may have some in a bag here.'

Estelle laughed. 'Icarus was a Greek god with wings made of wax, *Mother*.'

'*Sur* what would I know about Greek gods. I was wondering how you kept a good figure with such a sweet tooth.'

Estelle leaned forward, and gently hugged Marisa. 'I despair with you. Whenever I am about to win an argument, you sidestep me playing the innocent, simple old lady routine, while removing the ground from under me.'

Marisa peered over her shoulder and winked at

Lenka, who nodded and smiled back.

Five minutes later, Lenka entered the kitchen and announced she would join Klay on the convoy. Klay stood up and hugged her, while Foxy and Robert nodded reluctantly.

Lenka drew back, but left her hands on Klay's arms. 'Before we get the show on the road, Marisa and Estelle want to meet you. Come on.' She turned to the other two men. 'And you two. Come on. Upstairs.'

Ten minutes later, after Lenka had helped Robert up the stairs, everyone was gathered in Marisa's bedroom.

'I've never had a black man in my bedroom before,' welcomed Marisa, taking Klay's hand in hers.

Lenka and Estelle glared at Foxy, who responded with a cherubic grin and began whistling.

'Pleased to meet you Miss Ryan,' said Klay. 'I'm not too much of a shock, I hope?'

'Certainly not. I've never travelled, so I'm always delighted when the world comes to me. *Yer* must have raised a few eyebrows in town, though?'

'I've lived in Rio de Janeiro on and off for two

years. Its Portuguese history means that it's a mixture of all colours, so no one bats an eyelid. But I have to say, that since arriving in Ireland last night,' Klay said as he sat down, 'I've received as many wary looks as I did when I entered Romania.'

'Wary is a good word. I know nothing about Romania, but we're mostly a farming culture and prefer routine to change. Apart from a few fiery red heads, Ireland is as pale and white as you can get. But you will not find more welcoming people, once they get over the shock of a seven-foot black man walking down the High Street.'

'I'm only six foot one,' said the man, and smiled.

'Then it must be your character that makes you stand out,' said the elderly woman, before joining the man in laughter.

'An integrator of the highest order,' said Klay, smiling at Foxy.

'I told you. The softening-up process is complete, now for the knuckle-dusters.'

'What tosh,' said Marisa, looking up and smiling at Robert, who was sitting in the leather armchair in the far corner. 'I know it's not easy for you to climb the stairs, but I'm glad you have. Is Margaret looking after the children?' Robert nodded. 'What do you have to say on this matter of Lenka, leaving us again? At such times of war and even in peace, all thoughts are of those who go, but we must hear from those who are to hold the fort.'

Robert turned nervously towards Lenka who was standing by the window. *She was always the most popular girl in their school. The other girls admired her strength, determination and positivity, while the boys were shyly captivated by her feistiness and her beauty. But it was her kindness and her smile that won my love when we ate our jam sandwiches together in the playground.* Robert smiled at his friend. 'I never asked Lenka for counsel, but she always listened sympathetically when I talked. Now, it is my turn to do the same.'

Marisa nodded. 'Margaret said pretty much the same thing.' She looked over at Klay. 'Now, you have a smile that would melt an iceberg; tell us about what you have planned.'

For the next twenty minutes Klay outlined the details

of what they were taking, the route, and, after much probing, the dangers that lay ahead.

When he had finished, Marisa peered across at Estelle. The German woman leaned forward and shook her head. 'You know I am against Lenka going?'

Lenka walked over to Estelle and knelt in front of her, taking her hands in hers. 'I must do this. I can help get the convoy through. Foxy knows that, Klay knows that and now I know it, too.'

Estelle shook her head, then turned to Foxy. 'I cannot sanction this madness!'

Foxy sighed and looked sadly at Estelle. 'It is not our job to sanction what Lenka does. She is a woman,' he smiled, 'and has been for a long, long time. It is us who are in denial.'

'So we do not warn her of the danger and try to protect her?'

'We have done. But now she has made her decision,' he said as he walked over and sat on the end of the bed and took Estelle's hands in both of his. He stared out of the window and hoped that no one would see his watery eyes. 'Now, our role is to support her any way we can, because we love her.'

That night, when the lights were finally extinguished in the kitchen, some of the older children snuck out of Marisa's Arms. Philomena, Josie, Christine, Patrick, Peter, Davy and the others, waited until Ellen had wheeled Hannah into the barn to join them.

'Klay's a fantastic footballer,' continued Davy.

'*Yer* man is shite at hurling, though,' said Peter.

'He's my friend. I'll punch *yer* in the gob.'

'Klay's great,' replied Peter. 'But I'll punch *yer* in the gob before . . .'

'We're here to talk about supporting Margaret and Robert, and to see if we can do anything to help Lenka before she goes away in the morning,' said Hannah.

The two boys shrugged and nodded. 'Tomorrow is Valentine's Day,' said Josie. 'Maybe the boys can each draw her a card?'

All the boys shook their heads in horror, though each already carried a card in their pocket for Lenka.

'I don't think Lenka cares about us,' mumbled Christine. 'This is the second time she's left us.'

'Rubbish,' said Josie, opening a packet of custard

266

creams and sprinkling them out on the tablecloth that she had spread on the ground. 'We are not at risk, and Lenka is trying to help other children who are. She never takes holiday and looks after us all year round, even on her birthday. Anyway, she won't be away long.'

Everyone nodded, including Christine. 'Sorry.'

'I hope Estelle starts writing the Rogues comics again,' said Philomena. 'I want to read Lenka and Klay's stories.'

'You shouldn't be reading them, you're too young,' said Hannah.

'Nonsense, I'm nine,' replied Philomena.

'I've read them, too,' said Peter, proudly. 'They're full of sex and violence. They're brilliant!'

'What do you know about sex?' challenged Davy.

'I've kissed a girl.'

Everyone giggled, except Peter. '*Sur* I mean. I know what to do when I do kiss a girl.'

'Are there any black Rogue characters in '*em*?' asked Ellen.

'A few; a beautiful lady called Josephine and

Samuel. He was a war veteran. Fought in the Harlem Hillwalkers,' said Davy.

'Harlem Hellfighters, *yer* dick,' said Peter. 'Patrick, there's a secret stash of '*em* under Marisa's bed next to the pisspot.'

'How can she use a pisspot?' asked Patrick. 'She's bedridden.'

'*Sur*, it must be for guests,' said Davy.

Philomena shook her head. 'Morons!'

'Foxy's a ladies man according to the comics,' said Peter.

'Don't believe all *yer* read,' said Philomena.

'Most of the characters die,' said Christine, softly.

No one said another word. When the biscuits were finished, the children helped manoeuvre Hannah back into the unlit building.

Lenka watched from her window as the children returned to the house. She walked back to her bed and lifted her grandmother's diary from the dressing table. She turned to a well-thumbed entry.

13th January 1965

We're on the cattle boat to Holyhead now. There are so many children running around and throwing up that it makes Marisa's orphanage seem like a monastery. I am going to write about love and how I dealt with loss, because I just heard the voice of a man that reminded me of Sean.

I pray, granddaughter(s), that you never suffer the losses I have experienced. I was an orphan, raised in a home in Krakow. I never mourned my parents' death, because I never knew them or even who they were. But my greatest loss was Sean. Not a day goes by when I do not think of him bounding about, quick of movement and of temper. He was the only man I ever loved, though you would need a bus to carry the army of lovers I've had.

When he died, my heart was ripped from me. I had my adopted family, Marisa, Estelle and the children, but I wandered around like a zombie. But Sean's child was inside me, your father, Lock. His life filled the void left by Sean. Lock gave me a reason to live.

If you suffer the loss of either Kirsten or Lock, or God forbid both, or the one you have grown to love, mourn their loss but fill the emptiness. You may never find love again – I never found anyone who could match Sean, but I discovered love again when your father was born. Even though the cheeky little bastard never called me mother.

The only way you can avoid loss is never to experience love, which means you are not living. All this is hard for me to write. I write about sex and violence for the Rogues comics, but mushy sentiment is not really me.

In front of me are a couple of pints of oxygenated piss (I'll have to drink them both, as your mum is still sleeping), because I've decided that if my diary entry is to offer you guidance then I have to do the mushy stuff, as loss and emptiness is more than missing the frenzy of flailing limbs or suckling babies.

When you lose someone, either they die, are imprisoned or they walk away, they remain an ever-present ghost. You may have a day when you don't think of them, then you see someone with a similar hairstyle, pick up a scent that reminds you of them or hear a voice like I did, and their image and the memories of them will again flood your thoughts. It will not give you solace if you're lonely and will even make you feel isolated in a crowd, for only you will ever know that they are always present because you still love them . . . a little bastard has just thrown up his breakfast all over my boots. Which reminds me that more piss beer is to come, as the next stop is England.

4am, 14 February 1992, Cork

The following morning, Father Kent drew up outside the orphanage in his Morris Minor, with Klay squeezed in the passenger seat. Lenka was in Marisa's room and, though it was four in the morning, the elderly woman was awake. Lenka kissed her forehead.

'*Yer* said *yer* were not the woman *yer* were,' said Marisa. 'But you are off to help families fleeing from war. Sounds just like the Lenka I knew.' Lenka embraced Marisa, closed her eyes and prayed that the frail woman would still be there when she returned.

Estelle was waiting in the hall with Lenka's rucksack that she had carried down the stairs.

'It's not too late,' said Estelle, as she embraced Lenka, who was carrying a number of cards that she had discovered left outside her door.

Lenka felt her guardian's tears on her cheek. 'Be strong. We all need you, now more than ever.'

Estelle tried to smile, but failed, as she dabbed her eyes with a tissue from her sleeve.

Lenka opened the front door and discovered Foxy flopped down on the doorstep. Like everyone else in the household, he had not slept. More than anyone, he was racked with doubt. *It was my damn idea. I thought it would be good for her, it would give her purpose again. Like her parents and grandparents, she possesses the determination and focus to achieve the impossible. But I have placed her in the line of fire.* He knew Lenka well enough to know that she would never be deterred by his late pleas to stay.

Lenka did not try to squeeze into the small gap between Foxy and the doorframe, but crouched down behind him and wrapped her arms around his neck.

'When I drive off, I don't want to see your sad face,' said Lenka.

'I'll have Cedric take the rear-view mirror down,' muttered Foxy.

'Come on, don't sulk and don't blame yourself. You know that you did the right thing in asking Klay to call on my help.'

Foxy squeezed her hands, but his head remained bowed. 'After the death of your parents, I made a promise that nothing would ever harm you. But your heart is broken and now you're off to a war that even the armies of Britain and the United States dare not enter.' He wiped a tear from his cheek. 'What a pathetic guardian, I turned out to be.'

'You've organised the driving test for when we reach Cork Airport?'

'Yes, the instructor will be waiting with a hired truck. Are you sure you want to take the test? I can have some papers put together.'

'How am I to set an example for the children, if I circumvent the rules?'

'But if you fail?'

'I won't fail.'

Lenka kissed the crown of Foxy's bushel of wild silver hair. 'Look after everyone until I'm back, and tell the children that I had to leave early. I caused more than enough chaos the last time.' She gave Foxy one more squeeze, then stood up and threw her backpack over her shoulder and stepped over him.

Father Kent forced a smile as he opened the passenger door. Lenka threw her belongings onto the back seat and climbed in. Klay, who was sitting in the front passenger seat with his head wedged in under the roof, managed to turn around. 'Are you sure about this?' Lenka nodded. 'Okay, but if you want to pull out at any time, just say so. I haven't hidden the risks involved. Romania will be a picnic compared to what lies ahead.'

BOSNIA
1992

Chapter 14: Friends Reunited

11.20am, 23 February 1992, Prague, Czechoslovakia

Lenka and Klay entered the U Zlateho Tygra bar minutes from Wenceslas Square, having parked their vehicle in a secure military compound organised by Foxy. The bar was light and colourful and a fitting reflection of the atmosphere following the Velvet Revolution and the overthrow of the Communist government two and a half years earlier.

They were met with huge cheers from a table at the far end by the bar. Mary led the welcomes, a combination of kisses and hugs, followed by Sasha. Rat remained seated and tried to smile but failed.

'I'm so sorry for all the pain you suffered,' whispered Mary as she hugged Lenka tightly. Sasha was more reserved, but still whispered, 'Suffering is what us women have to endure, but we survive.'

Lenka was grateful for their words, but neither mentioned Simon.

Klay ordered two rounds of drinks, though Rat mumbled that he would not buy one in return as he refused to contribute to the capitalist system.

'Shame Connor isn't here, he'd call you a tight bastard,' said Klay. As the waitress deposited two trays of drinks on the table, Klay peered over at the empty stage in the corner. 'Any news of Connor?'

'Bollocks to Connor,' snapped Mary. 'Let's celebrate you getting married and having a kid,' she said as she raised her glass of quadruple Blue Vodka in a toast.

'And another on the way,' added Klay, raising his glass containing a double Jack Daniels.

Lenka and Sasha raised their bottles of *Pilsner Urquell* and, apart from Rat, all clinked their bottles and glasses. '*Na Zdravi!*'

'Jesus, two! Poor woman. Here's to Claude!' shouted Connor, taking a seat and grabbing Rat's redundant bottle of Pilsner.

'It's Claudia, you big, ignorant prick,' said Mary, laughing as she grabbed Connor in what appeared to be more like a headlock than a hug.

'God, I missed your feminine wiles,' said a muffled Connor. 'And clearly you missed me, you old bat!'

Mary bashed his forehead off the edge of the table, before releasing Connor and clasping her hands around her glass. 'Sorry, I'm a little emotional,' said Mary. 'It's just great to see you all.'

'The double vodkas probably helped,' grunted Rat.

Connor laughed as he ruffled Rat's spikey hair. 'Good, it looks like you'll be next to have your bonce bounced off the table.' He pulled Mary's baseball cap down over her eyes, swiped her drink and downed it in one. As Connor and Mary traded barbs, Lenka turned to Sasha. 'It's like we've never been away.'

The goth smiled and shook her matt-black hair streaked with red. 'Don't laugh, but you lot are the closest to a family I've ever known.'

'Seriously?' said Lenka.

'Put it this way, up to now the person who has shown me the most warmth has been,' and she nodded towards Rat. He sat motionless in the middle of the melee and looked like he had just discovered he was drinking arsenic.

'Oh dear,' said Lenka dispassionately, before looking at Klay, Mary and Connor, who were laughing and firing the drinks down. 'You mean family as in the Addams.'

Sasha clinked the neck of her bottle against Lenka's. 'You can call me Wednesday.'

Ten British army soldiers entered the bar followed by their commander.

The officer approached the table of Rogues. 'I'm Major Janus.'

'The pleasure is all yours,' said Connor as he shouted an order of drinks over to the surprised bar staff looking at the armed troops.

'Your passports please,' continued the officer.

Klay leaned back in his chair and folded his arms, Mary started whistling and Connor shouted over, 'Bollocks!'

'I ask only for the documents from those of you who are British citizens – which, apart from the lady here,' turning to Lenka, 'who resides in the Republic of Ireland, means all of you. And before you ask, I have special powers under the authority of Her Majesty's

Government when British citizens are deemed to be putting themselves at risk.'

'This special power fell out of a Christmas cracker, did it?' said Connor.

'No doubt you could all put up one hell of a fight. You might even win,' added the major. 'But one way or another, the police would be called to the scene and I'm sure would impound your vehicles and their contents until they had completed their enquiries. I can assure you that if I'm still breathing that would take some considerable time.'

'I've only just passed my heavy goods test,' spluttered Lenka.

'Exactly,' continued the major. 'It will be foolhardy to proceed on your own.'

'I have a powerful . . .' added Lenka.

'Viscount "Foxy" Foxborough,' said the major. 'He is why I'm here.' Lenka and Klay looked at each other. 'He told me of your mission.'

'Why?' asked Lenka.

'After the death of Captain Syrianus Trevelyan . . .'

'That prick screws it up even when he's dead,' said

Connor.

Lenka glared at him. 'You don't take prisoners, do you, Connor.'

'One of the signatories to the Geneva Convention was M.E Arse,' said Connor, without a smile. 'That was me.'

The major continued. 'Foxy and I agreed to share information. Foxy wanted to try and determine who killed the captain and to discover if the young woman here,' turning to Lenka to be met by an icy stare, 'was in any danger.'

'In return, Foxy kept you abreast of developments,' said Klay.

'Yes, and when he told me that a group of British citizens was heading into a war zone, I decided to intervene and stop you all from getting killed.'

'So this Foxy,' said Mary, 'confided in you and you betrayed him?'

'A British officer named after a two-faced god, betrays his friend. Well I never saw that coming,' mocked Connor.

'I'm not here to argue. Passports!' demanded the

British officer. Then to his surprise first Connor's, then Klay's, and finally Mary's, came flying from different directions towards his trousers along with the contents of three toppled glasses.

The major wiped his trousers with a bar-towel thrown across by a smiling Connor. 'Most kind,' said the major, handing the three passports to the sergeant who appeared at the table.

'And you two?' asked the major, looking across at the two goths. 'In the vehicle,' said Sasha. Rat folded his arms and with his jaw raised looked petulantly out of the window.

The major looked disappointedly at his stained uniform. 'I'm not overly worried about the Sex Pistols dragging us into a war,' he said, looking indifferently at Sasha and Rat. 'Just drop them into the British Embassy when you're ready.' He stood up. 'In a day or so, you can pick them up from the Austro-German-Swiss border post at Schwarzenberg am Böhmerwald on your way home.'

'How long will we have to wait?' asked Sasha.

'As long as it takes; you're not going anywhere.'

'The press will hear about what you have done today,' snapped Sasha.

'Not in the British press,' added the major as he walked towards the door followed by his men.

Connor raised his glass and began singing Elvis Costello's *Oliver's Army*.

After checking that the two trucks carrying the British troops and their commanding officer had headed off towards Charles Bridge, Connor and Klay returned to the bar.

Lenka met them with a shake of her head. 'I don't understand, you all just gave up your passports without even putting up an argument?'

Connor laid a British passport down on the table, then Klay added one, saying 'Snap!' and finally Mary, saying 'Snap!' even louder.

Lenka, Sasha and Rat exchanged looks.

'Rogues always carry a false passport in case the authorities wish to confiscate them,' said Klay. 'I've got another two back in the truck.'

'Me too,' added Mary. 'Plus, one Canadian and one Irish.'

'Actually, that's my last one,' said Connor sadly. 'But I know a little man with one bollock in Singapore who can ship me a few this week.'

'How do you know he has one testicle?' asked Klay.

'By his cough.'

6.35pm, 24 February 1992, London

Major Janus stepped crisply up the stairs of Brook's, a private gentlemen's club on Piccadilly's St James's Street, and disappeared into the dull yellow, Palladian-style building. In the grand reception hall, the smartly dressed elderly man, buttressed by a huge, unyielding, handlebar moustache, looked at the officer sternly. Due to the sweltering heat, the major had undone the second button down on his shirt, which was hidden behind his navy tie. The ex-Grenadier guardsman eyed the creases on the shirt on either side of the tie with disgust. 'I have an appointment with Viscount Foxborough,' said the major, standing to attention.

The man behind the desk released an extraordinarily welcoming smile. 'Ah, Foxy. I'll fill in the formalities; up you go to the Great Subscription

Room. It is up the stairs, first floor.' The major looked twice at the man who spun the ledger around and began to write, before setting off up the grand carpeted stairs.

Minutes later, the major entered the huge neo-classical hall. Foxy waved him towards the armchair opposite him in the farthest corner.

The major sat uncomfortably in the gigantic, English tweed-covered armchair. Around him sat retired heads of government departments snug behind various broadsheets and one elderly man in his late eighties rooted to a copy of Pravda. Of the twelve elderly men, the major recognised three retired commanders-in-chief from the special services and, from private conversations he was party to in the corridors of the Ministry of Defence, two former chiefs of Special Branch and a former head of M16. On the other side of the two-hundred-year-old, gilt-edged, walnut coffee table slouched Foxy, the club's most enigmatic member.

'Your message sounded most urgent, Major, and my instincts tells me that two of the club's finest brandies will be needed.'

'Only one, I'm still on duty.'

Foxy summoned the waiter and ordered two *Delord* vintage brandies but in one glass, and coffee for one. The waiter nodded, but seemed surprised that the order included a hot beverage.

Foxy reclined further back into the thick, ox-blood-red leather armchair as if he were settling in for the evening.

The major straightened up. 'I thought that after yesterday's events in Prague, I at least owed you an explanation.'

'For what?'

'What do you mean "For what?" For terminating the aid mission into Bosnia. Surely, your ward called you and dammed my name to the heavens?'

The furrows that appeared across Foxy's brow and the sudden blotches that erupted on his cheeks told the major that Foxy's surprise was genuine. The officer breathed out slowly and edged forward on his seat. 'You secured them a compound by the airport for their trucks. Can you call whoever is in charge there and check if they're still there?'

'They're not. I received a message last night that they left yesterday evening.'

'I don't understand,' confessed the major.

The expressionless waiter appeared with a silver tray bearing a tall, silver-plated coffee pot, one bone china cup, and a new vase-sized balloon glass, containing a generous measure of *Delord* 45-year-old Armagnac.

'Perhaps you better tell me what happened yesterday,' said Foxy, taking his drink from the tray. 'I fear I'm going to need this.'

Ten minutes later, the major had recounted an exact record of his meeting with the Rogues with the exception of Connor's remarks and choice of song.

'You well deserve your commission, major.'

'Meaning?'

'You're an idiot.'

Major Janus was expecting a derogatory comment of some kind. 'I care little for your opinion of me, but I would appreciate any insight into where the trucks might be.'

'On their way to Bosnia, and my guess is that they will not spare the horses and will arrive ahead of schedule.'

'Not without these,' the officer said as he produced three passports and threw them on the table.

Foxy screwed up his face, as if he had suddenly caught a whiff of *Murphy's Ruin*. 'Your problem, Major, is that you see the world solely from your perspective, as many in the services do. These men and women are Rogues. Trust me, I know the type. They do not play by your rules.'

'You mean they crossed the border without passports?'

Foxy shook his head disparagingly. 'The opposite; they have probably crossed the border with a deck of passports. How the hell do you think they have delivered aid across the world? I know Klay, and I'm sure the others are the same. They are usually the last port of call for charities large and small who have tried and failed to get aid to where it's needed. They are heading into Bosnia. Apart from the bravest like the doctors and nurses of Médecins Sans Frontières, medical staff can't enter, let alone trucks carrying aid.'

The major wiped his brow, but it was not due to the heat outside.

Foxy drained his glass. 'But you haven't told me why you tried to stop them; and don't try to spoon-feed me that "not allowing British citizens to endanger themselves" nonsense again.'

The major stared dejectedly up at the beautiful crystal chandelier. He summoned the waiter. 'Two more brandies, please.'

He paused, while Foxy watched tentatively without a word.

'Last month, we tapped into a Serbian Croatian telephone call between two opposing generals. The crux of the conversation was that they were trying to finalise a joint force to extinguish all resistance in a town in Bosnian territory. We checked. The village has not to our knowledge been part of any offensive, nor have any incidents of soldiers from any side been reported there. In fact, it's still ethnically mixed, between Serb, Croat and Bosnian Muslims. Naturally, we were alarmed that two opposing armies intended to join forces and turn their guns on the town.'

Foxy cradled the fresh glass in his hands. 'Nevertheless, we know that both governments have been colluding for some time to divide former Yugoslavia between them, so this can't be a surprise, surely?'

'True. Numerous calls followed, but they still could not agree on a coordinated attack. Then one side proposed a solution.'

'Which was?'

'"Send in the Wolves" were the exact words.'

Foxy threw his head back and for a moment lost his fingers within his explosion of silver strands.

'So these Wolves that I have been trying to find out about are operating in Bosnia. No more bullshit, or I swear I'll have you peeling enough potatoes to keep every chip shop on the British coast going for a decade.'

'I don't give a damn for your threats, but I do give a damn about British civilians becoming the targets of mercenaries.'

Foxy swirled the brandy around in the glass. *Was it*

an ominous omen that I ordered the same drink some twenty-five years earlier, when I brought 'Lock' (Lochran) to the club and we agreed to join forces and shared what we knew about a new, deadly legion of executioners known as The Alpha Wolves? He closed his eyes briefly. *Lock, the courageous and wily Samuel, the quiet but powerful giant Seamus, all were brutally murdered within a year. And Kirsten (Brett), my childhood friend and Lenka's mother, died, too. At least the elegant Josephine (Baker) died peacefully. Now, I am the last of the former Rogues. Memories are all I have.* He drew his hand slowly down his face. *Damn it man, "grow a pair" as Lock would say. Enough of this indulgent self-pity.*

Foxy opened his eyes. He said firmly. 'The games are over, major. Tell me all you know about these Wolves and why you think they pose a threat to Lenka and the others.'

8.45pm 27 February 1992, Split, Croatia

The convoy of Rogues' trucks rocked across the cobbled streets of the beautiful town situated on the eastern shore of the Adriatic Sea.

Connor waited for The Jam's *A Town Called Malice*

to finish on his cassette tape before he jumped down from the vehicle. He stretched his arms and rotated his upper body clockwise and then anti-clockwise. Mary joined him and bent down holding her knees. 'That was a straight fourteen-hour stretch up from the coast. I'm stiff!' She turned her head sharply up to Connor. 'And no smutty remarks from you.'

'Can't be arsed. Too tired. Let's find a bar and some food and then I'll do a few knob jokes, if you're lucky.'

'Shove that where the sun don't shine.'

Connor began to stretch Mary's arms and rotate them. He then started to knead the base of her spine with the heel of his hand. Slowly, she began to straighten up. 'Come on, my little Mary Whitehouse, let's help the others out of their trucks.'

Thirty minutes later, Lenka, Mary, Sasha, Klay, Rat and Connor were heading towards a bar on the corner of a neighbouring square, having removed the distributor caps from each truck, locked all the doors and added additional chains across the back ones.

Though the street was empty and quiet and most of the town's inhabitants were in bed, the bar was heaving.

'Christ, there's every form of life here,' said Connor, scanning the crowd, which was made up of soldiers, local militia and mercenaries, all in battle fatigues of various descriptions. All were armed with weapons, ranging from hand-pistols, to machetes strapped to belts loaded with cartridge shells, and even an M4 magazine-fed carbine, which was mounted on the bar fixed to its stand.

'This is like Mos Eisley,' said Lenka.

'I thought you'd never been beyond Dublin?' said Klay.

'I haven't. Mos Eisley is the bar in *Star Wars*. I took all the children to see it in '77.' She looked at the others' blank faces. 'Do any of you have a social life?'

Connor put his hand up. 'Anita and I sometimes have dinner whenever we turn up in the same country.'

Klay said proudly, 'I have every intention of getting back in time to be with Claudia for the birth of our next kid.' He added quietly, 'I missed Romeo's birth.'

'Jesus! You called him Romeo,' said Connor. 'Poor little bastard.'

'Convoys is all I have,' said Mary with resignation, while Rat looked at his feet and Sasha shrugged.

Lenka placed her black leather jacket over the back of a chair next to an empty table by the window, as the bar's customers preferred to be on their feet.

Connor looked up at the banner draped over the bar. 'An American football team do you think?'

'I think there was once a football team called The Los Angeles Wolves,' Klay said. 'I think they had a wolf's head as their symbol.'

7.10pm, 24 February 1992, London

'We've learnt that these modern-day Wolves model themselves on the infamous Alpha Wolves,' began Major Janus.

'The Nazis' elite assassins of the '30s,' said Foxy.

'No, the revamped ones who rose again in the '60s,' added the major. Foxy said nothing, racked by painful memories of the legion of professional killers. 'No doubt they originally adopted the Wolves' moniker to instill fear, but they have no need of it now.'

'Why?' asked Foxy.

'Over the last ten years, they've inflicted atrocities from Africa to South America. Now it's Europe's turn.'

'How and when did you learn this?' growled Foxy.

'After you expressed an interest in them, I made some enquiries through some international military contacts. They first came to prominence in Brazil in the '80s, after the government used local police to form death squads to eliminate slum children. When the international press exposed their crimes, another solution had to be found. Thus, the rise of the Wolves. Foreign mercenaries with no apparent link to the authorities. They became the spear head of the death squads.'

'"Zero-footprint" is the common terminology in modern warfare,' said Foxy. 'Are they still operating there?'

'Yes, but they also exported their murder squads to South Africa. However, since the fall of apartheid, their tentacles have spread elsewhere: Haiti, Afghanistan, Somalia, wherever there is money to be earned for killing en masse, you'll find them.'

'En masse?' queried Foxy.

'Unlike The Alpha Wolves of thirty years ago they do not usually target specific kills, but murder in bulk. Their current price is 10,000 deutschmarks per 100 dead – soldiers, civilians, women, children; it matters not.'

'Who are their paymasters in the Balkans?'

'Difficult to say. There is no direct link to any government and former Yugoslavia is not simply divided into three pieces, between the Serbs, Croats and Bosnians. There are militias, ranging from the Chechens to the Mujahidin. Usually, in civil wars it soon becomes clear who pays mercenaries, as they fight only for one side. But the Wolves really are non-partisan and are reported to have worked for opposing sides at the same time. Perversely, their business plan makes them doubly attractive to those wishing to secure their services as it's hard to pin down who their paymasters are.'

'But there must be someone they report to, or at least meet to hand over their bounty?' said Foxy. 'That would be one way to track their paymasters.'

'Not according to my contacts. Apparently, it's done through banks. Money is paid into an account along with the name of the target, though usually it's just a town.'

'That's it?'

'Intercepted telexes have picked up some negotiating on price, but there's never any names.'

'Someone has to recruit them.'

'Obviously! But they have one known stipulation. They keep their number at 100 and no more. New recruits can only join if one of them is killed. The 100, again adds to the elite nature of their operation, which they promote.'

'And how do they do this?' asked Foxy.

'In criminal circles the Wolves are often described as "the 100 deadliest killers on the planet". B-movie stuff, but in terms of making an impact it's memorable and, unfortunately, apparently true.'

Foxy rested his head back against the leather. 'Jesus! Now, I understand why you went halfway across Europe to stop Lenka and the others from heading into Bosnia. I'm embarrassed to say I know nothing of any of this. Who sanctioned your investigations and your intervention yesterday?'

'No one. I've broken every rule I have sworn to uphold. I just know – but for the life of me, I can't explain why – that this Wolves business will end in war and Britain will be dragged into it.'

'We will make a Rogue of you yet,' said Foxy, as he stared at the professional soldier who had acted on what he believed was right. Foxy leaned forward, nursing the empty glass in his hands. 'We can be certain of one thing; the nature of the Rogues and the Wolves will lead them on a collision course.'

The major shook his head and stared vacantly into his full glass. 'Unfortunately, there are two things we can be sure of.'

'What is that, Major?'

'When they do clash and against such numbers, there can only be one outcome – the Rogues will lose.'

9.10pm, 27 February 1992, Split, Croatia

Connor worked his way through the throng of fighters, greeted by menacing eye contact with three

297

before he reached the bar. 'Six beers,' he shouted, while holding up six fingers. The mean-looking barmaid gave him a sour look as she plonked the bottles on the bar. 'Thank you. Has anyone ever told you that you have a beautiful smile?'

'No,' she said, through clenched, chipped teeth.

'Thought not,' said Connor, scooping up the bottles.

He was shoved from behind, followed by '*Fuckin* big man. You smartass.' Connor detected that the voice was Latin American before he rested the bottles back on the bar and slowly turned around.

'Try me, you big *fuk*!' Connor did not look down at the swarthy, muscular man holding a serrated knife in his stumpy fingers.

'Who pushed me?' said Connor.

'Funny man,' said the mercenary raising the blade up to Connor's face.

'Christ! Oompa-Loompas do exist,' said Connor, following the point of the swaying blade.

'I'm Colombian and I'm going to slice you up so that even your whore of a mother won't recognise you.'

'I believe she was quite free with her favours, but she never charged to my knowledge, God rest her.'

The Colombian prodded the point of the blade he had taken from a Gurkha he had shot in the back, so it was millimetres from Connor's throat.

'One more move and you'll never be able to sit down with that kukri sticking out of your hairy arse.'

Klay's hand engulfed the Colombian's wrist. 'No need for this. It's late, everyone needs a drink and I'm buying.'

The Colombian slipped a knife from his belt and spun around. Connor grabbed his hand before he could plunge the dagger into Klay. The man suddenly stopped when he looked up at the huge black man staring down at him, as the rest of the fighters drew their weapons and locked them on Klay and Connor.

Connor heard the locking of a magazine behind him. He turned his head slowly and smiled at the barmaid who had loaded the carbine and was aiming the barrel at his head. 'You do have warm eyes, though,' said Connor, who was slowly raising his hands.

'Put down your weapons,' came a calm, but commanding voice from the open door.

The Rogues and Wolves focused on the man, wearing army fatigues, as he removed his black beret. A Glock 17 semi-automatic was on display tucked into his trousers. His four bodyguards, similarly attired, entered behind him and spread out along the perimeter of the bar without acknowledging their colleagues.

The packed room made a channel for the powerful man to make his way up to the bar. He looked up at the banner above the bar and turned to a man who was pointing a Beretta M9 semi-automatic at Connor's head. 'Take that down!'

The man walked slowly by the bar until he reached an open photo album resting on the bar. He began to flick through the pictures. He looked coldly at the Colombian whose hands were still restrained. 'Is this yours, Salvano?'

The Colombian nodded, as beads of sweat that had gathered on his chin dropped onto his khaki jacket. 'Yes, La . . .'

The taller man shook his head. 'So the reports were right. Good to see that my trip half-way around the world was not in vain.' He flicked through some more leaves. 'So, you've started to compile a photographic record of our kills.' He bent his head. 'Hmm, here's one of me in Rio. I look so young. Look at all those dead bodies,' he said and smiled across at Salvano. 'We worked so well together, my old friend.' He turned back and closed the album. 'We made some money that day.'

With the photo album tucked until his arm, the blonde-haired man walked slowly back towards Salvano, Klay and Connor. He nodded at Klay. 'You are right, my friend, let's draw a line under all this, but please, I will buy the drinks,' he said as he tossed a thick wad of deutschmarks towards the barmaid who released her hands from the trigger handles of the machine gun to catch it.

'May I join you?' asked the man.

'If I know how to introduce you,' replied Klay.

One of the founding members of the Wolves, and former US Navy SEAL, extended his hand. 'I'm known as Lazar, and you are?'

'Kenneth Clayton,' Klay said as he shook hands with the man, who, at six foot seven, appeared to have not an ounce of fat on him. With his harshly clipped military-style box-shaped haircut and overly developed muscular, square jaw, he looked like he had been fashioned from concrete with a stone-cutter.

'Once again, I'm sorry about all this needless hostility.' He turned and smiled at Connor. 'I didn't get your name?'

'I didn't give it,' said Connor.

Lazar nodded. 'Will you join us, please.'

Connor took a swig from one of the bottles. 'Someone would have to be a right fucker for me not to accept a drink from them.'

As Klay returned to the table, the leader of the mercenaries turned around and watched as Connor rested his arm on the bar. Lazar smirked and said, 'I have no doubt that we will meet again.'

When Lazar reached the table where the other Rogues were sitting, one of his men rushed forward with a chair. He smiled at the others as he took a seat, placed the photo album on the floor and rested his boots on top of it. The barmaid acknowledged Lazar with a nod, before placing the tray laden with bottles of opened *Pilsners* on the table.

'So you're all delivering aid,' said Lazar.

'How do you know that?' said Lenka.

'I noticed the vehicles around the corner. The menacing-looking, black rig marked Turkey Shoot. I take it, it's yours?' he said as he smiled without warmth at Sasha and Rat. Neither acknowledged him.

'So you're a mercenary and these are your men,' said Lenka, looking around at the muted mouths in the bar.

'We are all mercenaries; it's just that we're honest about our price.'

'How much per kill?' snapped Mary.

'Please let us not discuss such things tonight. If you are determined to clash with everyone who has a gun for hire, you will never reach your destination. This region is full of us: ex-soldiers and policemen following the end of apartheid; Chechens fleeing the Russians who for now have the upper hand; Irish and

Palestinian terrorists, South American killers, ex-American servicemen desperate to sate their cravings until the next war. Such a build-up of mercenaries has not been seen since the Napoleonic Wars.'

Klay looked over towards Connor, who was goading two other mercenaries at the bar.

'Don't worry,' said Lazar. 'Your friend could start a war in a monastery, but it will not escalate while I and my men are present.' A cup of tea appeared in front of him, as the barmaid returned to the bar.

'I thought you just arrived,' said Klay.

'I have to keep tabs on all our global operations. I am known here.' He took a sip of tea and smiled as he noticed that the others refused to touch the beer he had ordered. He replaced his cup in the centre of the saucer. 'Talking of our business model, we are always looking out for new recruits, as our turnover can be quite high.' He glanced over at Salvano who was no longer drinking, before turning back to Klay. 'You would be a suitable candidate, as a vacancy will shortly need to be filled.'

'Why, is someone leaving?' said Klay.

Lazar shook his head. 'Salvano was good. Professional, efficient, driven only by money and, surprisingly for a South American, he lacked emotion. Then his wife wanted a divorce.'

'Easy to see why,' said Mary, drily.

'You're so right,' said Lazar. 'And you are?'

'Poppins, Mary Poppins,' said Mary, as if Walt Disney had taken over the James Bond franchise.

Lazar grinned. 'Most amusing. Sadly, the passion that his wife missed was rekindled following her request for a divorce, though sadly not in the form she required.'

Lenka looked uncomfortably over at the subdued Colombian.

'He murdered their two daughters in front of his wife before cutting her throat with the curved knife he threatened you with, just now.'

'And you can have someone like that working for you?' said Lenka.

'Everyone here has a bloody history. Most are wanted by various governments and have a price on their heads. However, such a history is an essential prerequisite in the selection process to become a Wolf. The final test is determined by your ability to kill effectively.' The agitated Colombian stared over at Lazar, who returned the look with a cruel, cold smile. 'But recently, Salvano has let emotion and ego take control of him. The incriminating photo collection, the banner he hung over the bar and the silly testosterone game with your childish friend is merely further evidence of that.'

He smiled at Klay. 'But you demonstrated at the bar that nothing will divert you from your objective, in this case getting the aid through. And unlike your hot-headed friend you will even drink with me, the epitome of all you despise, so that nothing happens here tonight that impedes your mission. Tenacity is a quality that the Wolves will reward handsomely.'

Klay nodded. 'It is an offer that I will seriously consider. Perhaps, after the aid has been delivered, we could meet, just the two of us, away from here to discuss it further?'

Lenka and the others looked with shock at the man they all admired.

Lazar laughed loudly. 'I knew it was a long-shot considering your adopted line of work, but never let it be said that I didn't try to recruit you.' He caught Lenka's bemused look. 'If your friend really was interested, he would have jumped at the chance. Instead, after his mission is accomplished he wants to lure me away from my bodyguards and perhaps,' he raised his eyebrows and grinned at Klay, 'kill me?' Klay smiled back. 'Your friends here do not know you that well. They actually thought that you would continue to deliver aid and then return to discuss options on killing the recipients. Your choice of friends is poor.'

Klay pushed the bottle meant for him towards the Wolf. 'Well, now that we understand each other, shall we just leave things as they are and go our separate ways?'

'Yes, we can for now,' said Lazar, draining his cup. 'But Bosnia is a turbulent place and when we secure a major contract, we do not discern whether the target is military, civilian or, for that matter, an aid worker.'

Klay said nothing, but was looking above Lazar's head. Then he understood why, as Connor slammed his bottle onto the saucer, shattering it.

Lazar was not taken by surprise, as the argument at the bar had stopped seconds earlier, and the barrels of his bodyguards' weapons had followed Connor's approach.

'Have we got past the bullshit and ended up where we knew we would, anyway?' said Connor, his head bent down looking Lazar directly in the eyes.

'Ah, naturally the volatile child of the group was eavesdropping,' said Lazar, as he coldly watched Connor flop into the chair next to him. 'I could have sworn that your eyes were grey-green up at the bar. It is most unusual for me to get such details wrong.' He looked down at the tip of the US Navy SEAL knife in his left hand that was now resting against Connor's stomach. 'I would suggest you take a leaf out of the black giant's book and focus on your mission, or I will slice open your guts and invite the local dogs in for a late snack.'

'An animal lover, but they say so was Hitler,' said Connor, quickly flicking open the cut-throat, once owned by Bulla, and resting the blade just below

Lazar's neck. 'I'm going to make you famous.'

The mercenaries in the bar that had not aimed their weapons at Connor, now joined the others. Lazar raised his arm to stay their weapons. He tilted his head towards Connor's, seemingly oblivious to the blade cutting into his skin. His men stepped forward and aimed their automatics at Connor's head. Lazar continued to hold his arm up. He said nonchalantly, 'Famous for being the man who finally cut down The Englander, perhaps?'

'Not a name I've ever felt comfortable with,' replied Connor, hiding his surprise at the mentioned of his unwelcome *nom de guerre*.

'I'll have to remember that,' grinned Lazar. It's a name that has been mooted many times as a potential applicant for our elite organisation; your prowess in eliminating your enemies is well known. But you're a loose cannon, and money, apparently, holds little interest for you.' He raised his tepid drink. 'Without an enticement or an addiction, how could we control you? Of course, you do have one addiction, but alcohol is available anywhere.' He took a sip, grinned and replaced the cup back on the tablecloth. 'I take it that this fame I'm heading towards is to do with my demise?'

Connor beamed the man a huge smile and slapped his free hand excitedly on the table. 'You know me so well. Now this is what I'm thinking, so please be honest as I'd hate to build up your hopes of finally achieving something.'

'I'm all ears,' replied Lazar.

'That depends on if I can find them after our next meeting.' He leaned closer into the man, still holding the tip of the knife in the flesh wound. 'Let me explain. You see, shortly after our next meeting, I can visualise an exhibit of you in Madame Tussauds Chamber of Horrors.' Connor smiled. 'You'd like that wouldn't you,' he said, stretching his arm out towards the armed men. 'You love all the adulation that comes with all this *Wild Geese*, *Dogs of War* bullshit. You being head honcho, *en* all.'

'But I'm not the head. We have a collective, shall we say, management structure.' Lazar rested his free right hand on the table. 'I like your act, though. All this goading so I will divulge more about our organisation. Amateurish, but I'm happy to talk.' He looked at the faces around the table. 'But doesn't it worry you that I have been so open with you all?' He opened his arms. 'Perhaps, it is because I know you'll all be dead soon.'

Connor, Mary and Klay noticed the fear that this instilled in the younger Rogues. Connor slammed his hand on the table loudly again, causing Lazar's men to steady their aim. He shook his head sadly and pressed his bottom lip out. 'Shame you lost interest in your waxwork exhibit. What will make yours stand out from the other dummies on display is that what is left of you will be in a slop bucket. It will have a waxed model of a pig standing beside it turning its nose up at it. I thought it would be a funny metaphor and a welcome toilet break on the macabre tour.'

'You are dumb,' snarled Lazar. 'After all you heard, do you think I'm going to waste my time on a fight to *your* death for no financial reward?'

'That's why I know that we are not in your crosshairs,' said Connor, glancing at Lenka, Sasha and Rat. 'And that you're telling us everything because who in authority is going to listen to us. Plus, we're not the sort to stand in a witness box in a suit.' He smiled at Sasha and Rat's goth garb, 'Well, not these two, anyway.'

'You may be right, but you still have a blade wedged in my neck and I'm getting tired of your monologue,' growled Lazar.

Both men rose, their eyes and weapons still locked on each other.

Suddenly, each man locked his free hand on the other's holding the blade. Klay appeared and clamped his hands over the weapon-wielding wrists of both men. He looked at Connor. 'Not here; not now,' he said quietly, but firmly.

Connor nodded as he tilted his head towards Lazar. 'As I said, next time.'

The men sheathed their weapons.

Lazar held his finger up to his mouth and tapped his lips repeatedly. 'It might be worth me checking to see if there is a reward for your head. I'd be very surprised, if there isn't.' He wiped his finger across the nick to his throat and licked the blood from his finger.

'I do hope so and then we can do business after all.' As he was about to walk away, he stopped and turned: 'You clearly don't care about your own life, but what of your petrified friends here,' he said, scanning the faces of the other Rogues.

Mary yawned and started scratching her chest. 'I wish I knew why my tits get itchy when I'm bored.'

'Tuck *'em* into your socks,' mumbled Rat. 'That might help.'

Mary grabbed him by the back of his head, as if she were about to smack his head off the table. Instead, she leaned into his terrified face and growled loudly. Lenka and Sasha looked at each other, trying not to laugh.

'As you can see, they look after themselves,' said Connor.

'So I can see; a carefree, motley crew, indeed,' grunted Lazar.

'I'm not sure about this little fellow, though,' said Connor, turning the attention away from the others by placing his hand on Klay's shoulder.

'I'm a little weeping violet, me,' said Klay, shrugging

his shoulders.

'Connor Pierce,' continued Lazar. 'No parents, no siblings, no wife, and, until now,' he continued, looking and grinning at the other Rogues, 'no friends. Yes, I remember the story of The Englander, the "righter of wrongs". But we all have someone that we love more than ourselves; perhaps you just don't know it yet.'

Lenka looked up at Connor. He did not notice, but Lazar did.

Connor stepped forward. 'I guess with your lack of social skills, you don't have any love in your life, either.' He grinned. 'I've got it! Get yourself a pet pig. It will give the exhibit pathos.'

'Goodbye,' said Lazar to those sitting around the table, without exuding any warmth. 'I would suggest that you all turn back, or you may find yourself in the total column of my next invoice.'

'Who's your paymaster?' said Lenka.

'The names on the invoices change by the day,' said Lazar.

'You should get yourself a good accountant,' said

Lenka.

Lazar stared quizzically at the woman.

Mary released the neck of the bottle in her hand and let it crash to the floor, as she scanned the faces of the army of killers who returned their weapons to their holsters. She turned around but before she sat down, she saw that Sasha and Rat were supporting Lenka, who was about to fall to the floor.

'My God,' said Mary. 'What's happened?'

'I don't know. She just fell to the floor,' said Sasha.

'She has a weak heart,' said Klay.

Connor rushed around the table and tried to lift Lenka up in his arms.

'No,' said Lenka. 'Just support me and walk me out, please.'

The bar began to fill with flashing blue light as a number of police cars drew up outside.

'Come on, let's disappear out the back,' said Klay.

As the police entered the bar they were greeted as old friends by those inside, while the Rogues emerged onto the dark, cobbled street from the rear kitchen.

Lenka straightened up. 'Right, let's get back to the

315

trucks and get the hell out of here.'

The other Rogues looked at each other and then at the young woman who was running down the cobbled street.

Connor turned to Klay. 'It's not usual for someone to have a heart attack, then jump up and leg it like a greyhound, is it?'

'We've been had, again,' said Klay, rubbing his stubbly chin.

Before Lenka disappeared down the side turning, which led to the trucks, she lifted something from under the leather jacket up into the air. It looked like a photo album.

'Oh bollocks!' said Connor and Mary in unison, who, along with the others, took off after her as fast as they could.

Chapter 15: Bloody Legoland

7.55am, 1 March 1992, Mostar, Bosnia-Herzegovina

At one of the unofficial border posts that separated Croatia from Bosnia, a melee of international observers and reporters, standing underneath a rain-soaked canopy, trained their binoculars on the fires in the town ahead.

Connor was the first to leap down from the Rogues' vehicles as they drew in. He marched up past the fleet of Humvees and an army personnel carrier, hired for those under the tent. But before he opened his mouth, Sasha brushed past him.

'Have the people been evacuated?' she asked of no one in particular.

'No,' said a man with a press badge, who spoke with a Swedish accent.

A mortar shell was fired from a mountain in the distance and burst into one of the tall housing blocks in the centre of Mostar. 'This is unreal,' muttered

317

Sasha. 'It's hard to believe that people are trapped inside the buildings under attack.'

'Like a child with *Lego* bricks lobbing them at the village he's just built,' said Connor. Sasha stared up at his strained face. 'Can we do anything?'

'If our trucks were empty, we'd be straight in getting as many families out as we could.'

'No chance,' interjected another reporter, with what sounded like a Canadian accent. 'Every road is blocked, and snipers are picking off anyone going in or out.'

'Jesus,' said Lenka, with Sasha and Rat standing beside her.

'Have you got any room on your truck for my cargo?' asked Connor, as Klay approached.

'I'm packed to the rafters,' said Klay, shaking his head.

'Even if you got in, you'd just be making the job easier for the snipers guarding the road, by delivering their targets to them,' said a black man. He wore a press badge and was carrying a bottle of wine and a tower of plastic cups.

'It's never good to see you, Murray, for when we do, it means we're surrounded by carnage,' said Klay, relieving the man of the cups and shaking his hand.

'Murray,' said Connor, as the reporter started to fill the containers. 'How long has this been going on?'

'I arrived six days ago. The intensity of the bombing has been sporadic but unrelenting. If the booms don't drive the families over there insane, sleep deprivation will. The snipers in the surrounding hills are even bored and taking bets on their victims. On points, heavily pregnant women score the highest.'

'How many snipers?' growled Connor.

'Hard to say. Two hundred, maybe more,' said Murray, looking at Klay and Connor. 'Even you two couldn't take them on.' He shook his head. 'Unless, the United Nations intervenes, this will spread. We are witnessing the return of genocide in Europe.'

Lenka and Mary joined them but before they could say anything, another mortar landed on an outhouse in the town turning it to a grey powdery cloud.

'I'm Murray Grant, senior reporter for US World at One.'

'The first black international television news correspondent,' said Klay.

'No, there have been others,' said Murray.

'One of the rare few amongst the vultures around us, who is focused on the story and not on a Pulitzer,' said Connor, so that any eavesdropping journalists could hear.

'Is anyone doing anything? said Lenka.

'If we capture a story that riles the public, then the politicians may follow the outcry,' said Murray, shaking his head. 'I'd understand if you refuse to say, but where are you heading?'

'Tuzla,' said Klay.

'It will be tough, and you will have to traverse Snipers' Alley to reach it,' said Murray.

'There's nothing we can do here, let's get going,' snarled Connor, finishing his drink. 'What about you, Murray, are you staying here, with these overpaid dick-pullers?'

'No, I'll head into Mostar at dusk again with Lincoln, my cameraman, and film what we can. Maybe we will find an image that will get our viewers to sit up.'

'I can't stand reporters,' snapped Mary, 'so just make bloody sure you do.'

'I promise,' said Murray, with a nod.

Klay turned to Lenka. 'Murray, we may have something of interest to your viewers.'

Lenka shook her head.

'But Murray is a good guy, a friend . . .' added Connor.

Lenka again shook her head.

Murray shrugged at Lenka. 'Okay, but I'm happy to help if I can, with whatever it is.'

'I'll explain another time, but this is not the time,' said Lenka, shaking his hand.

But just as the Rogues were about to return to their trucks, a tall, determined-looking woman in battle fatigues blocked their path.

'Holey Mary, passing judgment on everyone as usual.'

'Of course, I should have known. As there's a camera, you had to be here.'

Sasha whispered to Connor, 'Is that who I think it

is?'

'How the hell do I know who you think it is? But that is Christina Pitchsmith, she's Swiss, and calls herself "The Children's Saviour".'

'She is one impressive woman,' said Lenka, quietly. 'I've watched her building hospitals on the news. Africa, Asia, Latin American, wherever children are in peril, she's there. In my country she's viewed as a saint.'

'She builds fuck all,' said Mary, turning her head towards Lenka, making no attempt to lower her voice. 'But when the work is done, she appears and presses her snout against the camera lens.'

'I don't do it for myself,' shouted Pitchsmith, in the direction of the reporters, 'but to raise the money to save children.'

'Slickdick, I thought the advert you did for baby milk powder was lovely,' said Connor. 'I'm sure the fee went straight to your charity rather than to build another swimming pool on your little hovel in Aspen.'

'Fuck off, Connor!' snapped Pitchsmith, but softly so she was not overheard.

'Gladly, Slickdick,' he replied without glancing at her, only to have a microphone hovering an inch from his sharp nose.

'Dolores Channing, Channel 24. A few words?' announced the glamorous reporter, with her make-up assistant just off camera.

'Not today, Farrah Fawcett,' said Connor, barging past and lifting himself up into his truck.

The frontline reporter held the door open and lifted the microphone up higher, as her cameraman zoomed in on Connor. 'What does the world need to know, now?'

'My cock is two-foot long when I fold it in half,' said Connor, looking directly into the camera, before slamming the door.

'Arsehole,' shouted back the reporter. She turned towards Mary, who was passing behind her. 'Sir, a few words for the world?'

'Oh yes. I'm a 'smashed-the-fucking-door-off-the-closet' lesbian! Got a problem with that, Barbie?' spat Mary, as she dragged herself up into the cabin of her battleship-grey van.

'Jesus!' said the reporter, before focusing on Rat, while Lenka and Sasha walked quickly towards their vehicles. 'You, Sir,' she shouted, regretting it immediately as Rat pulled back the hood of his black jacket, exposing his piercings, dirty spiky-hair and a chain leading from his left nostril to his left ear. He grabbed the microphone. 'Capitalism causes all wars. Kill the bloated, fat cats. Revolution now!' he shouted, raising his fist in the air.

Channing wrenched the microphone from his tattooed hands, pushing him firmly away. Then she saw Klay. 'You, black guy! What have you to say to the world?'

Klay smiled broadly into the camera. He then began to dance his fingers off his bottom lip quickly and howl, before placing his thumbs on the side of his head and wriggling his fingers like a jabbering child.

'Where the fuck did this freak show come from?' spat the reporter, as Klay jumped into the cabin of his truck.

The reporter turned dejectedly to the cameraman. 'None of that went out live, did it?'

The cameraman kept his head ducked behind the eyepiece of the camera lens to hide his smile. 'All of it, and I'm still filming.'

'Arsehole!' screamed the *Charlie's Angels* look-a-like.

As the Rogue trucks rocked back onto the dirt road and on past the road into Mostar, Pitchsmith walked up towards a dour-faced photographer. 'Did you get the photos?'

'Yes, one of you with the tough-looking guy and one of the black mountain on his own.'

'Head back to Split and send the roll of film express by overnight courier to the Herald.'

'Storyline?'

'Christina "The Children's Saviour" Pitchsmith Confronts International Mercenaries. Add the names Connor "The Englander" Pierce and Kenneth "Klay" Clayton. The tabloids will pick a good front page banner headline out of all that.'

'What about the women and the punk rocker? I've got images of all of them.'

'Did you get one of the classy blonde?'

The photographer smiled. 'Actually, I've got quite a

few of her.'

The woman did not smile. 'Focus on the men. I don't need the competition.'

Chapter 16: Every Inch the Hero?

6.35pm, 3 March 1992, 22 kilometres north-east of Mostar

'How far to Snipers' Alley?' asked Klay, steering the recently sprayed, dull gunmetal-grey artic through the winding mountain roads. Mary's battleship-grey pick-up was leading the convoy, followed by the black truck, which still had Turkey Shoot daubed on both sides, then Klay's truck and finally Connor's white turbo truck.

Lenka was map reading diligently. 'Are we waiting until nightfall before we enter the valley?'

'After we do a reconnaissance,' Klay said, pointing at the Redfield rifle sight lying on the dashboard. 'We can work out how best to negotiate the road and how much time it will take. According to the map, we are exposed to the hills for about two miles. I'd say we head off in a couple of hours before first light, that's if there's no burnt-out trucks, landslides or the road hasn't been blown up. Say, around 3.30am, which hopefully will be when most of the snipers in the hills are asleep.'

'But if there is anything on the road, we set off sooner?'

'Yep, the most important thing is that we're through before daylight, or the hills will light up like a Christmas tree.' Then Klay added quietly, 'One of us will walk ahead to check the road.'

Lenka relaxed her clammy hands so as not to ruin the map and looked up at Klay, whose face remained fixed on the winding road. 'And check for mines?'

'Yes, as we can't have the headlights on, and we can't risk using a torch.'

Lenka nodded and kept her eyes forlornly on Klay, who continued to avoid her gaze. 'Then that's me. I will guide us through. Everyone else has to drive their rigs.'

'Bloody knew you'd say that,' said Klay, biting his lip. 'Look, if it was simply trying to divert the trucks around any obstacles in the dark, then Rat or Sasha could equally do it, as the other can drive. But this is not just about being a scout. Whoever does it will have to check every rock, every piece of debris for mines. They may have to disarm them if . . .' He paused as he steered the truck to the right, around the hairpin bend.

'What is it?' asked Lenka.

'Look, you can drive this thing. You would only be moving five miles an hour at most, and you'd be between Sasha and Connor's vehicles.'

'I could, but why?'

'I know more about traps and mines. Best I do it. You know how to reverse this thing, don't you?' he added almost matter-of-factly.

'You've given me quite a few lessons.' She smiled at Klay, and gripped his hand resting on the steering wheel while he steered the vehicle to the left as it continued to climb the snaking trail. 'You are a good man, Klay.'

'Why say that now?'

'Because you're checking that if you get blown up, we can all get out.'

9.10pm, 3 March 1992, 31 kilometres north-east of Mostar

As darkness slipped its cowl over Hun Mountain, Mary

pulled her truck into a clearing off the road, as the moon stayed safely behind the sleepy, thick grey clouds. She had been looking out for a place to park the trucks for the night, and she selected a spot by a bombed-out house. The others began to creep off the dirt road behind her, and park up under the cover of the forest.

As quietly as they could, the Rogues unloaded utensils and canned food from boxes and made their way a few yards into the dense forest. Sasha, Lenka and Rat had offered to help gather what was needed, but Mary warned them to stay back because of the risk of landmines.

Connor and Mary moved carefully towards the burnt-out, roofless house, avoiding stepping on any scattered bricks or timber. When they reached the house, both used their knives to dismantle the top layer of bricks from a half wall, as there was less risk of triggering a booby-trap than picking a brick off the ground. As they loaded the bricks into their arms, they saw the charred body of a young girl lying in the debris. "'War, what is it good for?'" sang the man,' said

Mary solemnly, looking up at Connor's pained face in the dim moonlight.

'Parades, and the awarding of medals and honours,' said Connor, shaking his head. 'It doesn't rhyme, though,' he added bitterly.

Both Rogues knew that if a mine had been laid, it would be under what was left of the dead girl.

When Connor and Mary returned with the bricks, Klay began to build a wall around the kettle on the Calor gas stove as Lenka, Sasha and Rat began opening tin cans and filling the three pots with the contents. 'The smoke should blend in with that from the building, so shouldn't alert any snipers.'

'I'm a vegan,' said Rat.

'Me too,' added Sasha.

'Go and eat fucking grass,' snapped Connor. 'There's a war on.'

'They have principles, Connor,' said Lenka. 'What we see around us, is the result of people no longer having any.'

'Sorry, teach!' said Connor, with a shrug as he turned to the goths. 'I'll eat the spam out of the stew, if that helps.'

'Fascist!' mumbled Rat.

'They're up in the hills,' said Connor, sourly. 'Do you want some of this rice or not, Smiler? I'm doing enough for all of us.'

'I'll do some toast and I have tomatoes,' said Klay.

'I have tomatoes and rice in my truck,' interjected Lenka.

'We have rice, we'll just add in lentils and some mushrooms,' Sasha said, smiling.

Rat grumbled but nodded.

'We'll put ours on when you've all finished,' said Sasha.

'No, you bloody won't,' said Connor. 'We're a team,' he said as he rose and headed back to the bombed house to collect more bricks for a second fire.

An hour later, two kettles were happily spluttering away on top of the fires. There were few exchanges over dinner as everyone's thoughts were on those still trapped in Mostar.

Klay made coffee and passed around the warm, welcoming metal mugs, as the evening was turning cold. Connor opened six bottes of *Pilsner* and placed them in the middle of the Rogues before damping the fires.

'Where did you come across Christina Pitchsmith?' asked Lenka.

'Angola,' said Connor.

'Peru,' said Mary.

'Sudan,' said Klay.

'She must be doing some good,' pressed Lenka.

'It seemed personal between you and her,' said Sasha, looking at Connor.

'Did you shag her and dump her?' added Rat.

'Shut it and finish your carrot,' said Connor.

'I bet you did,' said Sasha. 'You come across as a bit of a slag.'

'You're about 10, shouldn't you be in bed by now? And I never talk about my relationships.'

'Actually, I heard he turned her down,' said Klay, laughing. 'That's why she hates him.'

'How do you know?' asked Connor.

'She told me,' said Klay. 'She was furious.'

'Oh, she told you. This wouldn't be in bed would

it? No, wait, I apologise, it wasn't in bed. Wasn't there a story and photos about her and a "black colossus", according to *The Sun*, being caught having a knee-trembler in a car park in Paris?'

Klay shrugged. 'Don't remind me. I found the police going through my truck the next day, in full view of the press.'

'She told me too, once when she was drunk,' muttered Mary, sheepishly.

'Told you what?' asked Connor.

'That she made advances on some flash Londoner, but he laughed and said, "He'd rather masturbate with a steak knife in his hand." I've only clicked now, but that sounds dumb enough to be you.'

'People can be so sensitive,' said Connor. Then he lifted his head suddenly and nearly clapped, before looking across at the dark hills. He quickly dropped his hands on his knees. 'Wait a minute! What a moment to savour, you slept with Slickdick too. Superb! He lifted his face to the heavens. 'For once I have the moral high ground between these two bookends.'

'A mixed metaphor,' clipped Lenka.

'Sorry teach. Apparently, there was a lot of mixing going on,' said Connor.

Lenka ran her fingers through her hair and bent forward. 'Do you think the world will step forward and save those people back in Mostar?'

'I'm not a politician,' replied Connor gruffly, taking a large gulp of lager.

The others said nothing.

'Are we just applying a sticking plaster?' said Lenka, staring into the fading flames.

'Yes,' said Mary, quietly.

In the distance thunder roared. Spears of lightning began to be traded by angry gods crouching behind the gathering clouds.

'We had better start putting our stuff back in the trucks,' nodded Connor. 'Ten, maybe fifteen minutes before the deluge reaches us.' Having downed two beers, he was now rolling a tin mug of coffee in his hands and looked across at Lenka. 'If you wanted a photo album for your birthday you only had to say, and I would have bought you one from *Woolworths* when we got back.' Lenka said nothing. He leaned forward on the tin box he was sitting on. 'Forgive me, but following your little theft in Split, there are professional assassins trying to hunt us down. I know I'm stating the obvious, and I'm trying to scare everyone, but that is what they do.' Connor looked up at Lenka. 'Why didn't you give it to Murray, back there? Klay and I vouched for him. It would have been on every channel by tonight.'

'That's why,' said Lenka.

'I don't get it,' said Klay.

'I do,' said Mary. 'They would have gone to ground, or been eliminated by their superiors.'

'And replaced,' said Sasha.

Connor turned to Rat. 'Had you worked this out too?' Rat shook his head. 'Sometimes, I think the only function men have in the world is to carry heavy equipment.'

'I'll get a wheelbarrow,' said Mary, smartly.

Klay and Sasha tried to muffle their laughter.

Connor gave Mary a brief insincere smile before returning to Lenka. 'What do you propose to do with the photo album?'

A crack of thunder roared loudly above, demanding to be heard. Everyone looked warily across at Lenka, who was sitting on a wooden crate with an untouched cup of coffee in her hands.

'We just acknowledged that all we are doing is applying sticking plasters. We may prolong a life, perhaps even save lives, but as long as there is this ruthless legion of killers out there – these Wolves – we are only delaying the inevitable for those we hope to save. But if the album reaches the right channels it may result in the arrest of what is probably the largest group of professional killers not just in the Balkans, but in the world.'

'Their crimes alone should warrant their arrest,' said Mary.

'You're right, but where is the evidence? They kill from afar. Only their comrades and those who pay the blood money know of their crimes, and they will not incriminate themselves.' She held up the photo album. 'But this could be Exhibit One in their trial. It is the equivalent of Al Capone's accountant's ledger. The FBI couldn't secure the evidence or the witnesses to bring him to trial for his crimes, but they finally nailed him for tax evasion.'

Klay shrugged and smiled at the others. 'She's right. If the album reaches the proper channels, she may save more lives than we would in a lifetime.'

'You've probably signed all our death warrants,' said Sasha. 'But you did the right thing. Have you gone through it all yet?'

'I've only had the stomach to look at the first few pages,' said Lenka. 'They're mostly of Asia and Africa. The Wolves gather around their victims like big game trophy hunters.'

'Any of our friends back in the bar in them?' asked Connor.

'None that I've recognised. But I'm going to go through the whole album, I promise.'

No one said anything as the flames sunk into the charcoal.

'You did the right thing,' said Klay, smiling.

'It's big stuff, and you were smart enough to keep your wits, while dickhead here,' said Mary, tilting her head towards Connor, 'did his best to get us all killed for nothing.'

Connor shrugged and nodded.

'His antics did distract Lazar, so I could grab the album,' said Lenka.

Klay raised his metal mug, savoured the coffee aroma and made a toast. 'To Lenka, who kept her head, while twats lost theirs!'

Everyone tapped their mugs gently against Lenka's, except Connor.

'You have a problem?' asked Klay. 'She did what we should have done.'

'Your toast was crap! This is the women who outwitted us and took on a Romanian crime lord, feigned a heart attack and swiped a document that could bring down the most lethal force in the Balkans, again right under their noses.' He raised his mug, bent forward and tapped it against Lenka's. 'To Lenka, the smartest of the Rogues!'

Torrential rain began violently slapping the leaves, tins and upturned saucepans.

Connor raised his face and welcomed the rain. *You made your entrance sooner than I thought. Good to see you old friend, try and keep those snipers' heads down, tomorrow.*

Lenka looked at the smiling faces of the others, including to her surprise Rat, as they began to erase any evidence that they had been there, but she hid her thoughts. *Sasha and Connor were right, I have signed all their death warrants.*

7.05am, 4 March 1992, 38 kilometres north east of Mostar

The next morning, as the others were washing themselves with hand towels in plastic bowls by their trucks, Lenka approached Connor. 'I've been waiting to find a quiet moment to talk to you.'

Connor lifted his head from his soapy hands and wiped a towel across his face. 'I'm all yours, well, at least the parts Anita doesn't want.'

'Where was your father born?'

'Oh, Christ! You're not composing my eulogy already?' he said, wiping the towel across his hairy chest.

'No, it's to do with your eyes.'

'Oh, the changing colour thing. Well, I don't know why that happens, and I don't know who my father is

340

either. My mum got pregnant with me and moved to Belfast, as that's where her sister lived.'

'Where was she before that?'

'Your hometown. She was a barmaid in a pub in Cork.'

'Cork! And you really have no idea who your father is?'

'None at all, and I don't care. She was a good woman and raised me the best way she could. I wanted for nothing.'

'Have you ever read the Rogues comics?'

'No, and this grasshopper conversation is now at a close. We've got to get to Snipers' Alley before nightfall.' He buttoned up his faded navy blue shirt, leapt up into his truck and its engine welcomed the day with a roar.

'I need to talk to you at the next stop,' said Lenka, before turning towards Klay's truck where he was sitting in the driver's seat. 'And thank you for the watch!' she said, pointing to the Rolex. Connor gave her a thumbs up.

Lenka stood still and ran her finger slowly across

the crack in its glass, which would never be repaired.

4.15pm, 4 March 1992, 45 kilometres south-west of Tuzla, Bosnia-Herzegovina

'Snipers' Alley,' said Klay, adjusting the aperture of his sniper's sight until the overturned truck lying on the only road in the valley ahead came into view.

'Quiet as a graveyard,' noted Connor, with his arms folded standing beside him.

'Your gallows humour couldn't be more appropriate,' said Klay grimly. 'The crows are feasting on two bodies lying on the road. They probably tried to make a run for it when the driver was killed.'

Klay handed his Redfield sight to Mary.

'No ground to manoeuvre around it,' sighed Mary. 'Either we blow it up or ram it.'

'Either way, all hell will break loose in the hills and we'll be cut to pieces,' said Klay.

'Not if they think one of their own took a pot shot at the petrol tank and blew it up,' said Connor.

'It's on its side; I'd doubt if it has fuel in its tank,' said Mary.

Connor squinted up at the sun. 'I have an idea. In

four hours' time, it will be turning dark. Let's crack open a few beers, get some rest and then we'll get to work.'

The three Rogues returned to the others standing by the trucks parked off the road. Lenka refused a drink and, after hearing Connor's plan, she walked over to a clearing looking over Snipers' Alley. She sat on a bare patch of road, carefully avoiding the log propped up on the edge. A few minutes later Sasha joined her.

'Are you scared?' asked Sasha.

'Terrified,' replied Lenka.

'Me too.'

Lenka began to laugh, quietly. 'Yes, I'm terrified.'

'Are you okay, Lenka?'

'Yes,' said Lenka, as she continued to chuckle. 'Yes, I think I am.'

Sasha looked nervously at the woman who was only a few years older than her. 'Do you need something to relax you? Rat keeps a First Aid box on the truck that's full of weed.'

'Apart from the odd beer, drugs are not my scene.

Thank you though, but seriously I'm fine. It's just that I've thought of something so ridiculous that it's hilarious.'

'I can see if Rat's got anything stronger?'

'No, Sasha. Really, everything is fine,' she said as she turned and smiled at the puzzled goth. 'A few weeks ago, though it seems like years, my guardian . . .'

'You have a guardian?'

'I have two, well, until I was eighteen. Anyway, each argued about whether I should join up with Klay on this trip. One of them, Foxy, thought that if I took on this challenge it would help me to recover after Simon's death.'

'I didn't know Simon that well, but when I heard he became your man, I thought he must have some good qualities.'

'Actually, I don't think anyone liked him. He wasn't warm or compassionate, not the kind of man I ever thought I would fall for. But I did. When he was killed, he was holding me.'

'Christ! I didn't know that.'

'I was covered in his blood. From that day until

around five minutes ago, I have tried to look like I'm in control, but I've been numb; empty; shallow; call it what you will but now . . .' she smiled and turned towards Sasha. 'I'm absolutely terrified.'

Sasha looked even more worried. 'I don't get it. Shall I get Mary? You might be having a breakdown. Not surprising, after all you've been through.'

Lenka smothered a laugh. 'What I am trying to say is that Foxy was, in a perverse way, right. I have woken up, I am alive again,' she said as she tried to suppress her laughter, 'because I'm scared.' Giggling, she took Sasha's hand. 'It's not a good feeling, but it is a feeling. And I haven't had one of those in a long time.'

Sasha shook her head. 'I still think you're having a breakdown, which is fine as that makes you as mad as the rest of us!'

Lenka smiled. 'If you're trying to comfort me, you might need to phrase it better.'

Sasha nodded and began to giggle, too. 'When I was getting drunk with Connor on the Hungarian-Romanian border two years back when I first met you all, he told me that 99% of the people who volunteer

345

to do this work need more therapy than the ones they're trying to help.' She muffled her laughter, 'and that the other 1%, like him, are beyond therapy.'

As the two women walked back towards the others, still giggling, Connor looked over his shoulder at Mary, Klay and Rat, 'Sometimes, I think I'm the only sane one here.'

The other three Rogues raised their eyebrows towards each other, before continuing to secure the five-gallon jerry can full of petrol onto Connor's back.

Four hours later, with still enough natural light to see ahead, Connor crept quietly through the thicket carrying two five-gallon drums filled with petrol and another strapped on his back. Fifty metres above him, Klay was making his way quickly but stealthily towards a ridge a hundred yards from the derelict truck. Both men knew that a broken stick would echo throughout the valley and bring gunfire raining down on them from the surrounding hills.

When Connor reached the edge of the road, he lowered the petrol cans onto the grass and untied the straps securing the other on his back. He began to crawl slowly across the road towards the truck, dragging one container at a time. The smell of the rotting corpses on the road was overpowering. He stopped briefly to look at the bodies and guessed that each man was maybe sixteen or seventeen but no more.

After he had placed all three containers under the fuselage, he tapped the fuel tank to see how much fuel it contained to calculate how far away he would need to be to give the signal to Klay. It had been drained. He crawled towards the front of the overturned truck and peered up into the cabin. Inside was the body of a woman dressed in overalls. She was riddled with bullets like the men – target practice, so the snipers could keep their eye in until the next target arrived.

Connor crawled off the road and gradually began to raise himself as he slowly made his way back through the dense forest.

Connor stopped when he calculated that he was approximately two hundred metres away from the road and in sight of the wooden hut up on the ridge, where Klay was to position himself to take the shot. He raised Rat's disposable cigarette lighter in front of the mirror from Lenka's compact face-powder case.

Klay knelt by the wooden hut and returned Connor's signal by shining the flame from another of Rat's never-ending supply of lighters across the lens of his Redfield sight. He removed the snub-nosed .38 Fitz Special from his jacket and began to gauge the trajectory of the bullet that, for all their sakes, had to hit the target.

Connor set off, not waiting for the explosion – even with a revolver and at such a distance he had no doubt that his friend would hit the target. It would take him over an hour to climb back up through the undergrowth to reach the others.

Klay lay down between the trees and supported his raised arm, holding the revolver with the other. He moved his hips and legs so that his body was at a more comfortable angle. He heard a click. For a second, he froze; then, he clenched his jaw. He began to regulate his breathing as he took aim at the black rectangular objects beneath the vehicle's fuel tank. He had calculated that he would only have one shot. The shot would attract fire, but towards the vehicle as he would have to be very unlucky for a sniper to have spotted the exchange of signals between him and Connor. If he were to take a second shot from the same position – a novice mistake that ended the careers of many snipers – he would be at the centre of a firestorm. Not that it mattered, now. His body was rigid, but comfortable, his breathing light and unhurried. He squeezed the trigger.

Flames engulfed the overturned truck.

The remaining Rogues lying in front of their vehicles, hidden by the densest clump of forest they could find, watched the sporadic gunfire from the mountains aimed at the burning truck. Several mortars landed, and one hit the truck, obliterating it.

'That's a bonus,' said Sasha.

After a few minutes the gunfire and shelling stopped.

'Good, they believe it was one of their trigger-happy colleagues,' said Lenka.

Twenty minutes later, Rat, who was training Klay's binoculars on the routes that Klay and Connor had taken, spotted Connor slowly making his way through the gorge. 'It will be another half-hour before he gets up here.'

'Where's Klay?' asked Lenka. 'He should be back by now.'

Rat shook his head. Mary lifted the lenses from Rat's hands and trained them on the path that Klay had taken.

'He might have been hit. I'm going down,' said Lenka. 'You three stay here.'

'But . . .' said Mary, before Lenka disappeared into the thicket that bordered the edge of the valley.

Twenty-five minutes later, Lenka had worked her way quickly, but stealthily, to avoid any rocks or covering on the path, and could now see the wooden shack. As she approached, she could see the outline of Klay's body lying flat on the ground. As she moved forward, Klay lifted his head.

'Thank God,' whispered Lenka.

As she drew nearer, he whispered, 'Stay back. I've triggered a mine.' Lenka froze, then moved slowly forward. 'Back, Lenka,' repeated Klay, but she continued her approach.

She crouched down beside Klay but could see nothing metallic protruding from under his body. 'Where is it?'

'Under my hip. I triggered it as I was getting into position. I could tell from the sound, a sharp click, that it's a pressure switch. As long as I don't move though, you'll be fine. I want you to do something for me.'

'What? Anything,' she trembled.

'I've written a note. I want you to send it to Claudia, please,' he said as he lifted up a petrol invoice that he had scrawled a message on with a small blue pen from a *William Hill* betting shop.

Lenka lifted it from his hands and then grasped them. 'Like, I'm going to leave you here.'

'There's nothing you can do. Look, for the last few weeks I've been teaching you how to drive my truck, and you've been a quick learner. Keep between

Connor and Mary and head back to the Mostar border post. Then Connor and Mary can take over and relay the contents of my truck into Tuzla. Now go,' he said firmly.'

'You've never seen *Raiders*, have you?'

'No time for baseball, but no doubt one day my sons will get into it,' he replied, trying to smother the trembling in his voice.

'So, you know the sex of your unborn child,' said Lenka.

'I called Claudia before we left Vienna; that's what the scan says.'

'And you still want to just sit here until you fall asleep and never wake again?'

Klay pondered, then nodded, as Lenka eased off his boots. 'If you're sure about this?'

Lenka smiled, then shook her head. 'Bloody hell! You've never seen *Raiders*. It's true none of you have a social life,' she said, as she leaned across the prostrate man and peered at the iron lip of the thick cylindrical plate buried beneath his hip. She saw a broken slat from a fence lying behind her on the ground and stretched across to grab it.

'Lenka!' cried Klay.

'Sorry, yes,' she said contritely. She began to ease a slat off the fence. 'Yes, this will do,' she muttered, weighing it in her hands. 'Right, I'm going to put my hand up your trouser leg.'

Klay laughed nervously. 'Probably a bit late for all that; you should have shown your feelings sooner.'

'You're as bad as Connor,' she said, shaking her head. 'Now, relax your leg, so I can edge this up and wedge it between your thigh and the trigger mechanism. Then slowly work your leg out of your trousers. As you do that, I'll pile more weight on top of the slat to keep the trigger pressed down.'

'It won't work, these things are sensitive and scatter bodies for miles. Best you go . . .'

'Scatter *our* bodies for miles. I'll not going without you,' she said as she tucked Klay's note into her shirt pocket.

For the next ten minutes, Lenka slipped three wooden slats up the leg of Klay's canvas combats and over the trigger of the landmine, as he gradually drew his legs out of his army fatigues. Klay tensed and relaxed his thighs regularly, as cramp was starting to set in, and he wanted to be able to grab Lenka and throw her away from the explosion.

When Klay's knee was just above the trigger, having diligently checked beneath it, Lenka rolled a heavy rock next to the edge of the mine. She took a deep breath as she was about to slip her hand over the wooden slats and press down with all her might.

Klay gripped her hand. 'Your weight may not be enough? I think it's best you don't do this.'

Lenka placed her hand on his clammy cheek. 'I'm a Rogue! It's what we do.'

Klay held her hand, smiled and nodded. 'See you on the other side.'

'We'll keep the Pearly Gates ajar in case Connor or Mary ever want to sneak upstairs with a beer.'

Gradually, Lenka pressed her full weight down on the edge of Klay's trouser leg above the trigger switch and slipped the rock over it, while Klay lifted his leg.

Minutes later, despite the fierce cramp in his legs, Klay was standing up, bent double, gripping his knees and breathing deeply, having ensured that the trigger was still pressed down after adding two more bricks over it. Lenka supported the powerful man, placing his arm over her shoulder.

As they walked away from the muted explosive, in the direction of the trucks, Klay turned to Lenka. 'This *Raiders*, this is some manual you read about how to deal with mines?'

'No, *Raiders of the Lost Ark*. It's a film I took the children to see at the Saturday matinee a few years back.' Klay was speechless. 'In the opening scene, Harrison Ford, who played the hero, places a bag of sand over a trigger mechanism to stop the whole underground chamber collapsing on him.'

'A film!' said Klay in disbelief. He ran his free hand through his clipped hair. 'Well, at least it worked.'

Lenka looked up apologetically. 'Actually, come to think of it, it didn't. It set off the booby traps and the whole temple came down on him."

As they approached the road leading to the Rogues convoy, Connor and Mary appeared.

'Where have you two . . .' said Connor, before

355

stopping to peer quizzically at Klay standing in his underpants with his arm still around Lenka's shoulders. 'Come on, guys, there's a time and place for all that,' he said, before smiling and turning back towards the trucks.

Mary shook her hydra-styled head of matted hair and beamed broadly before turning back. 'Even I know that, and my morals are lower than a snake's belly.'

9.20pm, 4 March 1992, London

'Foxy, a welcome surprise even at this late hour,' said Estelle, after she had checked through the spyhole and opened the door to her fashionable house on Chelsea's Kings Road. She led her old friend into the lounge.

'Can I get you a drink?' asked Estelle.

'Would the Pope refuse to hear a psalm?'

'What would you like?'

'A 12-year-old single malt, as long as it's a double, or a bottle of Pol Roger, I'm not fussy. I suggest you get a stiff drink for yourself too.'

Estelle looked pensively at Foxy, before she walked

over to the drinks cabinet. She returned with a tumbler of *The Macallan* ten-year-old single malt, along with the bottle for Foxy and a glass of Madeira for herself.

'No Victoria tonight?' asked Foxy.

'She's already asleep upstairs.'

'You didn't have to order in then.'

Estelle only performed domestic chores when she visited Marisa's orphanage. Her food was prepared by her partner, Victoria, who was also lead seamstress for her fashion house, *Haute Couture by Estelle*. Foxy once described his own domestic arrangements as 'non-interventionist', as The Savoy Hotel prepared his food and delivered it to his house in Westminster's Smith Square. Estelle and Foxy contributed financially to the orphanage but helping to prepare food on their visits was a personal ritual. It made them feel part of something good and worthy, and integral to the extended family that thrived in Marisa's Arms.

'You've been together, what, six years?' asked Foxy.

'Nearer eight,' Estelle said.

'It's good you found someone.'

Estelle adjusted her purple silk kimono and curled up

on the chaise longue. 'You had your moments, Foxy, but you're too much of a tart. Men in uniform were always your weakness. But you're not here to talk about relationships, are you? Or has a Grenadier guardsman broken your heart again? You never turn up without calling me first.'

'Lenka is all I have; I have grim news,' replied Foxy.

'What's happened?' said Estelle, sitting up and dropping her bare feet onto the wooden floor. 'Is she hurt?'

Foxy had trouble clasping the glass firmly in his hands and, after taking a large mouthful, he rested it on the glass coffee table. 'To be honest, I have no idea.'

'What have you learnt?' said Estelle quietly.

'I received a telephone call this evening from a Major Janus. He informed me that a man . . . no, let me be explicit, a mercenary called Gardo Salvano, was found murdered on the road leading to the Croatian town of Split.'

'And how is he linked to Lenka?'

'The night before, a blonde-haired woman in her

mid-twenties who matches Lenka's description, was in the bar where this man was drinking. The woman, who was reported to be Lenka, was accompanied by some friends. One of them matches Klay's description.'

'That confirms it then, as there can't be that many black men wandering around the Balkans,' said Estelle.

'One of Lenka's acquaintances, a man called Connor Pierce whom she met in Romania, got into an argument with this Salvano fellow. The mercenary drew a Gurkha kukri on Connor, who, according to a statement made by the English-speaking barmaid to the Croatian police, "threatened to 'stick it up his arse"'.'

'Have you checked out this Connor?'

Foxy reclined into the antique armchair. 'A Rogue for sure. Born in Belfast. Served in the Irish Army, deployed in various UN peacekeeping operations and was part of some covert exchange scheme with elite military units from other countries. What we do know, is that when he left the army, he returned to Belfast where he clashed with the IRA resulting in the death of quite a number of their key operatives.'

'The latter part, Lenka told me. A dangerous man,' pondered Estelle. 'But this Salvano was a mercenary; it doesn't mean that this Connor was the murderer. Mercenaries do get killed. It is the nature of their profession, after all.'

'Salvano had his throat slit with the kukri.'

'I take it they found the weapon?'

'Yes, they didn't have to go far; it was found stuck up the dead man's arse.'

'Ah,' said Estelle, shaking her head. 'If Connor poses a threat to Lenka, then at least Klay is there to protect her.'

'True, and Klay is not just a sniper, he is a trained martial arts expert. This Connor would meet his match.'

Foxy lifted the bottle of scotch unsteadily and topped up his glass.

'Do you think Connor is linked to the murder of McNamara and Simon?' asked Estelle.

'There must be a link.'

'After some gentle coaxing, Lenka once told me that Simon and this Connor clashed repeatedly.'

'I didn't know that. But though I know there must be a link to McNamara's death I can't make the link with Connor Pierce.'

'Do we know where Lenka and the others are now?'

'Last seen crossing into Serbian-Bosnian disputed territory.'

'You mean the war zone.'

'Furthermore, the men who were with Salvano in the bar and were no doubt mercenaries, were also last reported to have entered the war zone. The Croatian police believe they are in pursuit of Lenka and the others.'

'Revenge?'

'From what I have learnt of this group, they come from an organisation of professional killers called The Wolves. It seems that money is their only driver; they have no loyalty to each other. In fact, when a Wolf dies, they vie with each other to secure any outstanding marks and claim the bounty on their heads. They have no interest in vengeance.'

'Then the Rogues have something they want,' said

Estelle.

Foxy nodded and stared into his glass for a few minutes. Estelle looked over at the photo of her younger self with Lenka as a child sitting on her lap, laughing.

'I'm so sorry, Estelle,' said Foxy, quietly. 'This is all my fault. I pride myself on being a strategist and the government calls me in times of crisis.' He shook his head and looked up at his friend. 'Yet when it came to the one person whom we raised and swore to protect, I persuaded her to enter a war zone accompanied by trained killers.'

'You didn't make Lenka go,' said Estelle, grimly. 'She chose to go.'

'It was all my idea. An idea that you fervently, and rightly, opposed.'

Estelle knew that there was no point in arguing with Foxy or trying to lift his mood and topped up his glass.

They sat in silence. Seconds later, it was broken by the purring of the telephone. Estelle walked over and lifted the receiver. 'Yes. . . . That's okay, I was awake . .

. Yes, he's here.' She turned to Foxy. 'It's a Major Janus for you.'

Foxy staggered up and walked slowly over to take the receiver. He said nothing, only nodded, as Estelle returned to her seat and lifted her drink from the table. After a couple of minutes, Foxy thanked the officer and replaced the receiver. He returned to the armchair and crumpled into it.

'What is it? Have they found . . .' She swallowed hard. 'Have they found Lenka?'

'No.' Foxy raised his head and looked anxiously across at Estelle's pale face. 'But I believe we have finally established the link that connects all the deaths. With the murder of McNamara, a can of worms was opened and now the contents are crawling out into the light.'

'For God's sake, Foxy, what have you learnt?' said Estelle.

He refilled his glass and emptied it in one swallow. He lifted his head. 'Once again, I am proven to be wrong. Captain Simon Syrianus Trevelyan was not, as I originally thought, "every inch the hero".'

9.40pm, 4 March 1992, 45 kilometres south-west of Tuzla

'Bollocks!' said Mary, training Connor's binoculars onto the valley. 'The engine landed back in the middle of the road. It will need moving.'

Klay smiled up at Lenka, as she helped lower him onto the step of his truck. 'That means I'm chief scout. I'm built for heavy lifting,' said the most powerful of the Rogues.

'Hold on, Tonto,' said Connor. 'The Lone Ranger gets top billing. I have to go ahead of the trucks, or Hollywood will never make a film of it. Oh, and like I'm going to trust my life to someone who can't even hang on to their trousers.'

'Jim Brown gets top billing in a few films these days,' said Lenka.

'Jim Brown?' repeated both men.

Lenka sighed. '*The Dirty Dozen*, *Ice Station Zebra*, surely you've seen one of them at a Saturday morning matinee?' She looked at their expressionless faces. 'We're all going to the pictures with the kids when we get back.'

'Anyway, ke-mo sah-bee,' continued Klay. 'You stay on your horse and look cool, while I do all the work – that's how the colour divide works.'

'No chance,' said Connor. 'You can drive my truck. If someone triggers a mine, I'm the best person to deal with it.'

Klay turned to smile at Lenka. 'I wouldn't be too sure about that.' He turned back to Connor. 'We draw straws for the honour to spread our entrails over a vast area.'

Lenka picked three pieces of dried straw by her feet and shortened one.

'Three?' noted Connor.

'Soon Hollywood will be crying out for stories with black lead characters and female ones too,' said Lenka. 'Don't screw up the Rogues' franchise at this stage.'

A fourth straw appeared. 'And it's about time they started making films with a glamorous queer lead too,' added Mary.

'Glamorous?' said Connor, pulling on a loose thread from a hole in her jumper. He lifted his hand, extending his fingers upwards and turned it back and forth, 'Average.'

'Why do you do that? Is that a comment on your sexual prowess?' said Mary.

'Average!' beamed Connor. 'That's probably the best compliment a woman's ever made on my sexual performance. If I write that down, will you sign it?'

'Only after I flatten your nuts into pancakes,' said Mary.

'Your kindness knows no bounds,' said Connor, turning to Klay. 'Well, I fear my time as the leading man has passed.' He broke into a broad smile. 'And thank God for that, it's not been easy having to be the morally right, pillar of respectability among this team of miscreants.'

Klay stood up and threw his arm around Connor's shoulder. 'There will always be a role for a simple-headed white man.' He tweaked Connor's cheek. 'And look at that big dumb grin; you'll always find an audience in an institution of some sort.'

Connor, expressionless, said drily, 'Once again, your kind words are quite underwhelming.' Then as Sasha and Rat approached, he grabbed the sullen little man by the arm. 'Smiler here can be my straight man.'

Rat frowned.

Sasha leaned into Lenka and whispered. 'The usual nonsense, I take it?'

Lenka nodded as she looked at the others. *Tonight, we will enter Snipers' Alley, a road already strewn with bodies, and the Rogues are acting as if they were going on a daytrip to Barleycove Beach. What would my family and the children back in Cork make of them, if they ever came to Marisa's Arms? That would be a day.*

The Rogues could hear the faint din of an aircraft in the distance.

'We're too open here,' said Connor. 'We can draw straws later.'

'Right,' said Mary. 'And we need to make dinner. The smoke will draw fire from the hills. Three miles back I saw a good shady spot off the road. We'll make camp there, before heading into the valley when it's dark.'

Lenka grabbed Connor's arm. 'Not tonight, but when we reach Tuzla, I need to talk to you about your father.'

Connor looked wary. 'I don't need to know anything about him.'

'You do, Connor, you really do.'

Connor said nothing, as he turned and walked towards his vehicle.

Lenka turned and was met by Sasha. 'Have you looked at the photo album, Lenka?'

'I'm going to do it now, as we drive to the clearing.'

'If it's unsettling, we can do it together tonight.'

'Thanks Sasha. I'll flip through it in the truck. But later we can go through it properly together, and then work out how we can get it to Foxy.' Lenka weighed the heavy album in her hands. She looked at Sasha and said quietly, 'After what I've done, do you think our photo will be the next one to be added to the album?'

Sasha placed a hand on Lenka's shoulder. 'If I'm going to be in a group photo, do you think I should get my hair done?' pointing up at her spiky red-striped black hair.

'We need to get you to a doctor immediately. I fear you're showing the first symptoms of gallows humour, better known as Rogues humour.'

Sasha sighed, 'It comes from fear.'

The women embraced each other before jumping into their vehicles.

Ten minutes later, as Klay's truck rocked slowly back down the meandering dirt road, Lenka lifted the photo album from the glove compartment.

'Are you sure you can stomach that now?' said Klay, steering the truck around the sharp bend.

Lenka nodded before inhaling deeply. Six leaves into the album, she rested her forehead on her hand, before wiping away her tears and peering out of the window at nothing. The pages contained the smiling faces of men carrying guns and bloody knives, posing over dead families. The only difference between the photos was the backdrop. Sunny Latin American scenes were followed by the sandy plains of Africa and then the multi-coloured landscape of Asia. The macabre group shots were not in sequence, either by country or date, each, apparently, slotted in where a gap roughly fitted the frame.

Returning to the portfolio of atrocities, she tentatively turned over the next page. She froze.

'Lenka, is everything okay?' asked Klay. 'You're deathly pale. Is it your heart, do you need me to pull over?'

Lenka gingerly peeled back the transparent plastic covering the photos. Her trembling fingers began to pick at the corner of another photo of several men smiling and giving peace signs as they knelt above the bloody dead bodies of several children.

She peeled the photo away from the sticky sleeve and lifted it up to look at the handsome face of the man kneeling between Salvano and Lazar. He was the only one not smiling; instead, he wore that same unemotional look she had first noticed when he held the little girl in Carol's orphanage.

Klay pulled the truck off the road as soon as he cleared the bend. 'Lenka, what is it? Talk to me! What's wrong?'

Lenka rested her trembling fingers on the cracked face of her watch, as the photo of the handsome British officer floated slowly down onto the dirty floor.

Next, The Lenka Trilogy Part 2

Resilience

NOVELS BY JOHN RIGHTEN
ALL AVAILABLE ON AMAZON

The Rogues Trilogy: *Churchill's Rogue; The Gathering Storm* & *The Darkest Hour*

&

The Lochran Trilogy: *Churchill's Assassin; The Last Rogue* & *The Alpha Wolves*

&

The Lenka Trilogy: *Heartbreak; Resilience* & *Reflection*

&

The Englander

&

The Benevolence of Rogues

&

The Pane of Rejection

I hope you enjoyed my novel. Reviews are always welcome on Amazon. If you have posted a review, I have limited edition sets of postcards of The Rogues Trilogy,

The Lochran Trilogy and The Lenka Trilogy covers, plus *The Benevolence of Rogues* and *The Pane of Rejection*, which, stocks permitting, are available free of charge. If you would like a set, please send me a personal message via Facebook, Twitter or Instagram with the name of the novel you reviewed (so I know which set to send), your name/pseudonym and address, and subject to availability, I will send you the corresponding set of postcards, free of charge including p&p.

In the meantime, my other novels and what the critics said . . .

The Rogues Trilogy

Churchill's Rogue – The Rogues Trilogy Part 1
December 1937. Winston Churchill asks a former adversary, Sean Ryan, for his help to save a woman and her son. Ryan agrees to help, but on his own terms. They, and other refugees, are being hunted by a specially formed SS unit, The Alpha Wolves. They are led by Major Krak, a psychopath, known by his enemies – he has no friends – as Cerberus
Ryan encounters a formidable woman, Lenka, and other Rogues who have their own personal reasons for helping those trying to escape their Nazi pursuers. The Rogues were born of struggle, each forged in the flames of the Irish or Spanish Civil Wars, the Great Depression or the Russian Revolution. We learn how each fought, suffered or

lost those they loved.

Despite their bitter rivalries, the Rogues join forces in a desperate race to save as many families as they can. But for each of the Rogues the struggle comes at a terribly high price. Meanwhile, Churchill stands alone, ridiculed by governments desperate to appease the evil stealing towards them.

Thus, begins the story, leading up to the outbreak of war, of the men and women who dare to challenge the Nazis. *Churchill's Rogue* is the first in a rousing trilogy, followed by *The Gathering Storm* and *The Darkest Hour*, which chronicle the bloody encounters between the Rogues and Cerberus' executioners.

Churchill's Rogue review

"Sean Ryan grew up in Ireland during the 20th century's first quarter and so understands death and loss. He learnt to defend what he felt right during his time as a bodyguard for Michael Collins. Therefore, when Winston Churchill called upon his services in 1937 to bring a mother and child out of Germany, Ryan doesn't say no. However, Ryan soon discovers this is no easy escort duty. The mother and child in question are for some reason being hunted by an elite German force led by Cerberus, a code name for a sadist incarnate. On the plus side, Ryan soon discovers he's not alone. There are more like him across Europe; those with pasts that forged them into violent defenders of the vulnerable in an increasingly dangerous world. These are the Rogues and, this time, Ryan needs their help.

This is British author John Righten's debut novel following the first instalment of his non-fiction autobiography The Benevolence of Rogues which brought to the fore some of the real life 'Rogues' he's met during a multi-faceted life spent in some very dangerous places. John isn't someone who has just had an exciting, precariously balanced life; he also has a talent for transferring such existences to the page. Anyone doubting this should certainly read Churchill's Rogue – and hold onto your seats!

Churchill's involvement is interesting as, in an era when the UK and US were dithering as to whether the Nazis should be fought or be expeditiously befriended, the future Prime Minister was a lone voice of almost prophetic warning.

Although there are other factual characters appearing (e.g. Himmler and the Fuhrer himself) the most compelling are the fictionalised. Sean Ryan is almost a 1930s Irish Jack Reacher and yet, as much as I love Lee Child's work (and I do love it!), John Righten adds rugged, scream-curdling realism and a pace that would render Jack Reacher an asthmatic wreck.

Speaking of scream-curdling brings us to the most

wonderful baddie in the Earl Grey drinking Cerberus. His real name – Major Krak - may give rise to a smirk or two but we don't laugh for long. He enjoys torture and, to give him credit, he's certainly got an imagination for it.

Indeed, earlier I described the novel as 'bloody' and for a good reason; it's definitely not a story for the delicate. However, the intensity of violence isn't for gratification. It reminds us that in the real world shootings and explosions don't just produce a tidy red dot on victims' bodies; death can be a messy business!

The other thing we notice is that this is doesn't suffer from that usual first in series malady, set-up-lull. As we follow the pasts and presents of Australian, Russian, American and British Rogues we back-track them through other conflicts like the Spanish Civil War and the Russian Revolution. The more we come to know them, the more we can't help loving them while also realising why it's best not to get close to anyone in this line of work. We're at the mercy of an author who will kill at will (in literary terms) but having started on the emotional roller coaster, I don't want the series to end. Bring on *The Gathering Storm* – I'm braced and more than ready!"
The Bookbag (UK)

The Lochran Trilogy

Churchill's Assassin

New Year's Eve 1964 and a young Irishman, Lochran Ryan, is being transported by Special Branch to a secret rendezvous with Sir Winston Churchill. Just as he arrives, a sniper tries to kill the statesman. But why kill a man who the world knows is gravely ill? This is the first of many questions that Lochran tries to answer. His quest for the truth takes him from New York, to London and Moscow, where he encounters the most ruthless criminal gangs, including Delafury – a one-man execution squad – who warns Lochran that a new force is rising that will change the world.

Churchill's Assassin is the first in the Lochran Trilogy, an epic tale that will turn your blood to ice as the world's most notorious criminal masterminds gather to strike at the one man who may discover their secret.

Churchill's Assassin review

"A riveting political thriller. Due the strength of characterization and plotting, the story reels you in immediately. Although Ryan and Churchill make for strange bedfellows, the concept nevertheless works brilliantly. *Churchill's Assassin* is a fine mixture of historical detail, thrilling action, and detailed characterization, making for a riveting spin on one of the world's greatest statesman that will have

readers eager to pick up the next book in the series."
Editor, *Self-Publishing Review* (US)

The Benevolence of Rogues

The Benevolence of Rogues reviews
"Aid worker's missions find unlikely support from prison forgers, gangsters' henchmen and sympathetic police... John Righten has been in the wrong place at the right time since the 1980s. Then, he was in Romania, delivering medical supplies to orphans suffering from Aids. Subsequently, he was in Bosnia in the 90s, sneaking in medical supplies and in South America – Brazil, Chile and Peru – during the 2000s. Righten is now back and has put together his experiences in his autobiography, *The Benevolence of Rogues*."
Hampstead & Highgate Express (UK)

"This is not a memoir for the straight-laced, politically correct or faint of heart: massive quantities of alcohol are consumed, many teeth are knocked out and sarcasm is in generous supply."
Kirkus Independent (US)

Printed in Poland
by Amazon Fulfillment
Poland Sp. z o.o., Wrocław

51189613R00217